PRAISE FOR *NEW YORK T...* BESTSELLING AUTHOR ANNE FRASIER

"Frasier has perfected the art of making a reader's skin crawl."

—*Publishers Weekly*

"A master."

—*Star Tribune* (Minneapolis)

"Anne Frasier delivers thoroughly engrossing, completely riveting suspense."

—Lisa Gardner

"Frasier's writing is fast and furious."

—Jayne Ann Krentz

PRAISE FOR *THE BODY READER*

Winner of the International Thriller Writers 2017 Thriller Award for Best Paperback Original

"Absorbing."

—*Publishers Weekly*

"This is an electrifying murder mystery—one of the best of the year."

—Mysterious Reviews

"I see the name Anne Frasier on a book and I know I am in for a treat . . . I thought it was a very unique premise and coupled with the good characters, made for an almost non-stop read for me. I highly recommend this."

—Pure Textuality

PRAISE FOR *THE BODY COUNTER*

"I thoroughly suggest that you take your time with this book. If it's been a while, I would suggest you re-read *The Body Reader* so you can revisit the horror Jude Fontaine has already endured, before embarking on this journey. Truly, sit back and let Anne Frasier take you on a journey that can't be matched. I have never seen an author develop a character so vividly as Frasier does with the characters in these books. You feel their desperation, their isolation in their fight to survive, their will to live, not physically, but mentally. You feel their compassion that has managed to remain despite the evil they lived through."

—Reader

PRAISE FOR *PLAY DEAD*

"This is a truly creepy and thrilling book. Frasier's skill at exposing the dark emotions and motivations of individuals gives it a gripping edge."

—RT Book Reviews

"*Play Dead* is a compelling and memorable police procedural, made even better by the way the characters interact with one another. Anne Frasier will be appreciated by fans who like Kay Hooper, Iris Johansen and Lisa Gardner."

—Blether: The Book Review Site

"A nicely constructed combination of mystery and thriller. Frasier is a talented writer whose forte is probing into the psyches of her characters, and she produces a fast-paced novel with a finale containing many surprises."

—I Love a Mystery

"Has all the essentials of an edge-of-your-seat story. There is suspense, believable characters, an interesting setting, and just the right amount of details to keep the reader's eyes always moving forward . . . I recommend *Play Dead* as a great addition to any mystery library."

—Roundtable Reviews

PRAISE FOR *PRETTY DEAD*

"Besides being beautifully written and tightly plotted, this book was that sort of great read you need on a regular basis to restore your faith in a genre."

—Lynn Viehl, Paperback Writer (Book of the Month)

"By far the best of the three books. I couldn't put my Kindle down till I'd read every last page."

—NetGalley

PRAISE FOR *HUSH*

"This is far and away the best serial-killer story I've read in a long time . . . strong characters, with a truly twisted bad guy."

—Jayne Ann Krentz

"I couldn't put it down. Engrossing . . . scary . . . I loved it."

—Linda Howard

"A deeply engrossing read, *Hush* delivers a creepy villain, a chilling plot, and two remarkable investigators whose personal struggles are only equaled by their compelling need to stop a madman before he kills again. Warning: don't read this book if you are home alone."

—Lisa Gardner

"A wealth of procedural detail, a heart-thumping finale, and two scarred but indelible protagonists make this a first-rate read."

—*Publishers Weekly*

"Anne Frasier has crafted a taut and suspenseful thriller."

—Kay Hooper

"Well-realized characters and taut, suspenseful plotting."

—*Star Tribune* (Minneapolis)

PRAISE FOR *SLEEP TIGHT*

"Guaranteed to keep you awake at night."

—Lisa Jackson

"There'll be no sleeping after reading this one. Laced with forensic detail and psychological twists."

—Andrea Kane

"Gripping and intense . . . Along with a fine plot, Frasier delivers her characters as whole people, each trying to cope in the face of violence and jealousies."

—*Star Tribune* (Minneapolis)

"Enthralling. There's a lot more to this clever intrigue than graphic police procedures. Indeed, one of Frasier's many strengths is her ability to create characters and relationships that are as compelling as the mystery itself. Will linger with the reader after the killer is caught."

—*Publishers Weekly*

PRAISE FOR *THE ORCHARD*

"Eerie and atmospheric, this is an indie movie in print. You'll read and read to see where it is going, although it's clear early on that the future is not going to be kind to anyone involved. Weir's story is more proof that only love can break your heart."

—*Library Journal*

"A gripping account of divided loyalties, the real cost of farming and the shattered people on the front lines. Not since Jane Smiley's *A Thousand Acres* has there been so enrapturing a family drama percolating out from the back forty."

—*Maclean's*

"This poignant memoir of love, labor, and dangerous pesticides reveals the terrible true price."

—*Oprah Magazine* (Fall Book Pick)

"Equal parts moving love story and environmental warning."

—*Entertainment Weekly* (B+)

"While reading this extraordinarily moving memoir, I kept remembering the last two lines of Muriel Rukeyser's poem 'Kathe Kollwitz' ('What would happen if one woman told the truth about her life? / The world would split open'), for Weir proffers a worldview that is at once eloquent, sincere, and searing."

—*Library Journal* (Librarians' Best Books of 2011)

"She tells her story with grace, unflinching honesty and compassion all the while establishing a sense of place and time with a master story teller's perspective so engaging you forget it is a memoir."

—Calvin Crosby, Books Inc. (Berkeley, CA)

"One of my favorite reads of 2011, *The Orchard* is easily mistakable as a novel for its engaging, page-turning flow and its seemingly imaginative plot."

—Susan McBeth, founder and owner of Adventures by the Book, San Diego, CA

"Moving and surprising."

—The Next Chapter (Fall 2011 Top 20 Best Books)

"Searing . . . the past is artfully juxtaposed with the present in this finely wrought work. Its haunting passages will linger long after the last page is turned."

—*Boston Globe* (Pick of the Week)

"If a writing instructor wanted an excellent example of voice in a piece of writing, this would be a five-star choice!"

—*San Diego Union-Tribune* (Recommended Read)

"This book produced a string of emotions that had my hand flying up to my mouth time and again, and not only made me realize, 'This woman can write!' but also made me appreciate the importance of this book, and how it reaches far beyond Weir's own story."

—Linda Grana, Diesel, a Bookstore

"*The Orchard* is a lovely book in all the ways that really matter, one of those rare and wonderful memoirs in which people you've never met become your friends."

—Nicholas Sparks

"A hypnotic tale of place, people, and of Midwestern family roots that run deep, stubbornly hidden, and equally menacing."

—Jamie Ford, *New York Times* bestselling author of *Hotel on the Corner of Bitter and Sweet*

THE
BODY KEEPER

ALSO BY ANNE FRASIER

Detective Jude Fontaine Mysteries

The Body Reader
The Body Counter

The Elise Sandburg Series

Play Dead
Stay Dead
Pretty Dead
Truly Dead

Other Novels

Hush
Sleep Tight
Before I Wake
Pale Immortal
Garden of Darkness

Nonfiction (as Theresa Weir)

The Orchard: A Memoir
The Man Who Left

THE
BODY KEEPER

ANNE FRASIER

THOMAS & MERCER

Text copyright © 2019 by Theresa Weir

Published by Thomas & Mercer, Seattle

www.apub.com

Amazon, the Amazon logo, and Thomas & Mercer are trademarks of Amazon.com, Inc., or its affiliates.

ISBN-13: 9781542040242
ISBN-10: 1542040248

Cover design by PEPE *nymi*, Milano

Printed in the United States of America

THE
BODY KEEPER

CHAPTER 1

Minneapolis, mid-November

Once the bodies were loaded, she slid into the driver's seat, turned the ignition key—and heard nothing but a terrifying click. Her heart hammered as she panic-pumped the accelerator while twisting the key again. The cargo van shook and the engine sputtered, then fell silent. That was followed by the alarming scent of gasoline. All her instincts shouted to run, just run. Maybe catch a cab and then a plane to Mexico or someplace, anyplace.

She tried the key again.

The vehicle rocked and spewed black exhaust, but this time the engine caught. Without waiting for it to settle into a steady idle, she put it in gear and shot forward.

She took a side street. No interstate for her. Last thing she needed was to break down on a busy highway. She ended up winding through the Stevens Square neighborhood of Minneapolis, somehow ending up on Franklin Avenue. A right turn, an incline, a bridge spanning water, and the engine started coughing again, then died completely. She kept her foot off the brake pedal and coasted uphill, muttering, "Come on, come on, come on." But the vehicle didn't quite crest the center rise of the bridge before slowly coming to a complete stop. Then it began to roll backward. *Now* she slammed on the brakes, put the van in park, and tried to restart it. A few futile minutes later, a red light bounced off her side mirror.

A cop pulling up behind her.

With a flashlight in his hand, the officer got out of the squad car and approached. She lowered the window. The typical drill. She gave him her driver's license and registration, trying to keep her voice and hands steady, all the while aware of the bodies behind her seat, covered in a tarp.

"Cold night to be out so late," he said.

"I had some errands to run. A friend's in the hospital and I'm watching her dogs." She'd always been good at bullshitting. But this kind of thing had been easier when she was young and attractive. She could get out of any predicament back then.

He took her license to his squad car, then returned a couple of minutes later, passing it through the window. "Do you have someone coming to help you?"

"I called a tow truck."

"Would you like to wait in my car until he comes? It's below zero right now. I don't want you ending up in the hospital too."

"No, that's fine. They said ten minutes max."

"I'll be back in ten or fifteen to check on you. Don't try to walk anywhere. Always best to stay with your vehicle."

Once he was gone, she jumped out of the van and scanned the area. She was in one of those neighborhoods that existed deep in the city: oddly secluded, except she could hear Interstate 94. The houses were close, but not too close. And there were a lot of big evergreen trees. It would be tough for someone to see her from a window; plus it was dark, the nearest lights far off. She'd read that vandals had been shooting out streetlights, but Minneapolis was also a dark-sky-compliant city.

Scared shitless about the cop's promise to return, she hurried to the back of the van and dragged out one of the bodies, pulling it across ice and snow. Her heart was pumping so much adrenaline she probably could have lifted a truck over her head. No need. The edge of the bridge was low.

With what felt like very little effort and superhuman strength, she balanced the stiff body on the concrete ledge and raised the feet—like raising one end of a teeter-totter. It practically did the rest on its own, vanishing over the side into the blackness. But instead of the splash she expected, she heard a dull thud. She looked over and barely made out the dark shape lying on top of the ice.

Committed now, nothing else she could do, no way to get the body back, she returned to the van for the rest, disposing of them one after the other. Third time really was the charm because the ice cracked and the dark shapes disappeared. By the time she tossed the fourth body over, she heard the splash she'd been waiting for. Finished, she closed the van doors, climbed into the driver's seat, and called for roadside assistance.

True to his word, the cop swung past again. He seemed about to get out of his vehicle when the emergency lights of the tow truck appeared from around a curve in the road. The cop lowered his window, waved, shouted for her to have a nice night, and pulled away.

CHAPTER 2

Minneapolis, December 31

He was always careful. He'd never tried to kiss her, never touched her really, never even held eye contact too long. She'd been through a lot, and he figured right now she needed a friend more than a boyfriend. So he was surprised when he felt her hand brush his.

At first, he thought it was an accident. Maybe she'd flailed a little as they skated across the frozen city lake and had unintentionally gotten too close. But when it happened again, he knew it was deliberate. Before he could process the situation, they were holding hands. Really holding hands, as much as people wearing mittens could do. And even then, he told himself her grasp was for stability, but in truth he was the shitty skater, not her.

Loring Park, with the beautiful lake surrounded by brownstones, had been his idea for New Year's Eve. It was the last night of an event called Holidazzle—two weeks of outdoor holiday celebrations that included a block of food vendors and a heated beer tent. They were even showing *Frozen* on an outdoor screen while bundled-up families and couples sat on hay bales. You didn't get much more Minnesota than that. Off in the distance, an arched pedestrian bridge led across Interstate 94 to the Walker Art Center and *Spoonbridge and Cherry*—the giant sculpture that was every bit as iconic as the Mary Tyler Moore statue.

Elliot had been told Loring Park used to be one of the coolest areas of town, but the blackouts and subsequent crime wave of last year, along with artists moving to less expensive digs, had left the area grappling to retain its culturally significant spot in the city.

Didn't matter. He was from the flat, dry land of Texas, and Loring Park was as foreign to him as another country. He loved it. His heart swelled whenever he saw the tight streets packed with cars, the combination of narrow three-story Victorians and brownstones with curved entries that started at the sidewalk and ended at wooden doors built in the early 1900s. He even loved the way the tangled lanes of interstate dove into town, dropping into the Lowry Tunnel and its tiled walls, then turning sharply to converge in the no-longer-trendy Uptown.

This was Elliot's first real experience with winter. He'd moved to Minneapolis only a few months ago. He'd told his upstairs neighbor he was a student before later admitting he was writing a book about her. The well-known detective Jude Fontaine. Neither of those was the main reason he'd come to town, but while he waited for things to play out, he planned to actually write that book. And not just about Jude.

Beside him, Ava Germaine was still holding his hand. They were skating fast around the section of the lake that had been cleared of snow. The polished area was lit with torches, the sidewalks bordered by ornate streetlamps. Quaint ones, the kind that had gone up in gentrified areas to give them a sense of order and to fight the taint left from a power-grid issue that had plunged the city into darkness almost two years ago.

Ava's blond hair flowed out behind her, and she was smiling at him, the Basilica of Saint Mary at her back, strings of fairy lights in the branches of bare trees, the scent of woodsmoke from a vendor's grill, fireworks booming and bursting into the sky. Big ones. Purple and white. Ava looked happy. If a stranger noticed her, they'd never guess her history, the terrible things she'd been through.

Theirs hadn't been the typical meeting. He'd contacted her about
an interview. At first, she'd said no, but he could be charming and
relentless—his super strengths—and she'd finally agreed. And now,
a month later, here they were. A conflict of interest, some might say.
He'd even asked himself if deep down it was really about snagging an
exclusive on the mother-and-daughter story. He didn't think so, but
maybe he was just fooling himself. Maybe he was the ass some people
accused him of being.

As Ava watched him, her smile abruptly faded. She shouted his
name, her mouth a circle, eyes wide.

He corrected his course in time to keep from crashing into another
couple. He let go of Ava's hand, and the two of them broke apart, the
space between them expanding while their arms remained extended. At
first it was poetic, the separation of mittens, especially since his mittens
had been knitted by Ava and offered to him shyly, as a Christmas present. He'd given her a gift certificate to a coffee shop because he hadn't
wanted to be too forward. He'd regretted that afterward.

The poetry ended.

He let out a yelp as he went airborne, coming down and smacking
the ice with teeth-jarring impact. The spectacle didn't stop there. He
shot across the ice like a spinning bowling ball. People shouted and
jumped out of the way. It took forever, hours it seemed, but if anybody
had clocked it, he'd have guessed seconds. His momentum slowed, and
he finally came to a full stop.

Somewhere in the process of hurtling across the ice, he'd turned
belly-down. His wool coat was tangled around his torso, and his bare
stomach was pressed against the frozen lake. Behind him, Ava shouted
his name again. He heard her skates slicing the ice, heard her pull to a
hard hockey stop. That's how damn good she was.

"I'm not that great of a skater," she'd told him earlier.

And now he wondered about the hand-holding. And her professing
to not be a good skater. A ploy? He hoped so.

Her daughter, Octavia, caught up with them. He could see she was trying not to laugh. He might be hurt. But he understood the urge to laugh. He felt a little like laughing himself.

Octavia was an amazing kid. Not really a kid, almost twenty now, but she seemed younger. Some arrested development going on, he suspected. She'd been missing for three years, held against her will—a story not dissimilar to Jude's, except that in Octavia's case it was Jude's father who'd abducted her, the same thing he'd done to many other girls. After her rescue, Octavia had dropped back into a pretty normal life, but he knew that Ava, a former psychologist, was concerned she was in denial.

"You okay?" Ava was bent over him, her voice full of some really nice concern that didn't take the edge off his embarrassment.

He let his forehead fall to the ice. "I'm fine." Breathless, he propped himself on his elbows, hoping the gathering crowd would ungather as he took a few seconds to recover. He glanced at the curious faces, then back down at the ice just under his chin.

And saw a face looking up at him.

He blinked and rubbed a mittened fist against the ice, wondering if he'd hit his head during the fiasco, wondering if his breath had created a design on the ice that looked like a face.

He fumbled in his coat pocket, pulled out his phone, which thankfully had survived his slide across the lake, turned on the flashlight app, and shined it into the frozen ice. He hadn't imagined it. Someone was trapped in the ice.

Elliot's initial urge was to scramble away. Instead, he kept his arms braced over the face, not wanting Ava or Octavia to see it. They didn't need to add something like this, whatever *this* was, to mental wounds that were still healing.

He craned his neck to see mother and daughter standing there. Ava's hand was extended in an offer to help him up. Beyond her shoulder, a few concerned bystanders still stood, although thankfully most of them had dispersed once they realized he wasn't injured. He swiveled to sit cross-legged on the ice, covering the face with his ass.

"Just need to catch my breath." He worked to make his voice sound confident. He waved his hand at the people behind Octavia. *Nothing to see here.* The remaining crowd skated away, their conversations drifting behind them.

"He really hit hard," someone said. Another person laughed, but it was a laugh of sympathy, or so he hoped.

But the body.

The face had looked like it belonged to a child, or at least a young kid. And was it a body at all? Maybe it was just a mask. A dummy. Some sick joke. That would be a pretty good joke, he had to admit.

Octavia gave him a grin and skated off.

When it was obvious Ava wasn't going anywhere, Elliot tried to wave her away too. "I need a moment alone." Behind her, a particularly impressive firework shot into the night sky. It was white, with trails that exploded into stars and fell to the earth. "Go with Octavia. I'll be here waiting when you make a round."

With a puzzled look on her face, she nodded, turned, and skated away.

As soon as she was a good distance away, he rolled back to his stomach, engaged his flashlight app, and pointed it at the ice again. The light bounced back at him. He held the phone to one side. Now the face, if it was really a face, was a little more visible. Yes, it looked like a child.

He had to call Jude, but she didn't know he'd been hanging around with the Germaines. She might not take it well.

He called her. When she didn't answer, he sent a text.

I think I found a dead body. Loring Park skating rink. Come quick.

CHAPTER 3

Three-year-old Alice squirmed on Jude's lap, rearranging herself for the third time as she struggled to stay awake. Why were kids and animals attracted to people who just wanted to be left alone?

"She likes you," Chief Vivian Ortega said with a smile.

Vivian had dressed up for the evening in a sparkly red dress that looked good with her dark skin and red lipstick. Jude suspected her boss was trying to bring some sense of the ordinary into Jude's life by inviting her to participate in these family functions. She appreciated the concern, but being in the middle of such tradition made Jude feel even more alienated. This was not her world. She was more comfortable either in her small apartment with her cat, or working a high-priority homicide case. Either shut off or plugged in. There was no in-between for her.

Small talk was excruciating, and exposure to lives that were either lies or would never be for her created a dull, hollow ache in her belly. Better to stay away from reminders of the different path her life could have taken. Worse still were the reminders that people wanted her to have more, wanted to help her heal, reset her somehow. That wasn't going to happen. Jude had come to terms and wished everybody else would too.

Her partner, Detective Uriah Ashby, was one of the only people who didn't try to force her out of her comfort zone. And yet . . . What about tonight? Had he ever really planned to come?

The evening at the Ortega house was supposed to have included Uriah, but he'd canceled at the last minute, no excuse given. She'd been reluctantly okay with an evening spent with Vivian, Vivian's husband, two tolerable kids, and two dogs, because Uriah would have been there to take up the bulk of the socialization so she could hang back. She'd seen him around kids. He was great with them. Instead, she'd found herself helping with snacks and playing Pictionary. Jude's bad drawings had elicited much hilarity. Children liked to laugh. She didn't remember that about childhood.

A real Christmas tree with handmade decorations stood in front of the window, a gas fireplace put out heat on one side of the room, and mulled wine and popcorn waited on the table beside Jude's chair. Eight-year-old Joseph lay on a sleeping bag in the middle of the floor, coloring as he struggled to stay awake for the ball drop. Alice, her small head tucked into the crook of Jude's arm, smelled like strawberries, probably from the brightly colored bottle of shampoo Jude had noticed on the edge of the tub. She wore pink snowflake-print flannel pajamas and had bare feet, even though Vivian had told her to put her slippers back on.

Alice patted Jude's cheek. Her hand was so small and soft. "I like you."

Jude's breath caught, and her muscles tensed. How did a person respond to such a straightforward statement? With the distilled truth? *You make me uncomfortable, but I like the smell of your hair?* That was probably the best choice.

Jude looked up to see Vivian waiting raptly for her reaction. Even she knew that her child had pushed too much and too fast. They were all rescued by the vibration of Jude's phone.

Thank God.

Jude checked the screen.

I think I found a dead body. Loring Park skating rink. Come quick.

For most people, the word *body* would have been the star of the text. For Jude, it was the word *think*, and her downstairs neighbor's uncertainty about whether he'd found a body. She texted Elliot back, asking for more information. After a couple of minutes with no reply, she slipped Alice off her lap and said, "I'm going to have to go."

"You'll miss midnight!" the child said.

"That's okay." Jude hoped she didn't appear too relieved. "I've seen midnight before."

Alice stomped away, then dramatically tumbled onto the couch, arms at her sides.

Vivian rolled her eyes and walked Jude to the door, retrieving her coat from the closet and handing it to her. Jude slipped into it and tugged her black stocking cap from a pocket.

"Homicide?" Vivian asked.

"Not sure." Jude pulled on a pair of black gloves. "The text was from my neighbor. He thinks he might have found a body in Loring Park."

"Might?"

"My reaction too. I'll check it out and let you know."

"I'm sorry about Alice," Vivian said. "She's usually shy and doesn't have much to do with people she doesn't know."

"Maybe she pegged me as harmless."

"Trustworthy, more likely."

Not long ago, Vivian had apologized for not trying harder to find Jude when she'd been kidnapped. For three years, everyone had thought she was dead. Jude would have thought the same thing, and she blamed no one. But ever since the apology, she could see Vivian was subtly trying to fix things. It also explained why she'd allowed Jude back on the force so soon after her escape. She'd wanted to make things right,

wanted Jude to have some normalcy. But a homicide detective's existence would never be normal. Vivian tried and was doing a good job
with her own life, but she wasn't working scenes. The crimes weren't as
personal, and that was a good thing.

Outside in her car, Jude called Elliot rather than attempting another
text. He picked up, sounding surprised to hear from her.

Had his message been a joke? "Are you drunk?" she asked. If so,
he'd gotten her out of an uncomfortable evening. She could thank him
for that.

"Nope."

When he didn't elaborate or drop into an explanation, she prodded,
"I got your text."

"I think I found a dead body." His voice was low. She imagined him
cupping a hand over his cell phone for privacy.

"Why are you whispering?"

"I don't want Octavia to hear."

Octavia? It wasn't a very common name. "Octavia Germaine?"

"I've been hanging out with Ava." Talking fast, stammering a little,
sounding out of breath. "Both of them. I've been hanging out with
both of them."

"Is this for your book?" She pulled from the curb and began heading in the direction of Loring Park. The car she was driving was over
ten years old but new to her. She'd found it listed in a neighborhood
Facebook group. Elderly owner, stored in a garage for years. Low mile-
age, smelled like mothballs, heater wasn't the greatest, but it had been
cheap, and it got her from point A to B. But she missed riding her
motorcycle, and she was counting the days until it was warm enough
to get it back on the street. "Because I *really* don't like that."

A long pause. "I've interviewed them both."

She didn't know Elliot well, but what she did know wasn't reassur-
ing. He was an opportunist, and he would lie when it benefited him.

She didn't think he was an evil person, didn't think he was dangerous, but he always seemed to be working an angle.

"This has nothing to do with you," he said. "Not your business."

If you boiled it down, he was right, but Jude had saved Octavia's life, and finding her had cracked open the case against Jude's father. They had a connection, and Jude didn't want to see any man take advantage of the girl's trust again. "It *does* have to do with me," she said. "Especially since I'm going to guess you used my name to get a foot in the door. I know they weren't granting interviews. I even advised them not to."

His lack of response was telling.

She noticed she was coming upon her exit and realized the conversation had sidetracked her. She got his exact location and said, "Be there in five minutes."

At Loring Park, she found a spot to leave her car and strode toward the festivities, perusing the area as she walked. Hundreds of people crowded the sidewalks and skating rink. Finally spotting Elliot, Octavia, and Ava, she took a path across the ice that would intercept with theirs; her stride, while awkward on the slick surface, never wavered.

It struck her that the three of them looked like a family: smiling and talking while skating—the women, gracefully; Elliot a little more awkwardly, in the middle, his dark hair and medium skin tone contrasting with the two blonds. The speed with which he'd infiltrated their world was alarming.

Jude turned and stood with her legs braced and arms crossed, waiting for them to catch up. Elliot spotted her first, smiled, then flinched. Her face must have reflected more than the blankness she'd perfected during her years of imprisonment, because that flinch caused him to flounder and fall. Now, as he struggled back to his feet, she felt like a bully.

Beside him, Octavia and Ava cut to a stop, both women making small sounds of dismay at his accident while displaying near giddiness at Jude's unexpected appearance.

Her concern about Elliot was justified. He'd spied on her and had even taken secret photos of her, lining his bedroom walls with them, all the while pretending to be a photography student at the University of Minnesota when he was really a journalist working on a book about Jude. He'd planned to call it *The Detective Upstairs* or some such thing. Jude didn't care any longer what he said about her. He could write his story. But she did care what he said about innocent victims.

"Leave Octavia out of your book."

Ava looked at her in confusion, then at Elliot. "I thought you were friends," she said. To Jude: "He told me you two were friends."

Ah, a twist. Ava *liked* him liked him. That put another spin on things. "We live in the same apartment building." Jude certainly wouldn't say they were friends. Then again, she didn't know if she'd say that about anybody. Was Ava her friend? Octavia? Vivian? Uriah? She wasn't sure she felt comfortable thinking of any of them that way.

"Everything okay here?" a man asked, coming up behind them. He had the city logo—the Minneapolis skyline—on his jacket. Probably someone hired for the event. "Do I need to call the cops?"

Looking away from Elliot, Jude said, "I *am* the cops."

That announcement was followed by a surprised mutter and her name spoken under the man's breath. She'd been recognized. It happened more than she liked. She was tall, which meant she stood out. Combine that with her short white hair, partially covered with the knit cap at the moment, and a face that had been blasted on television screens around the world, and it was inevitable. Didn't mean she was okay with it, but she'd learned to block out the whispers and not make eye contact.

Elliot was struggling to stay in one place. She grabbed his arm, pulling him away from Ava and Octavia until they were out of earshot. "What about your message?"

He told her what had happened, then skated off, searching for the spot where he'd fallen. Jude followed on foot, feeling skeptical. The ice was dark; the torches around the perimeter of the skating area created a dancing light that confused the eyes.

She caught up with Elliot as he dropped to his knees and pulled out his phone, turning on the flashlight. "Here." He motioned Jude closer but told Ava and Octavia, who'd followed in their wake, to stay back. He was trying to protect the two women from seeing what might or might not be something disturbing. Jude would give him points for that.

A sudden barrage of fireworks lit up the sky, and skaters and people on the sidewalk cheered. Midnight. Jude wondered if Alice was still awake.

The area turned almost as bright as day, giving them a clearer view. Jude crouched down. Another large detonation, this one over the lake. Elliot shifted the glare of his flashlight.

Staring up at Jude was indeed a face.

The eyes were open, the mouth wide. It looked like a child, but it was hard to tell. The body lay maybe six inches below the surface, the ice itself cloudy and discolored. Was it a drowning victim? Had someone fallen through the ice when it wasn't yet safe to walk or skate on? People lost their lives every year in lakes all over the state. Her next thought was that it might not be a real body at all. Given the location, such a public place, it could very well be a hoax perpetrated by some talented students from a nearby art school.

Jude pulled out her phone. Even though there was zero proof they were dealing with a homicide or even a human, she called her partner. Uriah answered on the second ring.

She told him about the body. "The age of the possible victim appears to be anywhere from ten to fourteen. But it's hard to get a decent visual with the cloudy ice."

"Could it be a prank?"

"That's what I'm wondering. If so, someone is very talented."

"I'll be right there." She was about to disconnect when he asked, "How was the evening at Ortega's?"

"I had to play something called Apples to Apples, and Pictionary."

He laughed. She wouldn't even mention the child climbing onto her lap.

"Hold off calling anybody else," he said. "I'm on my way."

After disconnecting, she broke the news to Ava and Octavia. The women took it well. She was afraid nothing could deeply shock them anymore. Jude had this unfounded theory that once something unusual happened in your life, you became a magnet for more. There was no escaping it. That's what Elliot didn't understand. They were past shielding.

Uriah arrived fifteen minutes later, dressed for cold weather in a hip-length wool coat, gray scarf around his neck, and a gray knit cap pulled down over his dark curly hair. New accessories—possibly Christmas gifts, Jude noted.

She met him on the sidewalk, handing him the coffee she'd purchased from a nearby vendor as they moved toward the possible crime scene. Fireworks were still going off, but they were no longer part of the city display. These were private citizens shooting rockets from backyards and apartment balconies, some just as impressive as the ones she'd seen earlier. Jude hated the noise of fireworks, especially the mortars that created deep thuds in her chest, thuds that felt too close to fear, but she liked the visual displays.

"We're taking off," Elliot said. Ava and Octavia were walking away, side by side, Ava's arm around her daughter. "They're both a little freaked out, understandably."

Maybe they weren't immune after all.

The fewer people at the scene, the better. Right now there were no spectators nearby, but that could change if their actions drew too much curiosity. Jude nodded, thinking she'd question Elliot tomorrow about his intentions when it came to the two women. Set him straight if she had to. Warn them if she had to.

Uriah pulled out a Maglite and crouched over the body. He had the same problem with glare. It was like shining a light at a window. It just bounced back. And the brighter the light, the worse the bounce. By holding it at an angle, he was able to bring the white face into murky focus, enough to make out eyes that were opaque, a phenomenon sometimes seen postmortem. He finally clicked off the light and got to his feet.

Their actions were drawing attention. Uriah pulled out his phone and called Dispatch. "I'm going to need a couple of officers to guard a potential crime scene until morning," he said. "Make sure they're dressed warm. They're going to be outside. Detective Fontaine and I are waiting. Location: middle of Loring Park." To Jude he said, "What's this called? Loring Park Lake?"

"Loring Lake, but some people call it Loring Pond." It was big, but smaller than many of the other city lakes. Or maybe someone had simply thought *pond* sounded quainter than *lake*.

Uriah passed the info to the dispatcher. "That's right. Tell them to drive their vehicles across the sidewalk and onto the ice. They'll see us."

He pocketed his phone and took a drink of coffee. "What was your Pictionary word?"

"Horse."

"That should have been easy."

"It wasn't. The big guess was monkey."

He laughed discreetly. She waited for him to tell her why he hadn't come to the party, but he didn't.

He'd been sick not that long ago, and it had scared her. It had caused that sonic boom in her chest, that drop in her belly. She hoped his absence had nothing to do with his health, but it wasn't her business. Maybe he'd had a date. That new scarf . . .

Two police cars pulled across the frozen surface.

Yellow tape went up, marking a small perimeter, while Uriah gave the officers instructions. Then, to Jude, he said, "Let's call it a night. Tomorrow we'll contract with an ice cutter. We'll get the crime-scene team here, although there will be little for them to do but document the location. Once the body's in the morgue, once we find out what we're dealing with, we can continue with evidence collection if need be."

Jude planned to be out at first light. Maybe she could pick up on something then. She was good at reading body language, sometimes even the body language of the dead.

CHAPTER 4

The ice cutters arrived early in a convoy of heavy-duty trucks and a semi, streetlights glowing as snow began to fall. An hour ago, when Jude checked her weather app, she'd been dismayed to see a blizzard in the forecast, the brunt of it expected to hit tomorrow and continue over a period of days. There was a slight chance the front could work its way south, missing them, but since snow was already coming down, she wasn't feeling optimistic.

She and Uriah had arrived at approximately the same time, getting out of their cars, collars turned up against the flurries hitting the backs of their necks, and huddling under a streetlamp as if it could offer some warmth while they avoided eye contact with the press already on site with their cables and vans equipped with satellite dishes. The press were generally helpful in an investigation, but Jude had nothing to offer them right now other than what they already knew, social media having sounded the alert: a body in the ice that might or might not be a real person and that might or might not be a homicide. Everything was speculation at this point.

A man in brown canvas bib overalls and a red flannel shirt approached. Strapped to his insulated boots were metal crampons that rang out against the sidewalk. He was small, energetic, and introduced himself as Jerry "the Ice Man." "Third-generation ice harvester," he said.

"Been doing it my whole life, and I've found a lot of weird things. Dogs, deer, a wallet once, but a body is a first for me."

He was excited.

Jude had looked him up before leaving home. His company cut ice all winter, their biggest client being the Saint Paul Winter Carnival, where they harvested cubes from a lake up north and hauled them to the city for engineers, construction workers, and designers to build castles. It was a beautiful event, the magical combination of lights and clear ice something everyone should witness at least once.

Behind him, his crew waited inside idling diesel trucks. The semi was loaded with a single giant machine that looked something like a forklift with large tractor tires and a telescoping arm. It was strapped to the trailer bed, held down with chains as big around as an arm. Last night's celebration was over, and people had left behind a surprisingly small amount of trash that was already being collected by the event crew, who'd probably clocked in early to beat the storm.

The three of them walked across the ice, Jerry at an advantage due to the grip of the crampons, Jude and Uriah taking care with each step. The cops on site moved back, ready to leave after the long night but reluctant to miss the extraction.

Without the glare of flashlights, it was easier to see the face today, but the surface was still cloudy. Jerry let out a low whistle and said, "I can polish that up with a blowtorch once we get the block cut out." Seeing their skepticism, he followed up with, "So you can get a better look at what's inside. That's how we make ice for the castles transparent. It's like cleaning a foggy windshield."

He signaled for one of his crew to join him with a truck. From the bed, Jerry pulled out an auger, started the gas engine, and used the cutting tool to test the thickness of the ice. "Twenty-two inches," he announced, pleased. "That should hold the Lull." He pointed to the machine with the telescopic arm on the back of the semi, made a call to the crew onshore, and moments later the chains Jude had spotted earlier were clanging as they prepared to unload.

"Should?" Uriah asked.

"It usually stays onshore, so we're in untested territory."

Crime-scene investigators arrived. It was pretty obvious they thought their presence unnecessary, and it probably was. They'd rather be home, or in a coffee shop preparing for their day, but they couldn't relax protocol until they knew what they were dealing with.

Orange earplugs in, protective eyewear on, Jerry cranked up a small machine his boys had also unloaded. This one looked like a large tiller with a round blade. It took him a few tries to get it going. It coughed and spit black smoke before settling into a smooth rumble. Jerry worked alone, carefully and steadily cutting far from the body. Ice flew, mixing with the snow that was falling harder now. As he worked, smaller blocks were removed to free up space around the larger block while Uriah watched like a nervous grandmother. They needed to remove enough to get the actual lifting mechanism into the water.

The initial blocks were small enough for his crew to remove with giant metal tongs, two men grabbing and heaving them from the water, sliding the cubes across the ice. Once they had an opening slightly larger than a car, it was time for the star of the show, the Lull forklift waiting on the shore.

It crept across the ice, stopping a good ten feet from where the solid ice had been cut out to expose water. The hydraulic arm whined and telescoped, the operator inside the cab working the controls while Jerry used hand signals on the ground, the men pausing often to evaluate the position.

The phone in Jude's pocket vibrated. It was Elliot. Busy as she was, she answered.

"I'm over here, and there's a cop who won't let me come to the scene."

She turned and eyed the shoreline, spotting Elliot giving her a big wave, mittens on his hands, a uniformed cop standing next to him. He was a civilian, but he'd found the body. "Give him your phone." He did, and she told the cop to let him pass. A moment later, Elliot was ducking under yellow tape and moving awkwardly across the ice, camera around his neck.

The snow was coming down probably an inch an hour, making the ice even slicker. When Elliot reached her side, he tugged off his mittens with his teeth before uncapping his lens. She frowned, wondering where this photo would end up, and considered telling him he couldn't take pictures, but he was a good photographer and his images might be helpful.

He saw her looking at his camera. "I'm not going to sell them."

The machine was revving up again, the arm bobbing. She held her breath as it dipped into the square of open water. Jerry had calculated well, but it was close. With agonizingly slow speed, the giant metal arm sank into the darkness. Jerry shouted and held up a hand, then the fork moved forward, slid under the cube encasing the body, and scooped it out. The operator reversed until the ice block was no longer over open water. A cheer went up, including people waiting behind the police tape.

The operator lowered the fork, and Jerry produced the blowtorch he'd mentioned earlier. Using a small flint igniter that he pulled from a front pocket of his overalls, he lit the torch, adjusted the flame, and gave the top of the ice a delicate blast, melting away a thin layer of opaque ice. Shutting off the torch, he wiped the surface with his jacket sleeve, made a sound of quiet surprise, and stepped back so Jude and Uriah could move closer.

White eyes, like a fish with freezer burn, looked up at them. She was certain he was real. A boy, probably a few years older than Joseph, Vivian Ortega's son. Jude sensed a dismay in Uriah that mirrored her own. All death was hard, but the death of a child was especially demanding, and they had to hide their reactions and emotions from the watching public.

Jerry's trick of polishing the surface of the ice had helped clarify the face. Jude stared, trying to read something, anything from it. Maybe how much the boy had suffered, or how aware he'd been of dying . . .

"What's it telling you?" The voice was full of sarcasm.

Jude felt a jolt of surprise and looked up to see a man with a press pass clipped to his coat. She wasn't sure why the press had it in for her. Maybe because she hadn't granted interviews after she'd saved Octavia's life five months ago. Behind him, an assistant braced a handheld camera on one shoulder. This would be on the evening news. Somehow, maybe when all eyes had been on the block of ice being lifted from the lake, the two of them had gotten past the perimeter.

In the early days, Uriah had tried to protect her, cautioning that she keep her observations about the dead to herself. But things like that got out. Maybe someone had caught a whiff of her unconventional skill at a crime scene, or maybe one or more cops had witnessed it and shared the story with others, possibly laughing about it. Some reporters had even gone so far as to call her the "Body Reader," which was another kind of nonsense. She had no skill other than acute observation, and even that could fail her—and certainly *had* failed her and continued to fail her, especially when it came to socialization and relationships. But lately she'd found the lore of it could come in handy during interrogations. It made suspects nervous, so she didn't openly dispute it.

Ignoring the falling snow, she looked directly into the camera. With no expression that might hint at what was going on inside her head, she said, "We'll be holding a press conference once we have information to give you. Until then, I hope you'll refrain from sensationalism and speculation. And we'd like you to move back behind the barrier."

The guy stepped in the direction of the yellow tape, pausing for one last complaint. "He's not even press." He pointed to Elliot, who was snapping away, maneuvering around the block of ice, crouching, getting images from the side and top. Not a bad thing. And because he lived one floor down from her, his photos would be easier to confiscate as evidence if she had to. She and Uriah would take their own, but Elliot's would be better.

The wind increased, snow stinging her face, the sudden gale bringing a sense of urgency to the retrieval and transport. Jerry gave another of his hand signals that all looked the same to Jude. The forklift revved, the back-up alarm beeped, and the machine began a slow and careful crawl across the ice, returning to shore. Deep down, she'd expected a prank. But now she knew the forklift held something precious, most likely somebody's child.

The rest of the process went quickly. The block of ice was deposited carefully on the back of the flatbed, then attached with nylon straps and ratcheted tight.

"I'll follow it to the morgue," Uriah said with a somber tone.

Jude cast a glance around, spotted Elliot, waved for him to wait for her. "Go ahead," she told Uriah. "I'll meet you back at the office."

They broke apart.

News cameras were rolling, most focused on the departing trucks, but a couple zoomed in on Jude. She pulled her collar higher, shoved her hands in her pockets, and caught up with Elliot, who stood below the overhang of the small stone cottage, not in use today, where skaters warmed up. Park workers were unloading orange barricades and cones, placing them around the gaping hole left by the Lull. The remaining ice blocks stood in a semicircle, creating a strange alienscape. If the cold weather continued, the hole would be safe to skate on in a week or so.

"I'd like to see the photos you took," she said.

Elliot leaned over his camera to protect it from the falling snow and turned the viewing screen toward her.

"That one." She pointed to the clearest image of the face. "Send it to me right away so I can run it through our facial-recognition programs."

She hoped to get a hit from Minnesota Missing and Unidentified Persons Clearinghouse or NamUs, the national database. "Also, I want to talk to you about Ava."

"There's nothing to discuss. I like her. And I think she likes me." He closed his camera and tucked it back in the case. "I'm not using them, if that's what you think."

It was, or at least it was her concern. "You aren't going to write about her?"

"I can't promise that. Not if I have her consent. But I wouldn't do it without giving her a chance to read it first and give me her okay."

That was at least something. Maybe she'd overreacted. Maybe seeing them all skating around, looking like a family, had hit her wrong. "Don't forget to email the photo to me."

Her mind shifted back to the man with the press pass—and she realized she'd gotten no sense of anything when looking at the body trapped in the ice. Nothing.

◆ ◆ ◆

At Headquarters, Jude checked her email. The image she'd told Elliot to send was there, along with several others he'd taken. She opened, then dragged, the clearest photo of the face into the Minnesota missing persons facial-recognition database. California had the highest number of unsolved missing children cases, over six hundred last she'd looked. Minnesota was somewhere in the middle of national statistics. Two minutes in and she had a hit. Not a solid match, but a lead. Sixty-five percent. Once a hundred percent match couldn't be found, the software began searching for similar features. Add an unclear photo to the mix, and results could be even more unpredictable.

She read the bio and history of the missing child, a boy named Shaun Ford. The more she read, the more she felt it was a false lead, that this was not the boy in the ice, but it was a lead all the same, and it needed to be checked out.

Uriah wasn't back from the morgue. She called his cell phone.

"Got an image hit," she told him when he answered.

"Missing person?"

"Yeah, but it's only sixty-five percent. And I think you'll find this interesting. It's for a boy who went missing from Minneapolis twenty years ago."

CHAPTER 5

Gail Ford had given birth to her son when she was thirty. The pregnancy had been hard, and she'd had to quit working the last trimester because the baby was sucking the life out of her. She spent three months in bed, reading and watching television while trying to tell herself everything would be okay.

He was born healthy, but Gail ended up losing her job. She tried not to resent him for it, and she told her husband they'd figure something out. She could stay home with her son while her husband worked, keep a closer eye on the baby, protect him from danger. Because if anybody knew about danger, it was Gail. The world was full of bad people doing bad things. But as aware as she was about raising a child in that world, she'd never imagined that *her* child would one day be another statistic, one of those kids who vanished into thin air.

Gail and her husband had been the prime suspects. She didn't blame the cops for that. It was common to suspect the parents, especially in their case. No witnesses. Nobody saw anything. She would have suspected her too. But she always felt she'd see Shaun again, even long after her husband left and eventually died. If the phone rang in the middle of the night, she'd reach for it with a sense of expectation combined with dread. She never lost the feeling that one day a voice on the other end would call her Mom.

Deep in her heart, she knew his story. He wasn't dead. Instead, he'd been clothed and fed and cared for by a stranger, who might have even pretended to be his real father, someone who might not have abused him. In her mind, she created a safe haven for him where he'd been loved and cherished. In that idealized place, someone had taken loving care of her boy. Maybe even better care than he would have gotten with her.

When the doorbell rang in the middle of a heavy snowstorm, she had a feeling today would be different. This might be it. This might be him returning home. Gail was no longer young, and she worried about what he'd think when he saw her again. She was sixty-one, and stress had aged her another several years. Vain of her to even care, but she did.

The peephole revealed not her son, but a man and a woman wearing dark clothes and looking like a couple of crows against the whiteness of the world. She opened the door. The man pulled out a badge.

"Mrs. Ford? I'm homicide detective Uriah Ashby." Just like somebody in an old movie, he flicked the leather case closed and tucked his badge away. "And this is my partner, Detective Jude Fontaine."

Homicide. That wasn't right. That didn't fit.

"We're hoping you might be able to help us," Detective Fontaine said. "I don't know if you've been following the case of the body found in the lake, but we have a few questions we'd like to ask you."

What did that have to do with her? "I saw something about it this morning."

"Keep in mind that what we're going to propose is a highly unlikely scenario," Detective Ashby said. "We're just following up on a lead, checking things off our list. We ran a photo of the person found in the ice through facial-recognition software and came up with a sixty-five percent match. Sixty-five is not proof of anything. It's just a chance."

"The match was my son?"

"Yes."

Her heart beat erratically while her mind struggled with the logic of the situation. "He's been gone twenty years. He would no longer be a child. He'd be thirty-one now. I thought the news said it was a child."

Over the years, the police had hired composite artists to age her son. They'd run images on local news and national programs. But even at that, it had always been hard to think of him as a young man rather than a child.

"I know this is hard," the female detective said as Gail motioned them in and closed the door. "But we're hoping you can help us, maybe eliminate the chance of the body belonging to your son." She produced an image from somewhere, large, in color. "It's not very clear due to the ice." *Jude Fontaine.* Gail knew who she was. Fontaine had her own sad story. So many sad stories.

Gail held the photo in her hands, her heart pounding, then said quietly, "I think it's him."

They seemed surprised by her answer, and why wouldn't they?

"I have to see him in person to know for sure." She passed the photo back.

"We have other ways to do this," Detective Fontaine said. "Other ways for you to ID a body. You don't have to physically be there."

"I want to. I have to. I've been waiting twenty years."

"At least let us drive you," Detective Ashby said.

She agreed, grabbing her coat.

"It's still snowing," Fontaine said. "You'll need boots."

Gail looked down and saw she was wearing house slippers. She laughed nervously, changed, and struggled to open the door. "It sticks when we get rain or snow." After some tugging, the male detective was finally able to open it.

In the car, Ashby behind the wheel, Fontaine explained a little more about the frozen lake and ice-skaters. She sat sideways so she could look over the seat at Gail. "Thank you for doing this," she added once she'd gotten Gail up to speed. "I know it can't be easy."

Detective Ashby turned off Chicago Avenue and pulled into the parking lot behind the morgue, which sat in the shadows of the downtown Minnesota Vikings' stadium. Snow was still falling, and a small garden tractor with a blade was trying to keep the sidewalk clear.

Outside the building, Detective Fontaine spoke into the intercom system and a door unlocked, letting them in. They stomped off snow, then moved down a brightly lit hallway, all the while Gail wondering if it could be true. Was it Shaun? Had he been dead this whole time?

She took notice of strange things, like thick white paint chipped off door latches, and cages over ceiling lights, and how Ashby's skin had an unhealthy pallor, how he had a red scar on his forehead and perspiration on his upper lip. Suddenly they were in a metal-lined room, so cold their breath was a mingled cloud. There was a large stainless-steel table with wheels in the center, positioned over a floor drain. Drip, drip, drip. On top of the table was a block of ice. Inside the ice was a dark form.

Gail let out a little gasp, and her feet felt like they were nailed to the floor. But she wanted, needed to see. As if understanding, Fontaine gripped her elbow and gently urged her forward until Gail was looking down into the ice.

And she saw him.

Saw that face, his face.

"I don't believe it," she whispered, putting a shaking hand to her mouth. She let out a sob and bent forward, trying to get as close as she could to the body, pressing her own face against the ice. "I'm so sorry," she told him. "So sorry."

"Mrs. Ford?"

Time had become unimportant, and she gradually realized Fontaine was trying to get her attention. Gail looked at her.

"Do you think this might be your son?" the detective asked.

"It's him. It's my little boy."

Ashby made a sound of surprise and dismay, turned, and left the room. Gail thought about how pale he'd looked earlier and wondered about his strange exit, but she didn't care, really. That had nothing to do with her.

"This is a highly charged situation," Fontaine said. "Sometimes hope can make us believe things because we want to believe them so badly. Do you understand what I'm saying?"

Gail nodded.

"I'm sorry to tell you that we can't just take your word for it," Fontaine said softly, apologetically. "A visual ID is only part of the protocol." Her words might have seemed too blunt if not for the softness of her eyes and the compassion in her face. People like her were more in tune to the heartbreak of others. She understood pain and suffering.

"This is my child." Gail looked at the boy again, reached out, and ran her hand across the ice. "It wasn't supposed to end like this."

CHAPTER 6

Jude watched the mother stroke the ice with a gesture that managed to convey both longing and regret. Jude was sure that Gail Ford would have swept the child into her arms if she'd been able to. She gave the woman a few moments, then touched her shoulder, pulling her back from her grief, enough for her to understand that they needed to exit the cold locker even though she wanted to hold vigil, stay with the body. Impossible, even under normal conditions.

"I don't want to leave him," Gail said. She was standing up straight now, looking at Jude.

"You should go home while we work to establish the child's identity."

"Why do you need further proof? I've told you he's my son."

"You haven't seen him in twenty years," Jude reminded her gently.

"Haven't seen him in twenty years?" Gail's voice rose. "I've seen him every day and every moment of my life since he vanished."

Sometimes the dead or missing could be more real than the people right in front of you. Jude chose her next words carefully, hoping to avoid coming across as unsympathetic or patronizing. "We can't positively ID the body without proof from dental records, fingerprints, or DNA. Maybe all three. As you are probably aware, DNA is rarely collected for missing persons cases. And it would be hard and probably impossible to get any from old belongings. Right now, all we can do is follow protocol. Until then, the body is still considered a John Doe. But I promise to keep you updated as things progress. And you can call me if you have any questions or think of anything you'd like to tell us." Jude knew this wasn't the outcome any mother wanted, and a positive ID would bring Gail a fresh and raw kind of pain. "And going forward, I'd like to hope you can find at least a little bit of peace from the closure this will bring."

After Gail's DNA was collected, she was sent home from the morgue in a cab with an important assignment. Arrange for the transfer of her son's dental records, which a quick phone call had determined were still archived. The release would require contacting her dentist and signing consent forms, much faster than a court order. From there, Shaun Ford's X-rays could be emailed to the medical examiner's office, where Jude and Uriah would enlist the assistance of a forensic odontologist.

Once Gail was gone, Jude and Uriah returned to the walk-in cooler, this time with Chief Medical Examiner Ingrid Stevenson. The compartment was unusually large, the morgue a repurposed food-storage facility. It had been a great idea years ago—a single walk-in cooler that could store several bodies at once. Now it was no longer enough space. They were up to 1,400 autopsies a year. Almost everyone, from the mayor to morgue interns, agreed the facility had outgrown itself.

"I've called in a forensic paleoradiologist from Duluth who'll head to the cities when the snow lets up," Ingrid said. "According to the forecast, it looks like there'll be an eight-hour window between bands, so he's packed and waiting for that break." She bent close, hands in her pockets as she tried to peer through the ice, then straightened with a sigh. "A frozen body presents a multitude of challenges. None involve speed. The body has to be thawed slowly, over days and in stages. The paleoradiologist will help with that. His specialty is actually mummies, but he was instrumental in helping to identify a couple found in a northern lake a few years ago." She also related an incident of a man

who'd fallen off a boat into near-freezing water only to float to the surface perfectly preserved two years later.

There was nothing to do but wait, so Jude and Uriah left to head
back to the Homicide Department and upload reports. Outside, people
were holding vigil even though it was snowing. Battery-operated candles lined a low wall, along with bouquets of frozen flowers. Reporters
were set up in vans, waiting for the announcement.

"You might as well go home," Uriah said, repeating what Jude had
told Gail. "We don't expect to have a positive ID for days."

A few people let out a groan, but most seemed relieved to be able
to get out of the cold.

Back at Homicide, their colleagues were talking about the brunt of
the winter storm still heading their way. "Have you seen the footage?"
someone asked. "Snow up to the rooftops. People in South Dakota
stranded without food or water, no electricity. National Guard has been
called in."

Four hours later, long after most of the day shift had gone home
and the lights had automatically dimmed for evening, a coworker
announced that the parking ramp had closed due to the snow. "No
vehicles in or out, and the buses are going to quit running soon."

Jude grabbed her jacket off the back of her chair. "I have to get
home and feed my cat." Strange words, considering a few short months
ago she'd refused to risk any form of attachment.

Unable to retrieve her car, huddled under a streetlamp as she waited
for the bus, Jude was reminded of a similar snowy night when she'd
escaped from captivity almost a year ago. While in that intolerable situation, kept in a cell in the dark, she'd clung to the hope that there would
be better days ahead. Maybe not tomorrow or next week, but somewhere in her future. She wondered if that small spark of hope would
have continued to burn if she'd known these were the better days.

CHAPTER 7

The woman behind the wheel had hoped to beat the worst of it, but by the time she got the boy in the car, the snow was coming down so hard she could barely see out the windshield. She adjusted the vents and turned the heat all the way up.

With the car running, she slipped out to swipe at the snow. It was heavy and wet, the temperature around thirty degrees. She cleaned off the wiper blade, just on her side. By the time she was done, her gloves were soaked through. She pulled them off and tossed them in the back seat, then settled herself behind the wheel.

"Can I make a snowman?" the boy asked. He'd managed to buckle himself in while she was dealing with the wiper.

"No." He always asked that whenever he saw snow. She'd let him try a few times while she sat inside the house, smoking. He didn't know he had to start with a ball and roll it until it was big. She didn't bother to tell him. His snowmen were always small, just piles, really. But he didn't care. He was one of the happiest kids she'd ever been around. One time she even gave him a carrot for a nose, and he'd shoved it into the pile, then jumped up and down in excitement like it was the best damn day of his pathetic little life.

"It's dark. I can make a snowman in the dark, can't I? Please?"

Dark was the only time she let the boy go outside anymore. She'd learned her lesson about that fast. Early on, she'd taken him with her to public places, in the bright light of day, especially when he was an infant, figuring nobody would notice them. Wrong. Babies attracted attention.

And then one time in a department store, she almost ran into someone from a nearby farm, a woman she knew from church. That close call had been it for her. She decided it was best to leave him in the care of a boyfriend when she went out. But in truth, the kid was better off by himself. She'd learned that pretty fast too. She didn't have the best taste in men. So after the boyfriends didn't work out, she'd leave once the kid was asleep, and she'd usually get back before he woke up. But a few times she'd stepped into the house to hear him screaming at the top of his lungs, rattling his cage. Good thing nobody lived very close to them.

After being almost spotted that one time, she started driving far away to shop for anything related to children, like clothing and food kids liked to eat. She didn't buy much. If anybody asked, she could always say it was for a relative. No more toys. No books. He'd never even seen a doctor as far as she knew, not even at birth. Luckily he was a pretty healthy kid. Maybe because he hadn't been exposed to many germs. But sometimes she felt bad for him, and a few times she'd even taken him to a park to swing in the middle of the night.

"Stars, Nana! Stars!" he'd said like he was seeing magic for the first time.

"That's right, Boy. Stars."

He didn't have a name when he came to her, and she was told she could give him one, but she'd always just called him Boy. He didn't care, and it was better that way. Made it so she didn't feel as close to him in case the time ever came to set him free.

Like now.

He was a decent kid, and she'd probably miss him for a while. But her husband and loser boyfriends were long gone, and the guy who'd paid her to take care of the boy was dead. She couldn't afford to keep him anymore. Just the way it was. She'd been planning this awhile. It wouldn't be hard, and she was confident it would be okay. The boy wouldn't be able to tell anybody anything. Where he lived, who he lived with. Nana—that was all.

She'd considered and even attempted to kill him. Put him in a tub and held him down. She'd gotten close to finishing him off, but at the last minute she'd been unable to make herself hold him under the water long enough to do the trick. She'd started to shake and maybe even cry a little, to her shame.

"I don't want a bath," he started saying whenever she suggested it now. He'd cry, and she'd let it go. She couldn't remember when he'd last had a bath, poor kid. And then she'd come up with this plan. Nobody would be able to connect him to her. He was a blank slate, with no birth history and no medical records. No anything. He had no past. As far as anybody else was concerned, he didn't exist.

She'd deliberately chosen tonight. *Genius,* she thought. The snow would cover a lot of sins. Her make and model of car. Her plates. Not many people on the roads. Nobody out. Nobody to see her. It was a damn good idea.

As she drove into Minneapolis from the south, the city looked magical. She took Interstate 35 to the Crosstown, then the Cedar Avenue exit to an area called Powderhorn. Luckily, the GPS on her phone took her straight to the building she was looking for. It was dark, the street was empty, her wipers beating the window to death. She didn't pull to the curb, because the snow was deeper there, and she didn't want to risk getting stuck. God, that would mess things up for the rest of her life. So she stayed in the tracks someone else had made and put the car in park.

"See that door?" She pointed to the brick apartment building with the single light above the entry.

"Uh-huh." He was so little his feet didn't touch the floor.

"I want you to walk to that door and open it. Go inside and wait in there until someone comes."

"Not you?"

"Not me." Truth be told, she felt a little saintly and generous letting him go like this. He had a chance this way. To be somebody, to have a life outside the walls of her house.

"Where you going?" he asked. "Shopping?"

"Yeah, shopping. Can you wait? For as long as you have to?"

"I can, Nana."

She quizzed him. "What did I say?"

"Wait for you by the door."

Let him think she was coming back. "That's right."

She unfastened his seat belt, then reached across and opened the passenger door. Flakes swirled in. He giggled in delight. The snow was level with the floorboard. She had to get the hell out of there. "Go on, now." She briefly thought about giving him a hug, but that was a stupid idea. Where had it even come from? She'd never hugged him, not in the four years he'd been with her.

He slid out and stood there. She shooed him away. "Go on. Hurry!"

He turned and stopped, his back to her. Then he started walking. She closed the door and lowered the passenger window, the action cleaning the glass so she could see him. He looked so little in front of the big building. So little trudging through snow that was much deeper than his knees.

She'd planned to wait until he reached the entry, but she spotted headlights coming her direction. She put the car in gear and pulled away.

Taking care of the kid had been good, easy money while it had lasted. Sure, she'd had to learn to be thrifty. Shopping at the dollar store and Goodwill. Clipping coupons. But it had been worth it, not having to work anymore.

She considered circling the block to make sure the boy did what he'd been told, but that was a soft thing to do. What did she care, right? Not her boy, not her responsibility any longer. And he always obeyed her. He was a good kid.

Ten minutes into the drive home, she began to feel euphoric about unloading him. What a weight lifted from her. She was free. Fifteen minutes, and she had the radio blasting and was singing along to an Adele song.

A semi roared past her on the four-lane, the driver going too fast for conditions. She got sucked into his draft, then quickly released. She stopped wailing along with the radio, the moment ruined. She laid on the horn and threw the driver the finger even though he couldn't see her. That felt good for only a half second. She overcorrected, and the car began to slide.

Turn toward the skid.

She knew that, and she tried, but turning the wheel did nothing to change the direction of the vehicle as the twin beams of her headlights revealed a metal guardrail straight ahead. She hit it, the impact rocking her to her bones while metal shrieked against metal. Her seat belt pulled tight across her chest and the airbag inflated, hitting her in the face.

That wasn't the end of it. The car shot into the sky.

In that moment of flight, she thought everything might be okay. But with another jarring shudder, the car slammed to the ground, tires exploding, the vehicle rolling until it came to an abrupt halt, the seat belt digging into her waist as she hung upside down.

CHAPTER 8

Jude's bus made it a third of the way home before getting stuck. No amount of rocking back and forth, digging, or pushing by the passengers, Jude included, could unstick it. Belongings were collected and the riders disembarked, most with the intention of walking the rest of the way. Others spotted a café that was still open and aimed for the lights.

In front of the bus was a gridlock of cars also stuck in deep snow. It made sense for Jude to ask how someone like her, with reasonable intelligence, hadn't just remained at the police station. But she'd slept very little the night before, and it was true that her cat needed to be fed, and she really wanted to be alone in order to process the events of the past twenty-four hours. She could think better when she was by herself, in the solitude of her apartment. And she could recharge better when she was home. It had sort of made sense an hour ago, as long as the buses were running and streets were still open.

But the snow. The damn snow wasn't showing any sign of slowing. In fact, the wind was picking up, tunneling down streets, causing drifts to build quickly. And here they were, a handful of people without transportation; Jude was horrified at the prospect of offering strangers the use of her place to wait out the blizzard. "My apartment is about a mile away," she announced in a decent attempt to hide her reluctance to issue the invite. "If anybody needs a place to stay."

People looked down, mumbled thanks, and moved off.

Had they recognized her? Remembered that she'd killed her own father? Did they know a young girl had died in her apartment not long ago? It said a lot that they preferred a blizzard to her home. And yet she was relieved that none of them took her up on the offer.

"I hope you all have a place to go!" she shouted after the thinning crowd, making one final attempt. Because regardless of how she felt about company, she didn't want anybody to die tonight.

A man turned around. Walking backward, he said, "I'm heading for that bar." He pointed to a neon sign down the street. His knit cap was covered with a thick layer of snow. He was a big guy, and he'd pushed with the rest of them.

Another person: "Thanks, but I'm almost home."

She nodded and watched them disperse. Inside the bus, the driver sat behind the wheel, cell phone to her ear.

"What about you?" Jude asked through the open door.

The woman waved her on. "I'm staying! Plow is supposed to come through in another hour or two."

So Jude took off.

Head bent into the increasing wind, she trudged forward. The snow was almost to her thighs in spots, and walking was astonishingly hard, almost impossible. Back in the early 1900s, anthropologist Franz Boas claimed that Eskimos had dozens of words for the different forms of snow. She wondered what this form would be called. It was thick and heavy, almost like trying to walk through wet cement. There were times when she thought she must be almost home. She would squint through the whiteout, searching for a familiar landmark, only to find she'd barely gone a block. In her pocket, her phone vibrated, but she didn't check it.

Ten minutes into her journey, she was the only human left on the street. Businesses were closed, houses and apartment buildings dark and mysterious. Street-corner lights illuminated nothing but the immediate snowfall beneath the bulb.

Oddly enough, Jude felt her shoulders relax, felt the tension leave her. The snow, as deadly as it could be, created a buffer between herself and other people. And right now, this was her world. This beautiful hush. It kept everybody else away, and that was a good thing.

She took a moment to pause in the center of the street, breathing deeply, watching the snow fall. She thought a light might have flickered—an intrusion on her brief sense of calm. She shouldn't be afraid of a power outage. A power outage had saved her life. But she was aware enough of her own mind to know a blackout could trigger unwanted memories.

She trudged on, head down, while remaining aware of her surroundings. She picked out familiar landmarks and knew she had only a few blocks to go, when the silence was broken by a hum that grew louder until it finally stopped alongside her.

"Need a ride?" The question came from a man on a snowmobile dressed in full gear, his face hidden behind a shield.

Probably a Good Samaritan, but no. She would never get on or in a vehicle with a stranger. She told him she was okay, and he blasted away, searching for his next victim or person in need.

By the time she reached her apartment building, her leg muscles ached. A small and not very strong bulb illuminated the entry. Just below the light and etched into concrete was the year the dwelling had been constructed—1930. Within that alcove, snow had drifted high in front of the double glass doors.

She retrieved her key, thankful to be home, looking forward to tugging off her damp clothes, slipping into yoga pants and a sweatshirt, putting a frozen dinner in the microwave, and feeding Roof Cat.

A sudden nearby noise brought her to full alert.

It sounded like a whimper.

She fished out her phone and saw she had messages from Uriah, probably checking to see if she'd made it. She turned on the flashlight and passed the beam around the alcove. One of the drifts shifted, and she heard a repeat of the sound.

Animal?

She dragged her foot through the snow, breaking it down, uncovering a patch of fabric. Definitely not an animal. Maybe a homeless person. What an awful night to have no place to sleep. She dug quickly with her gloved hand, brushing snow away, aiming her light at the shape in the corner for a full reveal.

The figure in the corner was a child.

CHAPTER 9

Jude crouched beside the child. He or she whimpered again but was otherwise unresponsive. Speaking gently, she shook a small shoulder. Eyes opened and stared at her, a bottom lip trembled.

She didn't know much about kids. A boy? Maybe. Probably. This one could have been five. No, six. No, four. She had no idea. Too young to be on his own. That's all she did know.

She unlocked the entry door, propped it open with her leg, then scooped up the tiny human and carried him inside, brushing snow from him as she went. On the way to her apartment, she paused on the third floor and kicked at Elliot's door with a boot, shouting his name.

He appeared in jeans, a gray hooded sweatshirt, and slippers, his dark hair in a ponytail, eyes a little bleary.

"I need your help." Slightly out of breath, she shifted the boy and handed Elliot her keys. "I found a kid."

"Jesus."

Her apartment was on the top floor. He followed her up the remaining flight of stairs and unlocked her door. Inside, she put the snow-covered bundle on the couch and pulled back his hood, then tugged off her gloves to feel his face. Cold. No surprise there. His lips were tinged blue, but the eyes watching her were alert.

How long had he been there? Was he lost? Did he live in the building, or nearby? Had he wandered outside to play in the snow? Or maybe walked home from school and gotten disoriented?

She pulled off his mittens. "His hands look okay, I think." Dirty. The kind of dirt that took time to accumulate. She'd guess homeless or neglected. Or both. "I'm Jude, and this is Elliot." She untied his laces.

"Are you supposed to take off their boots?" Elliot asked. "I saw this show once where the guy's feet were frozen, and they took off his boot and—"

"Stop talking," Jude said in a calm, conversational voice. She didn't want to alarm their guest.

It seemed to take Elliot a moment to understand he'd been about to get graphic in front of a young child. "Oh, right."

She slowly pulled off the boots, dropping them to the floor. No socks. His feet were even filthier than his hands. She tested them. "Ice-cold."

Elliot made a sound of concern and hovered behind her.

Her place was small. Almost a year ago, she'd walked in with nothing but the few articles of clothing Uriah had brought to the hospital after her escape from captivity. It was interesting how belongings she used to care about meant nothing to her anymore. All she wanted was a secure space, privacy, and a bed. Nothing else really mattered. Nobody above her, one bedroom, living-room-and-kitchen combination separated by a breakfast counter and three stools. The previous tenant had skipped out on rent, leaving behind a nice vintage orange sofa, now faintly blood-stained from the recent murder that had taken place in that very room, midcentury modern coffee table, braided rug, Grain Belt beer poster, metal bottle opener shaped like Minnesota, along with dishes and pots and pans. The bloodstains, which had refused to come out completely no matter how much Jude scrubbed, hadn't bothered her before. But seeing the child sitting next to them caused her to inwardly wince.

She straightened, kicked off her own boots near the door, tossed her coat on a chair, and hurried to the kitchen in search of something big enough for the boy to put his feet in. She rarely cooked, and this was her first serious exploration of the lower cupboards. She was pleased to find a deep pan that might have been used for spaghetti. It was a tight fit, but she was able to get it in the sink to fill with lukewarm water. "The trick is to slowly warm the extremities." She carried the pan to the living room, placing it on the floor in front of the child.

"Should we call 911?" Elliot asked.

"I'm not sure they can get here, and I don't think he needs a hospital." To the child, she asked, "Honey, what's your name?"

"Honey is bee poop." The words were spoken one at a time in a strange singsong.

Elliot let out a snort, and the boy looked up at him with curiosity—a good sign.

"What's your name?" Jude repeated.

"Don't have a name."

"Everybody has a name."

"Nana says I don't need a name. She just calls me Boy because I'm a boy."

"Who's Nana?"

"Nana, Nana, Nan."

Was Nana short for *nanny*? But what kind of nanny didn't take care of her charge? "Keep your feet in the water," she told him when he tried to pull them out. He quickly put them back in. "Do you live in this building?" she asked.

He shook his head.

"Do you live around here?"

He shook his head.

"Where *do* you live?"

He pointed. "Over there." Somehow Jude discerned that the pointing and the words were in some vague reference to something that could be near or very far. He just didn't live *here*.

"Did you ride in a car from somewhere else?"

He nodded an exaggerated nod that was more like a head bob.

"Where is Nana now?"

"Gone."

"Did she walk away?" If the woman was out there in the blizzard, she might need help.

"Drove." He made driving motions with his fists.

"Maybe she stopped, and he opened the door and got out without her knowing it," Elliot said.

"Most cars have safety features to keep that from happening."

"Newer ones."

True.

"Did you get out of the car when you weren't supposed to?" Jude asked.

"No."

"Did a grown-up tell you to get out of the car?"

"Nana did."

"What did she tell you?"

"She said go to the door and wait. So I waited."

He could be confused. Children often got things mixed up, but if he wasn't . . .

"We need to check with all the tenants and see if anybody was expecting him," she told Elliot. Maybe he was supposed to have been buzzed in. Horribly neglectful, regardless. Leaving a small child to tackle the intricacies of an intercom. She also zeroed in on the idea of someone deliberately abandoning him. Like an infant left on church steps. And not only abandoning him, but doing it during a snowstorm. There were cases of overwhelmed mothers murdering their own children. It happened too much. Maybe to an unstable mind, abandoning a child in a snowstorm seemed less horrible, unlike the preferred methods of poisoning or drowning.

Elliot looked up from his phone. "I just sent a group text to all the residents to see if anybody is expecting him or missing him."

"You know everybody in the building?" How was that possible? She spent most of her time trying to avoid them.

"It's not that hard. There are sixteen apartments, and only six of them are occupied. This isn't a prime location, which I'm guessing is why you moved here."

Jude straightened and revisited the kitchen, this time to fill a plastic pitcher with hot water. When she returned, Elliot was eyeing an unopened letter from her lawyer lying on the coffee table. It had been there awhile now.

She held the pitcher out to him. He jumped a little and took it.

She hadn't opened the envelope, because it could contain confirmation of a DNA match. People had come out of the woodwork to try to claim they were heirs to her dead father's estate. Let them have it. She wanted nothing to do with any of it. She'd made that clear, and she wished the lawyers would leave her alone. But a small part of her was also curious because it could mean she had a sibling out there. But she wasn't curious enough to read the letter yet.

"Gradually increase the water while I try to contact Child Protection Services," she said.

"Nobody will be able to pick him up tonight."

She mouthed the next words. *He can't stay with me.*

"I think he might have to."

She felt a rush of panic, worse than the panic she'd felt when she offered the bus riders the use of her home. She couldn't take care of a child.

Maybe he could go to Elliot's.

In the privacy of her bedroom, door closed, Roof Cat purring under the bed, she took a few moments to check Uriah's texts, then replied to let him know she was home. She would explain about the boy later. After that, she made the call to Child Protection Services and got the news she'd expected.

"Under normal conditions, we'd have someone out there within an hour, but with the roads closed, nobody can come for him tonight," said a woman who introduced herself as one of the staff handling off-hours and emergency calls.

Jude was afraid the streets might be even worse by morning. She was so panicked at the thought of the child staying with her all night that she started thinking of ridiculous ways to get rid of him sooner. Someone could come on a snowmobile. Or a horse.

"We can start a file in the morning," the woman said, "but it'll be sparse until we're able to gather more information. If you can keep him tonight, hopefully someone can take him off your hands tomorrow. But I have to also say that our foster families are booked solid."

"I can't keep him any longer than overnight."

"We'll figure something out."

"Thanks. I'll be in touch."

Next, Jude contacted someone in the local Missing Persons department. She didn't need the boy in front of her for specifics like hair and eye color, but she returned to the living room to take a photo and question him about his age.

"How old are you?" she asked.

The boy shrugged and smiled.

"Do you like birthdays?" Elliot said. "I'll bet you do. When you eat cake."

"I like cake."

Jude gave the man at the other end of the line what information she could, got his secure email address so she could send him the photo of the child, told him she'd contact him again tomorrow, and disconnected. Back in the bedroom, she dug out dry socks that would be too big, grabbed a blanket off her bed, and towels from the bathroom.

"Nobody was expecting him." Elliot held up his phone with the replies to his message, then put the device on the table and asked the boy, "You hungry?"

She hadn't even thought about feeding him. That's how good she was when it came to kids.

"I like pancakes."

"His feet are warm and have color." Elliot looked up at Jude. "His hands are warm too. He must not have been out there too long."

"It's going to be difficult to find anybody who saw anything." Jude wondered if she had ingredients to make pancakes. Unlikely. She checked the refrigerator. "Grilled cheese. Do you like grilled cheese sandwiches?"

"Nana makes that for me sometimes."

That must mean he could at least tolerate them. "That's what we'll have, then."

"Any more news about the"—Elliot mouthed the word *body*—"in the lake?"

"We might have a lead, but I can't elaborate on it. Sorry."

"That's okay." But he looked a little hurt. He'd helped with a previous case, and he had this grand idea that he was now an honorary detective and part of the team. He'd even talked about opening his own detective agency. She was trying to discourage that simply because he didn't know anything about it and seemed to feel proximity to her made him more than a novice and gave him cred.

Elliot cooked three sandwiches while Jude focused on the child. No real name, no age, no birthday, no mother, just someone he called Nana. And no socks. She didn't know why that bothered her so much. Just demonstrated the level of neglect, she supposed. And now that he was beginning to warm up, he was emitting a strong odor of unwashed body.

"This is kind of nice," Elliot said, putting three plates of sandwiches on the coffee table. Pan of water pushed to the side, socks on his feet, blanket around his shoulders, the boy sat on the couch, legs dangling, eating a grilled cheese and drinking milk from a glass that was too big for his hands while Elliot perched on the opposite end of the couch and Jude stood leaning against a wall, ignoring her sandwich, still trying to solve at least a little of the mystery of this child.

"Do you go to school?" she asked.

He shook his head.

"What kind of TV shows do you like to watch?"

"*Thomas the Tank Engine.*"

"What kind of games do you like to play?"

"Cards. Nana plays cards with me."

The lights flickered, and the boy dropped his sandwich, seeming more startled than scared.

Elliot whipped out his phone and turned on the flashlight app. Glancing up at Jude, he asked, "Got anything for emergencies?"

She was already moving toward the kitchen to return with three half-melted candles that had also been in the apartment when she'd moved in. The lights were back and weren't flickering, but for how long?

The boy's attention shifted when Roof Cat came slinking past, trying to race through the living room to the kitchen, where his dry food was waiting and where he was normally served canned cat food every evening.

"Kitty!" the boy shrieked in excitement.

Roof Cat jumped and gave up any attempt to sneak around the corner. He hissed and skidded back into the bedroom and probably into the box springs that had become his safe haven.

"He needs a bath," Jude said.

"I agree." Elliot waved a hand in front of his nose as he carried his plate to the kitchen. "I'm going to check out the family on the second floor. They've got a couple of kids. I'll see if they have any clothes we can borrow for him. Then I've got an article to finish before the power goes out completely."

"Maybe you can come back when you're done." Normally good at keeping her expression neutral, her unease at being left alone with a child must have shown.

Elliot smiled and glanced at the boy, who was looking sleepy, then back at Jude. "And here I thought you were fearless."

CHAPTER 10

Uriah was at his desk in Homicide. The lights had automatically dimmed for the night shift, courtesy of their new timer-controlled system that was supposed to be circadian-friendly. Along with that, Chief Ortega encouraged detectives to make their desks feel more like home. Many were decorated with plants, some a few feet tall, and photos. Uriah's even had a lamp with an amber shade, now casting a glow that reflected in the floor-to-ceiling windows overlooking the city street below. He'd gotten sucked down the rabbit hole known as Missing Persons, and now too much time had passed for him to make it home easily and safely. The roads had gotten so bad that the light rail shut down, and he couldn't recall that ever happening. A few night-shift officers sat at desks or moved back and forth in the room, shuffling papers, clicking keyboards. He liked Homicide at night.

Everyone was operating under the assumption that the child in the morgue was Shaun Ford due to Gail Ford's visual ID. Uriah was careful not to accept that until they had more information. People sometimes needed something so badly they could trick themselves into seeing what they wanted to see. Not that Ford wanted her son dead, but she wanted *something*, some connection to him.

Uriah planned to wait for solid confirmation, but none of his doubt had stopped him from looking up the case of the boy who'd gone missing twenty years ago. And as always with an investigation, that case led to similar cases and before he knew it, a couple of hours had passed as he followed virtual trails leading far from the Twin Cities.

Databases had improved over the past twenty years. Previously isolated counties were now connected to a bigger network instead of working independently. Information wasn't hoarded; it was shared. And what he was finding was interesting as well as disconcerting. He'd started by focusing on missing children in the state of Minnesota, then expanded to the bordering states of Wisconsin, Iowa, and South Dakota. He was especially interested in missing young white males about the same age as their John Doe.

The overheads and the amber lamp on his desk flickered. His monitor went blank, then just as quickly came back online. The building had emergency generators, but with the city's recent history, flickering lights made him uneasy. The blackouts had changed the people of Minneapolis. They now understood what detectives had always known. That the world, while beautiful and full of good, was also made of opportunists and predators. Not an easy thing for anybody to swallow, not even a homicide detective who saw the worst of humanity. Before the blackouts, Uriah had told himself he worked in a bubble of badness, and his job was to keep that bubble and badness from spreading and hurting innocent people. The bubble had popped.

His cell phone rang. He checked the screen and groaned. His doctor. He got up from his desk, found a quiet and private corner, and answered.

"Just calling to remind you about your appointment tomorrow."

"I know you're a busy man, but have you looked outside?" As Uriah asked the question, he did just that, glancing past his own reflection, through the window, to the street two stories below. Not a single car was moving, and not a single person was out. The wind was blowing so hard signs were wobbling. From where he stood, he could see drifts close to three feet deep. "I'm not sure I'm going to make it."

"You have to stick to protocol. Each of the three treatments needs to be a week apart. Are you having more issues?"

"The anti-nausea medication seems to be helping part of the time, but last night was rough." And today at the morgue. The lights, the body in the ice, and Gail Ford's emotional response had brought on a wave of queasiness.

"Are you at work? You shouldn't be working. We talked about your high-stress job and what could possibly happen."

A vessel in his brain could rupture, and he could bleed out. That was it in a nutshell. During a case they called the Fibonacci murders, he'd started getting migraines that had increased in frequency and intensity. At first, he'd thought his childhood leukemia might have returned. It hadn't. That was the good news. But an MRI revealed a benign brain tumor. It seemed to be growing slowly. The real danger? A hemorrhage. So the idea was to shrink and remove it, but unfortunately shrinking required a few rounds of chemo. Uriah wished he'd never started the treatment, especially now. It might not shrink enough for surgery. Without surgery, he might die. But he might not. He might be fine.

"Have you told anybody yet?"

"No."

He thought Jude suspected something, that she hadn't been convinced by his claim that his MRIs had been clean and the migraines had just been exacerbated by overwork and dehydration. But she hadn't pressed him about it yet. It wasn't that he was ashamed of having a health issue. He just didn't like to be fussed over, which his parents would do, so he hadn't told them the truth either. And he didn't want his health to distract from any ongoing investigations. He'd planned to tell Jude once things slowed down, but it didn't look like slowing down was going to happen anytime soon.

"It's not my business, but as your doctor I think this would go a lot more smoothly if you had a support group. I met your parents. I feel they would be more than willing to help. And they'll find out eventually anyway."

Not if he stopped the treatment. Not if he didn't go in tomorrow.

"Is it the hair? You have a great head of hair. I wish I had that hair. Is that it? It'll grow back. And with the chemo we've got you on, you might not even lose it."

"It's not the hair. I'll deal with that if it happens." But to be honest, it kinda was the hair, along with everything else.

"Tomorrow. Next day at the very latest. Then I want you to go home and rest."

"Thanks for the reminder."

Uriah ended the call, stuck the phone in his pocket, and looked out at the snow again. The beauty of it almost took his breath away, but the rapid arrival of deep winter also reminded him of the passage of time and a dark date creeping steadily closer—the two-year anniversary of his wife's death. The day she chose to end her life.

A minute later, he was back at his desk, going through the database, creating a spreadsheet of kidnap location, race, age, plus eye and hair color of male children who'd gone missing as far back as twenty-five years.

CHAPTER 11

Elliot had been right. Jude didn't like being alone with the boy. He was warm and fed now, and didn't seem to have any kind of lasting damage to his fingers or toes. But he still smelled.

"Let's get you into the tub," she said.

"No bath."

"It'll be fine." She reached for him. "Come on."

He slipped his hand in hers and reluctantly came along, dragging his feet and looking down at the floor. The bathroom was toasty, hot steam gurgling through the pipes, the finned radiator putting out more heat than the small space required. His demeanor changed when he spotted the claw-foot tub.

He laughed and pointed. "Feet."

"It does have feet."

"And painted toenails. That's funny."

They were red. Maybe even done with polish. Not applied very well, and Jude had always imagined some young woman doing her nails, then deciding to give the claws a manicure.

She filled the tub with about ten inches of water, felt it to make sure it wasn't too hot, and put a towel on the hexagon-tile floor so his feet wouldn't get cold. "Can you undress yourself?"

"No bath."

Crouching in front of him, she said, "You really need one." She wrinkled her nose. "And the tub has feet. It'll protect you."

He hung his head. "Okay." His bottom lip trembled.

She wondered if he'd had a bad experience in a tub. Maybe this wasn't such a good idea. "You know what? Why don't we forget the bath? Not a big deal. We'll just wash you up a little, and you won't have to even get in." The tub seemed to be what was really worrying him.

But he'd accepted his fate. "Take a bath." He began worming his way out of his long-sleeved shirt. He got his head caught, and she pulled the fabric free. Under such bright light, she could see that his skin was very pale, with no lines to indicate he'd ever been in the sun.

She touched a raised area on his collarbone. She knew a healed fracture when she saw one but asked anyway. "What's this?"

"Nana calls it my wing."

"Hmm." He had more old injuries. A forearm that had been broken and maybe set at home. Scars that were as bad as the ones she had on her body. She felt a combination of fury at the person or persons who'd done this, and overwhelming sadness for the boy.

Off came his pants and underpants and socks. The tub was too tall for him to get in by himself, so she lifted him over the edge. When his toes hit the water, she asked, "Does that feel okay?"

He nodded, and she lowered him the rest of the way.

"Do you have toys?" he asked.

He was still trying to be brave as he looked up at her with glistening eyes. Brave and terrified. Maybe he'd been hit for crying. Maybe he'd been beaten for not taking a bath or taking a bath or just being alive. She was sorry she'd ever suggested the tub but hoped she could somehow turn it around and make it something not scary.

"Let me look." She opened a cupboard, dug in the back, and pulled out a couple of pet toys Roof Cat hadn't had any interest in. A pink plastic worm attached to a string, and a goldfish that she squeaked. She tossed it in the water and handed him the worm wand. "You can go fishing."

He laughed and bobbed the worm in the water. "Hi, fish."

His current behavior was so normal . . .

A knock sounded on the bathroom door. She opened it a few inches so the heat wouldn't escape, and Elliot passed in a pair of gray jogging pants, underwear, and a striped shirt.

"Thanks."

"What's wrong?"

Her eyes burned, her throat tightened. She pressed her lips together and shook her head, meaning she'd tell him later. About the boy's "wing" and the other signs of breaks that hadn't been attended, and scars that told a horrible story. An hour earlier, she'd wanted to get rid of the boy as quickly as possible, but now she wanted to keep him until she was sure he would be safe and live an unharmed life. Such a horrible thing to find yourself wishing for something every child deserved no matter who they were or where they came from or what color their skin was.

An unharmed life.

"We're fine." The boy was talking to the fish, giving it a narrative, not paying attention to the adults. She whispered to Elliot, "He's so trusting. It's like he's a wild animal who's never been around strangers and doesn't know they can be dangerous."

"Poor guy." Elliot gave her a sad smile. "I'll be downstairs. Holler if you need anything."

"Maybe you should stay and help him take a bath."

"You're doing fine." He paused as if trying to decide whether he wanted to share something. "You understand people. He's a kid, but he's still people. I know some say you read bodies, but I don't believe that." He seemed to search for his next words. "You know how when you sneeze, guitar strings can vibrate from across the room?"

She shook her head. She'd never owned a guitar.

"It's called sympathetic resonance. You have it. I think because of what you went through, you almost get into the skin of certain people. You feel what others are feeling even if you aren't aware of it."

She wasn't sure about that. She'd misread his signals early on. "Are you trying to—" She pointed from him to her.

He glanced toward the living room and back. "Oh, hell no."

Behind her, the boy said "Hell no!" to the fish.

"Sorry." Elliot grimaced, started to leave, then returned to cling to the doorframe. "I meant what I said about Ava. I don't know if it will go anywhere, but I like her. It's nice that you look out for everybody, but you don't have to worry about her where I'm concerned. I know she and Octavia have been through a lot, and I know they're both important to you."

"Okay." She believed him.

Sometimes it felt like she was supporting everybody else when she could hardly support herself. She wasn't blind. There was something going on with Uriah. He hadn't seemed well lately, he'd missed the New Year's Eve party, and at the morgue earlier he'd looked ready to pass out.

"I've got to get to work." Elliot slapped his hand against the doorframe. "You'll be fine. You always are."

He left.

Behind her, the boy was still lost in his world of play, and the fish and worm on a string were having a great adventure. Jude rubbed a wet washcloth with a bar of soap, building up a lather, and tried to pass the cloth to him.

He was busy with his play. "You do it."

Kneeling next to the tub, she washed him, gently moving over his scarred flesh. Some of the scars had been caused by cigarette burns. She paused and closed her eyes a moment.

"I'm bad sometimes," he said in a happy voice, making whooshing sounds as the fish took a deep dive.

"Who says you're bad? Nana?"

"Nana makes me better."

"Let's wash your hair." She began easing him back in the tub. "Lie down."

"No, no, no!" he shrieked, his thin arms taut as he reached for something to grab, clinging to her.

She quickly pulled him upright, her heart pounding. "You're okay, you're okay," she said, trying to reassure him. "We won't do that." He finally calmed down and began playing with the toys again, distracted enough for her to rub his hair and scalp with the wet washcloth, just trying to clean them a little. Deciding a little clean was all she'd achieve, not wanting to risk upsetting him again, she went to work on his hands, scrubbing between his fingers, then his feet and toes, getting out some but not all of the embedded dirt, the water in the tub turning a dark brown.

For most of his short visit, he'd been docile and had obeyed without question. But he'd obviously had a traumatic experience in a tub. Maybe a near drowning. She'd have to be sure and include that trigger with the information she gave CPS when they picked him up.

"Soap smells like flowers."

It was lavender. "What do you know about flowers?"

"They're pretty. They smell good."

"Where have you seen them?" She was hoping she might get any small detail of his life that would fill in some blanks, maybe even a clue about where he lived.

"Nana brings them in the house. She says flowers make her happy."

So, this Nana made him feel better when he was hurt, brought flowers in the house, and had dropped him off at Jude's door. She really wanted to know if Nana was the person who'd also hurt him, but she didn't want to push him too hard. That would be a question for another time.

She lifted him from the tub—he probably didn't weigh over thirty-five pounds—dried him off, rubbed his hair until it stuck straight up, and helped him into the borrowed clothes that could also serve as pajamas.

He picked at the blue-and-green-striped shirt. "Not mine."

"I'm going to wash yours. These belong to a boy who lives in the building. He said you could use them." She opened the medicine cabinet and pulled out an unused, packaged toothbrush she'd bought for the girl who'd been killed in her apartment. She opened it, wet the bristles, applied toothpaste, and handed it to him.

He seemed to know what to do with it. If not a clue, it was at least another piece of his life. He didn't bathe, but he knew how to brush his teeth. A minute later, she was holding him high enough to spit into the sink.

"You can sleep in my bed tonight," she told him. "I'll sleep on the couch." She'd leave a light on. And she would probably stay awake all night.

Interesting that he wasn't afraid of her or Elliot. And he didn't question why he was in her apartment or feel nervous to be there without his people, as bad as those people might be. He'd perhaps adapted from a very early age to whatever life delivered. Accepted and didn't question, didn't argue, did what he was told—unless he was told to do something that truly terrified him. She knew and understood that form of self-protection. She'd employed it herself. You turned off, you obeyed, you found solace in things no one should find solace in. Like a cat toy.

But a child . . .

It broke her heart.

Her bedroom was small and dark, with a narrow window overlooking the street, long burgundy curtains that fell and pooled on the hardwood floor, a full bed, and a small white dresser, all of which had been there when she'd moved in. She hadn't even bothered to get new sheets or a new comforter. These were sufficient. The location of the apartment building—far from the more popular areas of town—the flat roof she'd slept on shortly after getting out of captivity, and no need to

shop for a single household item had all been positive reasons for signing a lease. She had no desire to leave her stamp on anything or to nest
or surround herself with pretty objects that served no purpose. Maybe
one day that would change and the domesticity she'd felt in her old life
would return. And if it didn't, no problem.

Uriah had once said she was like someone who'd lived before television and cars and certainly cell phones, before retail therapy and con-
sumer culture. She wanted nothing. A psychiatrist would probably call
that a state of mild depression. Jude would argue about that. This was
how she coped, by calming her mind and removing all wants. And this
was who she was now. Maybe one day she'd also care enough to get rid
of the bloodstained couch and buy some cute cups and plates. But if
she didn't, that was okay.

She put the boy to bed and covered him with a blanket.

"Where's the kitty?" he asked.

"He's gone to bed too." The closet door was open, and she suspected
he was hiding inside and would sneak out once the child was quiet.
"What do you usually do before you go to sleep?" she asked.

"Close my eyes."

Cute as hell. She didn't know kids could be so cute. She had the
urge to call Uriah and tell him what the boy had just said, then remembered Uriah didn't know about this new development. "Before you close
your eyes," she explained. "Do you get a drink? Do you read a book?"

"I look at books."

"Does anybody read to you?"

"Sometimes."

Still digging for information, she asked, "Who?"

"Nana."

Nana seemed to be the constant in his life. "What are some of the
books you like?"

"Cylopedia."

"Encyclopedia?" No kids' books?

He nodded, hugging the covers to his chest. "*A.* Just *A.*"

"I don't have that book," Jude told him. And the box of books she'd picked up from her old boyfriend's house, the boyfriend she'd been dating before she'd been abducted, had been given to Uriah for his collection.

"A-na-ta-mee is my favorite pictures."

Anatomy. Yes. The old encyclopedias contained transparent pages. "What about Dr. Seuss?"

He shook his head. Didn't ring a bell.

"*Cat in the Hat?*"

"Kitty." He glanced around the room, looking for Roof Cat again.

"Okay." She gave up. Apparently, he wasn't familiar with any children's books. How many people had actual physical encyclopedias anymore? She tried to picture this Nana in her head and kept imagining someone very old. It wasn't good for a detective to make those kinds of assumptions. Nothing he'd said had indicated age other than the book he liked to look at.

He fell asleep quickly.

In the living room, she curled her feet under her and was just getting ready to call Uriah when he beat her to it.

"I have something I want to tell you," he said.

"I might have a bigger story."

"Let's hear it."

Was it her imagination, or did he sound relieved? "I have a kid. Here in my apartment."

"Wow. Was not expecting that."

She relayed how she'd found him outside the entryway of her building.

"Send me a photo."

She did. That was followed by clicking keys. "I'm entering the image in the National Center for Missing and Exploited Children database." He punched some more keys. "I don't see anything."

"Uriah?" Her voice dropped. "My tinfoil hat moment? I think someone might have been trying to passively kill the boy. And beyond that, there's something very strange and unsettling about him. He doesn't seem to know much about common things. Oh, and the big thing? He can't tell me his real name or how old he is."

"Maybe he just doesn't have the capacity to relay that information."

"He seems bright otherwise. But then again, I don't know anything about kids." She laughed and related what he'd said when he went to bed. Then she told him about the physical abuse.

Uriah let out a low curse.

"What were you going to tell me?" Jude asked.

"I don't think I can compete with that."

"It's not a competition. Are you still at Homicide? I'll bet you are."

"And it looks like I'll be staying the night here."

"Sleep in the break room."

"I think someone beat me to it."

"Sleep on the floor." That sounded unappealing, but he had a penchant for sleeping at his desk. The floor was better.

The power flickered again, then went out completely. "Oh shit," they both said in unison.

"I've gotta go." She hung up.

In the bedroom, her flashlight app on, she found the boy curled in the corner on the floor, using his hands for a pillow and seemingly unaffected by the darkness. "What are you doing down there?"

"Want my spot."

She tried to coax him back to the bed, but he began to whimper. She gave up, pulled a cushion from the couch, snow-damp, blood-stained side down, and placed it on the floor in the corner, with a pillow and a blanket. He curled up like a puppy on a dog bed and was asleep within minutes.

CHAPTER 12

"Where's Nana? When's Nana coming back?"

The boy sat on a stool at Jude's kitchen counter, a bowl of un-kid-friendly microwave oatmeal in front of him, gripping a spoon with a fist, milk on his chin. It was morning, but the storm and the lack of sunlight made it feel more like evening. Wind howled around windows and shook glass panes as the temperature outside continued to drop, snow continued to fall, and residents were warned to stay inside. But oddly enough, the power was on.

Checking the local news that morning, Jude hadn't been surprised to hear schools and even shopping malls, including the Mall of America, were closed. Casualties were being reported, most from people losing their way in the blizzard, or by car accidents. The biggest story of the morning was about a near fatality that took place south of Minneapolis. A woman driving on Interstate 35 had been run off the road by a semi. She'd lost control of her car, sailed over a guardrail, flipped, and had landed upside down. Trapped by her seat belt, she was unable to reach her phone, and nobody spotted her headlights for a few hours. Luckily, last night's temperatures hadn't been that bad by Minnesota standards. Jude expected to continue hearing similar stories until the storm was over and streets were passable. The woman was lucky. She had some broken bones but was expected to live.

Jude poured a glass of orange juice and set it beside the boy's bowl of oatmeal. "I'm not sure when you'll see Nana." And with the unimproved weather, she wondered how much longer she was going to have a guest. Anxious to have her space to herself, Jude ducked into the bedroom, pulled out her cell phone, and called CPS again.

"We don't usually operate like this," the woman said in an apologetic voice. "Our protocol is to get the child, no matter what time it is, day or night. So please understand when I say we have no one to pick him up today due to the road conditions. Maybe tomorrow. I'll let you know. In the meantime, I'm confident he's safe or safer with you than he would be anywhere."

To follow up, Jude called their local Missing Persons again to see if there had been any overnight reports that hadn't yet been entered into the database. Then she made a call to the National Center for Missing and Exploited Children that Uriah had accessed online the night before. She gave them the information she had, got an email address, and promised to send a photo of the boy once she was off the phone.

Back in the kitchen, she poured herself another cup of coffee and leaned a hip against the counter, arms crossed. "What does Nana look like?" she asked.

"Like a lady," he said, scraping the bottom of his bowl. The orange juice was still there.

"Like me?"

He laughed. "No."

"Is her skin the same color as mine?" Jude extended her arm.

"Maybe."

"Is she skinny?"

He shook his head. "She feels like a pillow."

"Does she work for your mom or your dad?"

"No."

"Do you have a mom or dad?"

"She's my mom and dad."

"Okay." She decided on another approach. "What do you like to do? After you eat breakfast?"

"Sometimes I color."

"I like that idea. I'll bet you could draw a nice picture of a house and maybe the people who live there."

"Yeah."

"Did she make the marks on your back?"

"He did."

"Nana's husband?"

"A man."

"Does the man have a name?"

He didn't answer. He was losing interest in the conversation.

"Let's go wash your clothes."

Jude considered taking the elevator to the basement and the washer and dryer the tenants shared, but after the trauma of the tub, she didn't know how he'd react to a confined and disorienting space, so she chose the stairs. It took forever, one arm around the laundry basket, one hand holding his as he clambered down steps that had obviously been built for adults and not children. All the while, he kept up a monologue about everything he observed, like, "Funny walls." They were brick. "Pretty steps." They were marble. "Does the kitty live here too?" A bag of litter with a picture of a cat on it that Elliot might have left in the storage area.

Once the machine was going with everything they'd removed from him, including his coat and mittens, she picked him up for the return to her fourth-floor apartment. Halfway there, her phone rang. She pulled it from her sweatshirt pocket.

"Just got a call from Detective Valentine," Uriah said as she continued to climb, boy on her hip and phone in her hand, like a pro. "Got some fresh news about Loring Park."

"Don't tell me someone fell through the hole left by the ice cutters." It could have happened easily during the blizzard. Even though barriers had been set up, they, along with the warning signs, would have been covered in snow.

"That was my first thought when I got the call, but no. Another body's been found."

CHAPTER 13

I nside her apartment, Jude lowered the boy to the floor and walked to a window to check conditions outside.

"Did you hear me?" Uriah asked through the phone.

Snow was still falling, not as heavily now, but it didn't look like a plow had given her street a single pass yet. "I'm not sure if I'm going to get out of here," Jude said. "I might be able to walk, but it was hard going a mile last night, and the snow is deeper now." She pulled up a mental map and estimated the lake to be around three miles away. Dropping her voice, she added, "And he's still here. The boy."

"Can someone in your building watch him? Elliot, maybe? Don't worry about getting to the scene. I'll come and pick you up. Be there in thirty minutes." A pause. "Oh, and dress warm."

She called Elliot. "I need a favor." She didn't like asking anybody for anything, but this was different since it was for the child. "Can you keep an eye on the boy? I have to attend to a possible crime scene." She didn't go into details.

"Sure, I can watch the little dude. Bring him down."

She explained about the laundry and the need for crayons. He promised to find something.

"Are you going to make a snowman?" the boy asked when he saw her getting dressed for outdoors. Heavy wool socks on her feet, two hooded sweatshirts, and a black down coat with a puffy hood, along with insulated boots that were supposed to be good to thirty below zero.

"Not today."

"Can I make a snowman?"

"It's too cold out. And the snow won't stick together." She zipped her coat. "Right now, you're going to stay with Elliot. He'll have paper and something for you to color with."

"And we'll wait for Nana."

Oh man. He was breaking her heart. She dropped into that overused reply. "We'll see."

She took him downstairs to Elliot's apartment, reminding Elliot about the clothes in the washer. "If someone arrives looking for him, you're not to let him leave. No matter who they say they are." She wanted to be there when CPS came.

"When we go downstairs, we'll go as a team," Elliot said cheerfully, more to the boy than Jude. He put out his hand, palm up. "Give me a team slap. Come on. Right here." He demonstrated the silly game, slapping his own hand. Things clicked, the boy understood, and slapped his palm against Elliot's. Elliot made a dramatic face and the boy giggled. "I hear you like to draw and color," Elliot said. "I do too. And I just so happen to have some colored markers."

"I like crayons."

One of the few child-centric things he'd mentioned.

"These markers are pretty awesome. I think they might even be scented. What's your favorite color?"

"Red. No, purple."

"I like both of those too."

"I mean it, Elliot," Jude said.

He glanced up, then back at the boy. "I know you do. Nobody's getting close to this kid."

"Okay."

"I like to play cards too," the boy said, wandering around Elliot's apartment, spotting Blackie, Elliot's cat, and going straight for him. The animal didn't run away, and the boy was able to squat in front of him. "Hi."

The cat stared at him.

"Can you talk?"

Elliot crouched beside him. "He likes to be petted like this." He moved his hand over the cat's head. The cat stretched to meet Elliot's hand and began purring loudly.

The child laughed and tried it himself.

Jude backed out of the apartment and closed the door.

Her phone rang. It was Uriah. "I'm here."

She found him sitting on a black-and-white snowmobile that had the department logo and *Minneapolis Police Department* across the front. The sidewalk he'd parked on was still covered in deep snow and etched with trails where people had passed on foot. He wore a puffy gray coat, jeans, and heavy boots, along with a black half helmet with the partial face shield up. She shouldn't have been surprised. One area of the garage where the squad and unmarked cars were kept was specifically designated for the department's snowmobiles. Most years they were hardly used, but other times, like now, they could be one of the only ways for officers to get around a paralyzed city.

He handed her a helmet. She put it on and adjusted the strap under her chin. "Why does this seem so odd to me?"

"Because we're detectives?"

"No."

"Because we're going to ride down sidewalks and the middle of a city street?"

"No."

"Because I'm driving a snowmobile?"

"That's it." She swung her leg over the machine and settled on the seat behind him.

"I was driving a snowmobile by the time I was eight."

"Doesn't sound safe."

"I'm still here. Only one concussion."

"That explains a few things."

"Hang on." He dropped his face shield and she did the same. Then he gunned the engine and they leapt forward.

The snowmobile was loud, but not as annoying as it would have been if she hadn't been riding on it. Like any other intrusive sound—vacuuming, leaf-blowing—it was more irritating to be the innocent victim of the roar. Was there a word for that?

The noise left no opportunity for conversation. It was probably a testament to the growth of their relationship, but she didn't feel uncomfortable sitting close to him, and she didn't mind that he was driving the snowmobile and she wasn't. That didn't mean she was wrapped around him. Her hands inside black gloves gripped a leather seat strap behind her. Even when he turned sharply, she didn't give in to the reflex to grab his shoulders and hang on.

Uriah slowed at intersections but didn't stop for red lights. Even a snowmobile could get bogged down in deep snow, and there were very few vehicles to be cautious of. She spotted a couple of people trying to walk dogs dressed in knit sweaters and booties, but for the most part the streets were empty, and only a rare business had an open sign in the window. The ride might have actually been enjoyable except for the howling wind and near-whiteout conditions. It almost could have felt like a day off, a snow day, an interesting ride around the sleeping city, until she spotted Loring Park from around Uriah's shoulder.

So far, they'd gotten almost two feet of snow, but oddly enough there were areas of the frozen lake that were polished clear from strong winds. Some of the equipment trucked in to cut and remove the ice containing the body of John Doe was still there, its removal possibly hampered by the weather. Police vehicles and unmarked cars from their department were parked haphazardly on the ice. Uriah drove the

snowmobile across the lake and stopped near the cluster of unoccupied vehicles and yellow crime-scene tape strung between metal poles
that had been driven into the ice. Jude stepped from the machine and
flipped her face shield to the top of her helmet. Uriah did the same.

The blocks removed from the lake by the harvesters were still there,
sections managing to catch rays of faint sunlight and reflect it back,
monolithic and alien in their stark beauty. On site was a crew attempting to set up a tent, the kind of thing erected for the purpose of containing a crime scene when conditions were harsh. A man and a woman
pounded metal spikes into the ice as others struggled to keep the large
sheets of snapping and popping canvas from pulling them across the
lake like parasails.

Detective Valentine approached. He was a competent detective and
a relatively new hire from Chicago. Even in the aftermath of a blizzard,
he was well dressed in a long black coat, black snow boots, and black
leather gloves. His only concession to the brutality of the weather was
the fur-lined cap with earflaps, yet he somehow managed to make that
look fashionable. With a grim expression, Valentine motioned for them
to follow him. Officers backed away so the detectives could assess the
scene.

A hazy sun hung in the sky above, black trees stood at the shoreline,
and the snow that circled and swirled no longer fell from the sky but
instead was swept up and carried through the air to be redeposited when
it found a drift to cling to. From somewhere in the distance came the
sound of snowplows: the thud as the blade was lowered, followed by the
revving engine, then the back-up alert. Accompanying it was a lower
whir as citizens dug their way out of garages and fired up snowblowers.

Directly below Jude's feet, while nature amazed and paralyzed,
another body slept. The repeat of the scene wasn't lost on her. The
murky ice, the size and shape of the body several inches below. This time
the surface was clear, polished by snow and wind. The victim looked

like a male child, dressed in jeans and a blue T-shirt, sneakers. White face, blue lips, and light hair.

She looked up at Uriah. "What the hell is going on?"

"Wish I knew."

She scanned the expanse of ice. Off in the distance, officers were walking back and forth in a weak grid formation. "They're looking for more."

"Just making sure," Valentine said. "A thorough search will be conducted now that the weather is clearing."

"Who found him?" Jude asked.

"The ice cutters returned to remove the rest of their machinery, and in the process spotted him. Probably because the blowing wind cleaned and polished the ice enough to make him more visible. That's the theory anyway." He glanced up and saw an officer juggling carryout cups from a nearby café. "Excuse me." He shot off for the coffee. Before Jude could emotionally or visually process the scene, she got a text from Elliot.

It's always night in his drawings.

It took her a second to realize Elliot was talking about the boy. He included a drawing of a stick figure and what might have been a snowman. His observation was true. The background was black.

After a moment, she dropped to her knees to get a closer look at the body. The lake wasn't deep. Probably ten or fifteen feet in the center. Here, maybe eight. The victim was about a foot below the surface. Frozen beside him were plants: pondweed, muskgrass, and lacy milfoil. Years ago at her family's cabin up north, they'd used a special wheeled rake to remove the growth when it got so thick people could no longer swim without getting caught. One time she'd gotten so tangled, she'd almost drowned. She'd screamed, and her mother had come running.

Uriah crouched beside her.

"I gave the boy a bath last night," she said. "He was terrified of the tub."

"That tub is kind of freaky."

"He loved the toenails."

"Maybe he's never been in one."

"Pretty sure he has. That was the problem. He was okay until I tried to make him lie back to wash his hair."

"Another sign of abuse?"

"Maybe. I hope Child Protection Services picks him up soon. I don't like feeling this way. Responsible for upsetting him with unknown triggers." And worrying about him when she wasn't there. "Why would anybody want to be a parent? I think it must always hurt. I don't mean childbirth, obviously, but this—" She meant where they were and what they were looking at. Everything about parenthood seemed rife with pain, but to lose a child in such a way . . . Most mothers would die for their children. But then there were others . . .

Instead of the pep talk she'd expected, Uriah was quiet a moment before saying, "I think that's true. And maybe why I try to protect my mother from the bad things in my life."

She thought about his hospitalization last fall. He was keeping something to himself, and now he'd given her a possible reason.

She took a few photos, her fingers aching from the cold. When she was done, she stuck her phone away, slipped her gloves back on, and got to her feet. "Two dead bodies, both about the same age. It's like somebody put in an order for blond boys, then changed his mind and threw them away."

CHAPTER 14

At Headquarters, Jude checked in to make sure everything was going okay with Elliot and the boy. She and Uriah had left the frozen lake two hours ago, with Valentine still in charge. There would be a repeat of the previous ice harvest, but this time the company planned to leave all equipment on site until it was confirmed that no more bodies were to be found.

"We're making chocolate chip cookies," Elliot told her.

The boy's photo had been run through all the databases, including the Polly Klaas Foundation. No match. A couple of people at the police department were raking through NamUs, but the sheer volume was daunting. Every forty seconds a child in the US went missing. *Every forty seconds.*

"Really homemade this time?" she asked Elliot, recalling a plate of Oreos he'd left at her door.

"We're lacking some ingredients, so we'll see."

"I'll try to be back in a few hours."

"Don't worry. We're fine."

After she hung up, Uriah motioned to her. "I want you to see something. I was going to tell you about this last night before the power outage." He was sitting at his desk, hand on a mouse as he stared at his monitor, the glow turning his face a pasty blue. She rolled her chair close and sat down to view the screen.

"I've been going through all available records," he said, "and we've got missing young boys the age of Shaun Ford going back a helluva lot of years."

Not that odd, unfortunately, but she waited to see what he found so interesting.

He clicked the mouse. "I pulled up images of several, and the weird thing is many of them are pretty similar in physical characteristics. I made a spreadsheet. Missing persons, twelve-year-old blond boys with blue eyes." Another series of clicks. "Just sent it to you so you'll have a copy."

She looked at the spreadsheet open on his screen. "You've been busy." There were hundreds of names and dates. "How far do these go back?"

"Twenty-five years, but they could go back even further because old information has to be added post-case. The farther back in time we go, the more likely we don't have complete reports or we have missing reports. It's all just a weird coincidence, right? If you go back far enough, you're bound to find similarities, right?"

"It's uncanny and definitely bears deeper investigation." Her phone rang. Child Protection Services. She answered.

After a brief catch-up, the caller said, "Some streets have been reopened, and we should be able to pick up the child around seven tonight."

Jude experienced the expected relief, accompanied by a flash of anxiety.

Later, before retrieving her car from the police department garage, she walked two blocks to a department store that had reopened after the blizzard. Shelves of food were empty, but she was interested in toys and children's clothing. She wanted the boy to have some things to take with him when he left.

CHAPTER 15

Jude buzzed in the people from Child Protection Services. After climbing three flights of stairs, they were in her apartment, introducing themselves as they unwound long knit scarves from their necks. Jenny Hill, who was fairly young, maybe in her twenties, and Kim Tharp, a woman around fifty, with long dreadlocks. She seemed to be in charge. They sat on the couch, shrugging out of coats and hats and gloves.

The child sat on the floor, playing with the toys Jude had purchased a few hours earlier. She'd also bought two stuffed animals—a panda and an orange cat—some items of clothing, and a backpack with cartoon characters. She'd gotten a little carried away. The boy didn't appear interested in the visitors and hadn't even glanced up at them. He was fixated on a tyrannosaurus that had come in a small red suitcase with several other dinosaurs. What was it with boys and dinosaurs?

"Like you, we've been in touch with Missing Persons," Kim said as Jenny slipped to the floor in what would probably prove to be a futile attempt to engage the boy, considering how distracted he was by the toys. "With their input, we've decided to release the child's photo to local TV stations and also post it to our Facebook page. The situation is a little unusual since he's more of a found child than a missing one. But someone is missing him. Going public puts him in a more vulnerable position, but I think at this point it's a step we need to take."

Jude agreed.

"We have a physician on call who will document"—her words trailed off as she looked at the boy—"everything."

Jude had been there herself after her escape and knew what it would involve.

"We try to make it as easy as possible. We also have a child psychologist who'll see him tomorrow. I know you mentioned drawings, and we'll employ that technique and others. The good news is that we might have found a nice foster family for him. I'll let you know."

Jenny was walking a stegosaurus across the floor. Even the boy's dinosaur would not engage with hers. Jude silently signaled for Kim to follow her several steps away to the adjoining kitchen.

"I'll be watching this case closely," Jude whispered, glancing at the interaction, or rather lack of, taking place a few yards away. "Please make sure he doesn't go back where he was. I don't want this story to end tragically."

"We don't either. But that doesn't mean we won't do our best to find his mother or guardian so we can evaluate the situation. Was this Nana the abuser? Maybe, but maybe she protected him. And maybe leaving him at your door was an extension of that. We'll also be determining the current home situation. Can we do anything to help? Can we make it better? These are just a few of the questions we ask ourselves as we process a case."

Footsteps and a knock at the door. Elliot showing up to say goodbye. He glanced at the people in the room, said hello, then crouched in front of the boy as Jenny gave up attempting to interact and moved away.

"Hey, buddy. I hear you're taking a car ride."

"To see Nana?"

Interesting that he responded to Elliot after ignoring the women.

"These ladies are going to try to find her." He packed up the dinosaurs in the little plastic suitcase, but the boy clung to the tyrannosaurus.

Jude helped him into his snow boots and clean coat, zipped the coat, and put the stocking cap on his head. With the dinosaur in one hand, Jenny holding the other, and Kim carrying the backpack with his new clothes, toys, and stuffed animals, they left. The dinosaur bopped along the banister as the trio descended the stairs. The boy paused and glanced up at Jude, then continued with the two women. Once they were out of sight, Jude stepped back into her apartment.

Elliot plopped down on the couch. "I'll miss that weird little guy."

The place already felt emptier. "I'm going to miss him too." His strange presence. Wounded without even knowing it. There was something compelling and heartbreaking and innocently brave about that. She hoped his foster family would treat him well.

Now that the boy was gone, Roof Cat made an appearance. Jude opened a can of cat food, spooned the contents into a ceramic bowl with a drawing of a yellow cat wearing a bib, and placed it on the floor. "I used to think I wanted kids, but not anymore." She understood her limitations. She was too removed and shut off to be a mother.

"Don't sell yourself short. You were good with him."

"You and your mother are close, aren't you?" He always acted odd whenever she mentioned his mother. He practically squirmed.

"Yeah."

"You don't sound positive about that."

"She can be a little . . . judgmental. Let's just say that."

Elliot left abruptly for his apartment at the same time Jude received a group text from the medical examiner.

We were able to take dental X-rays of John Doe today. Please meet me and the forensic odontologist at the morgue tomorrow morning.

CHAPTER 16

The next morning, residents were still digging out their cars from city streets that were narrow but passable. Jude drove her vehicle back downtown, fishtailing and bottoming out in a couple of intersections where snow was still deep and surfaces were slick from traffic.

At the morgue, she was a little surprised to see two media vans in the parking lot. Because of the weather and the inability of people to get around, news of the second body, which was now safely ensconced inside the building, had gone almost unnoticed. Word must have been getting out. Detective Valentine continued to oversee the lake operation, but at this point no new bodies had turned up.

Jude parked near Uriah's sedan and was buzzed in the back door of the morgue, where she caught up with her partner. The woman at the desk gave them a smile and a nod. "Dr. Stevenson is waiting in her office."

They knew where to go. As they walked side by side down the white fluorescent hallway, Jude stuffed her gloves in her pocket and pulled off her knit cap. A tap on Ingrid's door, and they were told to come in. Coats were tossed over hard plastic chairs while the ME introduced them to the forensic odontologist, who attached a cable to a display port and mirrored her laptop to the monitor on the wall.

The comparison of unique dental features was an accepted method of victim identification and was often used to prosecute killers. That's how reliable it was. Not quite on the level of DNA, because it required someone specifically trained in forensic dentistry. In spite of advances in DNA profiling, fingerprints, and facial reconstruction, the comparison of dental records still played a significant role in the identification of bodies. Even if the antemortem dental records weren't available for comparison, a forensic odontologist might be able to determine age and sex from the teeth themselves. Here, they had dental records and a fairly well-preserved body.

Ingrid stood to one side, arms crossed, and let the specialist run the show.

A few key clicks and they were looking at two sets of dental X-rays, one clearly labeled twenty-two years ago; the other with yesterday's date, time, and location. Even to Jude's untrained eye, things did not look good. She glanced at Uriah and saw he was thinking the same thing. The outcome was so obvious that they really didn't need a specialist, and yet her role was vastly important because she would ground and validate their claims.

Uriah cut right to it. "These are not the same people."

"I agree," the specialist said. "I know you were expecting a different answer."

Ingrid stepped forward. "Since this is such a surprise, given the mother's input, I thought it would be good to go over the details before we present the information to the press."

Using a mouse, the specialist circled all the various areas of discrepancies between the two sets of X-rays, explaining as she went.

"What about age?" Jude asked.

"The second molars have erupted. From that, we can determine the victim from the lake was eleven to fourteen years of age. More likely twelve or thirteen."

"It might make things go smoother if you could actually attend the press conference," Uriah said. "Reporters are going to have a lot of questions."

"Happy to."

The focus shifted from the press conference back to the John Does still in the cooler. "So the first victim didn't die twenty years ago." Uriah sounded baffled.

"That's debatable," Ingrid said. "The body isn't completely thawed, so I'm still waiting to perform the autopsy. I'm seeing signs of decomposition that don't mesh with a death that might have occurred, say . . . last month, before the lake was safe to walk on. During autopsy, I should be able to tell if the body has gone through partial thaws over time. I'll be looking for cell breakage. When a body is frozen and thawed, blood cells rupture and leak intracellular fluid. It's a pretty obvious clue if you're looking for it. I'm also seeing clothing that looks dated."

"Vintage clothing is popular," Jude pointed out.

"But not typically with young kids," Uriah said.

Jude looked up at him, noting the circles under his eyes, feeling a fresh pang of worry. "Might not have been a style choice but an economical choice."

"How much longer before the autopsy?" Uriah asked.

"I'm hoping tomorrow." Ingrid seemed to be eyeing him a little closely too. "Since we have media camping right outside the doors, why not share this information with them immediately?"

"I'd rather schedule an official press conference," Uriah said. "I'll let the reporters outside know. Police department in thirty minutes?"

Jude didn't like that idea. "I need to speak to Mrs. Ford before this goes public."

Uriah checked his watch. "Okay, let's make it an hour."

An hour was going to be a challenge. It took Jude thirty minutes to get to Gail Ford's house. She didn't like the way they'd rushed the press conference, and had been surprised that Uriah had agreed to hold it so quickly with little or no prep. With the current road conditions, it didn't look like she was going to make it back in time. She tried to call him. No answer, so she followed up with a text.

The street Gail lived on had been given a quick pass with a plow, just enough for a car to drive through. Jude didn't want to get stuck, so she parked a few feet from the curb, barely leaving room for another car to squeeze by. She'd have to make this quick.

Gail's sidewalk had been cleared with a snowblower. Jude could tell by the pattern in the shallow layer of remaining snow, and the precision of the cut. She knocked, and a curtain moved in the picture window. Seconds later she heard footsteps and the front door opened.

With no hello, Gail said, "You have news."

"Yes."

"My neighbor cleared my walk." She motioned for Jude to step inside. "Everybody has been so nice since the story broke. Bringing food, asking if I need any help."

Jude stopped on the entry rug. She didn't want to get the hardwood floors wet.

"Don't worry about the snow."

"The forensic odontologist met with us today." Jude remained where she was. Minnesota nice. There was no way to ease into this slowly, and Gail knew something was up. "I'm sorry, but the records your dentist supplied did not match the dental X-rays taken of the body found in the lake three days ago." She paused, then added a final sentence for clarity. "The boy from the lake is not your son."

Gail stared, hands clasped in front of her, nodding, looking as if she understood what Jude had said.

"When can I have his body picked up? I need to plan a funeral."

"Mrs. Ford. Listen carefully. Are you with me?"

"Yes."

Jude looked directly into the woman's eyes. "The body found in the lake?"

"Yes." She nodded.

"Does not belong to your son."

"Does not belong to my son." Before Gail finished the sentence, she began to shake.

Jude kicked off her boots and led the grieving mother to the couch. The woman dropped down heavily, mouth open, eyes glistening. "I could have sworn . . ."

"I'm sorry," Jude said. "I'm very sorry."

"Can you tell me that again?"

"The body from the lake is not your son."

Gail sat in a daze as a clock in a distant room ticked loudly. "That's impossible." She came around pretty quickly, got brave, blinked, and sat up straighter, coming in for a verbal attack and blame. "You did something wrong. Run the tests again. Get another specialist. Do whatever you have to do. Do your job. Whatever you did, whatever you compared, do it over because that's my son."

"We can send the files to another specialist," Jude said. "I have no problem putting in that request. But I've seen the X-rays, and I can assure you the results will be the same."

"I was planning a funeral. I was going to have closure. I wanted to tell him I was sorry for being such a bad mother."

"Everybody has regrets when they lose someone," Jude said. "But you did the best you could do at the time. Remember that."

Gail started crying softly.

"Is there someone I can call?" Jude asked. "A neighbor, maybe? A relative?"

"I don't want to talk to any of them now. I already told them my son had been found. They were so happy for me. I can't face telling them otherwise."

Jude padded to the kitchen in her wool socks, where she filled a glass with water from the tap. In the living room, Gail took the glass with shaking hands, drank a little, and put it on the coffee table. Jude sat down at the other end of the couch.

The house was like a cave. She wanted to open the curtains to let in some light. From outside, laughter carried across the street as kids enjoyed the second snow day in a row. Maybe they were making a snowman. She hadn't gotten the chance to make one with the boy. She felt bad about that.

"This means my son could still be alive," Gail suddenly announced.

"It's possible," Jude said carefully.

"So, I'll keep waiting."

In truth, her son had probably been murdered twenty years ago, and the body might never be found. Gail might never have the closure she needed to get at least a little of her life back. "I have to tell you something else," Jude said. "Something you'll be hearing about soon."

"I hope it's not bad news. I don't know if I can take any more of that."

Life was cruel. "This hasn't been released to the press, but we found another body in the lake very near where the previous one was discovered. And as far as we can tell, it's another young boy with blond hair."

Gail sniffled and dabbed at her eyes with her sleeve. "Do you have a photo?"

Jude pulled out her phone and scrolled to one of the pictures she'd taken the day before at the lake. Gail looked intently at the screen, then shook her head. With a sob, she said, "That's not my son either."

Either. At least she'd said *either*, which meant she was beginning to accept the painful truth.

◆ ◆ ◆

The roads were no better on Jude's return drive. By the time she parked and was inside the police department building, the press conference was under way in one of their large meeting rooms. Rows of tables and chairs. An elevated platform under blinding lights, the US and Minnesota state flags flanking the podium. She was surprised to see Ortega and Valentine running the show, along with Ingrid and the forensic odontologist. No sign of Uriah.

When they broke the news about the original John Doe, the noise level of the room exploded. Hands were raised, and questions were shouted. They were told about the second body, and all hell broke loose.

Someone spotted Jude and shoved a microphone in her face. She declined to comment but made her way through the throng of reporters. At the podium, she removed her knit cap and unzipped her jacket. Where the hell was Uriah? Times like these, the press really wanted to talk to the head of Homicide. She picked up his slack, dropped into media mode, going over topics most likely already covered. But her presence and words seemed to bring some reassurance to the crowd. She ended by asking for the public's help.

Conference over, she sent another text to Uriah, asking him where he was.

His reply raised more questions than it answered.

Be back soon. Followed by a thumbs-up.

CHAPTER 17

Awareness brought pain. Simple as that. Nan had never been much into drugs. Surprising, since she liked oblivion. But her preference had always been hard liquor. That was until she started coughing up blood and had to quit for good. Bleeding ulcers weren't fun. The pain, the blood, anemia so bad she'd lived in bed for a while and slept most of the hours away. But quitting drinking . . . it was harder than she'd expected. She'd never even thought of herself as having a problem, but the withdrawal had been tough. And once she beat it, she missed the blur and buffer alcohol gave her. The numbness that had gotten her through many years.

But this floaty stuff was nice. And now that she thought about it, it was the first real mental relief she'd had since she quit drinking. She wanted to float forever, and she didn't like it when the nurses came in and talked and tried to move her around, bathe her.

"Ms. Perkins?"

Was she dreaming? Or was someone really in the room?

"Ms. Perkins? We're going to remove your IV tomorrow. That means you're only going to have the PCA pump one more day."

PCA pump—meaning the narcotic she was able to administer to herself with the push of a magic button. To demonstrate that she wasn't ready for such a drastic measure, Nan moaned and repeatedly pressed the button cradled in the palm of her hand.

"That won't do any good. You can press it a million times, but it won't deliver medication more than once every twenty minutes."

Nan opened her eyes a crack. It was daytime, the windows letting in the kind of bright and blinding light that came with snow-covered roofs and ground—that harsh bounced brilliance that was almost worse than the fluorescents overhead. Not only was the room torture, the nurse's face was too friendly for the seriousness of Nan's situation. She was like a clown at a funeral.

"How about trying to drink something? I've brought some ice water and apple juice." The girl set a plastic pitcher and a bottle of apple juice on the narrow wheeled table. "And I'm going to turn on the TV." The wall-mounted flat-screen responded to the click of a remote. "Sometimes it helps to have a little something to distract you from pain." The nurse went through channels, stopping on a soap opera. She demonstrated how to use the control for the television, the lights, the bed, and to call for help, before clipping it to the railing just inches from Nan's hand.

Soap operas. What the hell? Did she look like someone who watched soap operas? Maybe she did. That was depressing.

"Anything else I can get you?"

The nurse was young, maybe in her twenties, straight dark hair, pretty. Annoying. And now she was moving around the room, collecting things, smoothing the thin white blanket over Nan's uninjured leg, the other leg suspended in the air by a little hammock, her toes popping out of the end of the cast like fat sausages. The crash had shattered her tibia, and surgery had resulted in pins and screws and metal plates.

As if the girl had read her mind, she said, "Doctors say you're lucky to be alive." She shook her head. "That accident. I saw pictures of it. And it's amazing you were found."

"Would've been better if I'd died." How would she afford the medical bills? How would she get anywhere now that she didn't have a car? What a stupid idea. Driving to Minneapolis in a blizzard. All for a damn kid who was just like any other damn kid. Nothing special about him. Her first mistake had been making him her pet.

"Don't say that!" the nurse said. "Life is precious."

Precious.

That deserved a loud snort, but Nan didn't have the energy. These were the kinds of situations that reinforced her feeling of being different. *Life is precious.* That was some bullshit right there. Thinking those glittery thoughts had gotten her into this mess. And thinking life was precious was what had screwed things up so badly for her in the past. Why hadn't she learned her lesson? Why had she fallen into the trap of thinking the kid deserved to live? Thinking he was at least semiprecious? That boy was just a body, just blood and bones and skin. Disposable. Replaceable.

Nan grunted and grabbed the television remote, quickly thumbing through channels, wanting the foolish girl to see she had better things to do than waste her time on soap operas. Nature channels were soothing and informative. She especially liked the ones about faraway places like Africa. Nothing more entertaining than watching a big cat bring down a gazelle.

In her search for a bearable channel, she paused briefly on the local news. The morning crew. They weren't as proficient as the people in the evening and always looked a little like they'd just stumbled in from a long night on the town.

Right now, the male and female anchors at the desk were discussing the recent blizzard and the upcoming Winter Carnival. Rather than being the promised distraction, the sound of their tinny voices worked like some kind of trigger, causing fresh pain. And once that pain got a foothold . . . It started deep and radiated out, causing her to produce mental images of metal pins drilled and anchored into meaty bones, scraping against swollen muscle. Her teeth clenched, and the pain increased rapidly. Soon she was panting.

Her hand dropped the remote, and her fingers blindly searched for the magic button. She found and pressed it several times in a row, fast, like a madwoman, even though only one press would supply her fix. It beeped, and she let out a sigh just knowing the drug was being released into her veins and relief would come soon.

Within a couple of minutes, her breathing leveled out and her jaw began to unclench. The episode was proof of how inhumane it was to take her off the pump.

While the newscasters droned on, her eyes fluttered closed and she began to dream. She remained in that limbo state of pain-masked stupor and half sleep for a minute or two. Maybe through a commercial, then the news was back.

"We're looking for the public's help in solving a mystery that took place the night of the recent blizzard," the man said.

They bounced the story back and forth; now it was the woman's turn.

"This is sure to capture the heart of the nation and beyond. Two nights ago, a small, innocent child was discovered abandoned in a snowbank on a Minneapolis doorstep during one of the worst blizzards this city has ever seen. What's even sadder, the child is unable to tell police or CPS who he is or how he got on that doorstep. The final tragedy? Nobody has reported him missing. Nobody seems to be looking for this poor child."

No, it couldn't be. Could it?

"Given the severity of the storm," the guy said, "this might have had a dark ending, but luckily the child was rescued by none other than Detective Jude Fontaine."

Nan pressed her elbows into the mattress and strained to sit taller despite her trapped leg. "Boy," Nan whispered in disbelief. Then louder, "Boy."

"The police and Child Protection Services are reaching out to the public in hopes that someone might know something," the woman said with cheerful sadness.

A photo of a familiar face appeared on the left side of the screen while the woman at the desk kept talking.

She'd told him to go inside the building. Why hadn't he gone inside the building? She would never have abandoned him in a snowbank.

Now it had become some ridiculous drama, the story of the day, and she was being made out to be a horrible person, when the truth was she'd been saving him. Saving him!

The guy was talking now. "If you have any information about a missing child or if you recognize this child, call the number on the bottom of the screen. You can also visit our website for updated information as it comes in."

"At this point," the woman said, "the only name he's given his rescuers is Boy."

Nan heard a gasp and turned her head. The nurse was still in the room, watching television along with her. And now she was staring at Nan, eyes big, mouth open.

Nan tried to rouse her sluggish brain. Normally good at covering her ass, she said the first thing she could think of. "I saw the same news earlier today."

"Your TV hasn't been on," the nurse said. "I had to give you the control and show you how to use it."

"The drugs are confusing me. I just pushed the button. Don't pay any attention to me." She glanced back at the photo on the mounted TV. "I mean, he's a boy. That's what I meant." She rallied somewhat and managed a shrug. "What's the big deal?"

The nurse pulled a phone from her pocket. The number was still on the television. She poked at her device. Nan would have knocked it from her hand, but she was too far away. She looked for a weapon, found the plastic apple juice bottle, threw it. The nurse ducked. Juice exploded against the wall. "I'm just watching television," Nan said. "I just made an innocent comment."

The nurse lifted the phone to her ear. A moment later, arm crossed over her stomach and supporting an elbow as she kept an eye on Nan, she began talking to someone at the other end. "I might have information about the boy who was found in the blizzard."

CHAPTER 18

At her desk, Jude ran a search for a woman named Nanette Perkins. A few key clicks and she was on her feet, grabbing her jacket from the back of the chair. "I'm going to follow a lead," she told Uriah. The car accident had occurred south of Minneapolis. Lucky for the victim, the hospital was a good one.

He swiveled and looked up from his monitor, hands behind his head. No line between his brows, no pallor or shallow breathing. She felt a rush of relief, telling herself she was worrying too much. He was fine. He had no secrets.

"Need me to come?" he asked.

"This is about the kid who showed up at my place, not the frozen bodies. I'll try not to take long." She explained that the tip line had gotten a call from a nurse at Fairview Southdale Hospital, where the accident victim was being cared for. "The woman who ran her car off the road south of town. The nurse claimed the woman spoke the word *boy* upon seeing the child on the news. The woman's name? Nanette."

He raised his eyebrows.

Yep. Thanks to the local press, it was looking like they might have found the mysterious Nana. Just hours ago, she'd learned CPS had been able to place the boy in emergency foster care with a family in the neighborhood of Richfield. She should have felt good about that, but instead the news made her uneasy.

"Why are you getting information on that case?" Uriah asked. "Missing Persons should be dealing with it."

"I wanted to be kept in the loop."

He dropped his hands and swiveled back to his monitor. "Understandable." His response was surprising considering their caseload and his past reactions to her drifting too far from Homicide.

"Be back as soon as I can."

After exiting the police department parking ramp in her own car rather than a department vehicle, she took I-35 south. It was a sunny day, made almost blinding by the banks of snow everywhere. The interstate was clear, but even in the upscale town of Edina, the side streets were still a mess. Intersections were slick and slushy, and streets were enclosed by claustrophobic walls of snow being scraped away with front-end loaders and emptied into dump trucks waiting to haul it to designated lots.

She parked in the hospital ramp and took the walkway across France Avenue to the hospital. With her badge and introduction, she was given the location of Nanette Perkins's room. Avoiding the elevator, she hurried up the stairs to the third floor and knocked on the open door. Not waiting for an invitation, Jude stepped in, and the patient turned off the television.

Even though this might be their mysterious Nana, it wasn't hard to feel sympathy and even empathy for the person in the hospital bed, her foot suspended from a sling, bare toes swollen. It wasn't long ago that Jude had spent days in a hospital before furtively slipping out and escaping into city streets like some criminal.

Because of the swelling due to facial injuries sustained in the crash, it was hard to get a read on the woman. The only real expression came from the one eye that wasn't swollen shut.

Jude introduced herself.

"I know who you are."

Not a surprise. A bigger surprise came when people didn't recognize her. That's how much her face had been on TV and in grocery-store checkout lanes. "It's a little hard to fly under the radar," she admitted.

Sometimes Jude could observe and input information from a person's grooming and self-care, from the way the skin looked and whether nails were trimmed. That wasn't effective with a car-crash victim, so she worked with what she had. The woman was medium height, a little on the heavy side, but not much. Her dark hair was shoulder-length and matted from the accident, the surgery, and the bed. From Jude's earlier record search, she knew Nanette Perkins was forty-three and a young widow living on a farm south of town. Those things spoke of a hard life. But that one unswollen, brilliant-green eye watched with a sharpness that was surprising, especially given that she was gripping a narcotic pump button so tightly.

The tip-line caller had reported that Ms. Perkins had violently tossed a bottle of apple juice at her head. A miss, but the juice had exploded against a wall. Looked like the mess had been cleaned up, but Jude could still smell a lingering fruity vinegar under the scents of antiseptic and cotton blankets dried at a high temperature.

"Guess I should be flattered they called you about my little tantrum," the woman said. "But it seems a bit out of your line of work. Aren't you a homicide detective? Or are you moonlighting as a therapist?" She pushed her fists against the mattress, trying to sit up a little higher despite her leg being in a sling.

"Would you like me to adjust your bed?" Jude asked.

"I can do it." Perkins grabbed the control, and the bed groaned. "And I was kidding about the therapist. I know why you're really here. I was watching TV, and the nurse thought I said something about that missing kid." She squinted and glanced at the window beside her.

"That's what we were told." Jude crossed the room and pulled the curtains closed, cutting the brightness in half. The fluorescents overhead were still intolerable. Not only the light they emitted, but the sound.

A person might not notice it at first, not with all the other stimuli, but when you focused, you could hear a hum. "You understand that we have to follow up on any possible leads. We can't overlook anything. But rest assured, we're just doing our job." She made it sound as if this was just one of many tedious visits in her day. "The hotline has generated a lot of calls."

"Still, homicide?"

"I'm helping out. We do that sometimes." A half truth.

The woman relaxed.

Jude tugged a small spiral notebook from her messenger bag. She often liked to use real paper and a pen, even though it meant having to spend more time entering the information in the database later. Paper and pen gave her focus as she mentally composed her questions. Sometimes she didn't even write at all. Along with the notebook, she pulled out a photo and placed it on the narrow hospital table, then rolled the open-ended contraption over the bed and in front of the woman so she could get a good look at the eight-by-ten of the boy. Not the one Jude had captured in her apartment, but a more professional image taken by CPS, the one they were using for the tip line.

"I've seen him on the news," Perkins said. "Not much else to do here but watch TV."

"Do you know his name?"

"They said it was Boy. I guess the kid told somebody that. Said it was Boy."

"That's a strange name, don't you agree?" Jude watched her closely.

"He's a kid. Kids get confused. I'm sure you know that."

"So, was earlier today the first time you ever saw this boy?"

"Yes."

Perkins was beginning to sweat. Just a sheen of perspiration on her upper lip. Not necessarily a tell. Pain could cause a similar response.

Jude set her tablet aside and grabbed her phone. "Would you mind if I took a photo of you? For our records?"

"Hell no. No pictures." Like someone trying to avoid the paparazzi, the woman raised a hand in front of her face, palm out.

Jude put the phone away. "Why no photos? That makes me think you're hiding something."

"I look terrible." Perkins attempted to smooth her tangled hair. It didn't help. When Jude had gotten out of the hospital, she'd had such knots she chopped off her hair, leaving about an inch behind. Easier than the alternative. "No woman would want a photo taken of her in a hospital bed, unless maybe she was holding a baby or something," Perkins said.

"Not a problem. I was able to find some photos of you online. They weren't that recent, but recent enough. You don't really have much of an internet presence. No Facebook or Twitter or Instagram that I could find."

"I'm not into social media."

"Me either." Jude redirected the discussion. "Did you know the child was left at my apartment building?"

The woman blinked. "That's what I heard."

"I wonder if that was just some random thing. What do you think?"

She shrugged. "You're the cop."

"I'm not sure. If it was by choice, then why? That's my next question. Maybe someone was trying to get him to safety."

"Maybe."

"And even though the snowstorm wasn't the most ideal way to dump a child, maybe the person doing it was desperate."

"I could see that. You might be onto something."

Jude dug into her messenger bag again and pulled out three more photos she'd enlarged. She placed them on the narrow table along with the boy's headshot. "These are close-ups of the physical damage to the child, inflicted over a period of years. Well, he's only about four, but you get the idea."

The woman glanced at the images, then away, then back again. Jude watched her closely, watched her hands begin to shake as they hovered over the photos, like someone reading tarot cards and not liking the fortune in front of her.

"Broken bones that were never set," Jude explained casually. "That's what it looks like to me. What does it look like to you?"

"Why are you showing me these awful things about a boy I don't even know?" She glared up with that one eye. "You need to leave."

"I'm wondering about the circumstances that might lead to such a thing." She gathered her notebook and pen. "It might not have been abuse. People immediately think that, but there are many reasons for a child to end up in such dire circumstances, the biggest one being financial." Of course the injuries weren't accidental, but Jude was trying to put Ms. Perkins at ease and open up a conversation. "A child falls down, breaks an arm, breaks a collarbone. It costs a lot of money to repair those kinds of injuries if you don't have health insurance. And even if you do."

The woman nodded. "That's true. I have no idea how I'll ever pay for this." She looked around the room.

"But these . . ." Jude pulled out another color eight-by-ten. "This wasn't caused by a financial crisis or neglect. This was abuse." She placed the photo on top of another image, directly in front of Ms. Perkins. "What does this look like to you?"

No reply.

"I'm going to say cigarette burns. Wouldn't you agree?"

"They could be anything. Bugbite scars, I'd say. Have you ever seen a spider bite? They leave a round scar."

"True, but cigarette burns are highly specific and easily recognizable. I have a lot of data on cigarette burns." She tossed the tablet and pen aside, slipped off her jacket, and unbuttoned the top three buttons of her shirt, pulling it open enough to expose her shoulder, turning so the woman in bed could see it. "Some tormentors like to hold cigarettes against a person's back," Jude explained. "My theory is they want to hear the screams, but they don't want to watch the victim's face. It's just a little too much. But others get off on seeing the reaction and the pain they're causing." She turned and pulled up her shirt to reveal the midsection of her stomach. "As you can see, cigarette burns all look alike. They leave a precise scar." Pause for effect. "I know a cigarette burn when I see one."

The woman made an angry choking sound and swept the photos off the table to the floor. "This has nothing to do with me. Get out of here. Now. And don't come back."

Jude continued to watch the woman in the bed. She was in pain—real pain, not emotional pain. Jude felt bad about that. But Perkins knew something about the boy. No doubt about it.

She buttoned her shirt and put on her jacket. She picked up the photos with care and returned them safely to her bag. Perkins was lying back, eyes closed, fumbling for her pain pump. Jude stepped forward and put it in her hand. "I hope you feel better soon. Oh, and Ms. Perkins? I'll be back." After she visited the boy at his foster home to show him a photo of Nanette Perkins.

CHAPTER 19

Twenty years earlier . . .

The alarm woke her at three a.m. Nan had set it to go off every hour so she could keep tabs on the outdoor temperature.

"Lyle." She shook her husband's shoulder. "Get up."

He groaned and she shook him again.

"It's twenty below. You need to put heaters out there."

Like a sleepwalker, he tossed back the covers and shuffled away. She heard the jingle of his belt as he pulled on his jeans, heard the zip of his jacket and the metal click of his lighter, followed by a whiff of cigarette smoke. Then the door slammed, and she dropped off again. At some point he returned to bed, shivering, saying something about how damn cold it was, his arm hugging her waist, his legs like ice.

They both fell back asleep.

Several hours later, she woke to howling wind rattling the farmhouse. She checked the RadioShack temperature gauge next to the bed. It had a cord that ran along the baseboard and out a window. Still twenty below, but at least it hadn't gotten any colder. She recalled some worse nights.

A cold front had blown in late yesterday, and she and the rest of the team had come to the last-minute decision to wait on making their next delivery until morning because of the threat of black ice on the roads.

No sense risking lives and their valuable merchandise. Nan didn't like it when things didn't go smoothly, and the weather in the Midwest was especially challenging. Plus, they had a reputation to maintain. Their isolated farmhouse served as the national hub for smuggled goods, and a fast and effortless delivery was of utmost importance.

She got out of bed and put on layers of clothing. Jeans, sweatshirt, wool socks, heavy insulated boots. In the living room, she turned up the thermostat a couple of degrees, muttering to herself about their move to Minnesota. A few years ago, they'd had some merchandise go bad in the Oklahoma heat, and they'd thought moving north might be a good idea. "Nobody will be looking for us in rural Minnesota." It was true, and not a bad move except for the winters. There was no way she could have been prepared for this. Sure, she watched the news, knew it got cold, but a person really had to live it to understand what kind of hell it truly was.

In the kitchen, she turned on the coffeemaker. While it spit liquid into the glass pot, she laid out twenty pieces of white bread on the kitchen table and began scooping generic peanut butter from a big plastic jar. The bathroom door slammed, and Lyle appeared, tucking in his flannel shirt, a red cap on his head that advertised a popular tractor brand.

Everything was about blending in. They were just a couple in their twenties interested in working a few hundred acres. Luckily, Lyle had worked on a farm before deciding to go into the family business and knew how to make it look official. For the last two years, he'd even sold the corn crop they'd raised. In the summer, Nan had a stand at a market in the city where she sold eggs, and she'd started making strawberry jam that wasn't half-bad. It was easy to get sucked into the life and almost start believing it yourself.

Lyle looped an index finger through the handles of two mugs and filled them as liquid from the machine sizzled onto the warming plate. With a clatter, he replaced the carafe, set a cup of coffee near her, tapped and dumped two cigarettes from the pack on the table, and pulled a lighter from his pocket. Without a word, he lit both cigarettes and passed one over.

Their routine, his silent little love song to her.

This was something they did together. Drank coffee and hard liquor and smoked. But the smoking was the real glue in their relationship. A lot of couples bonded over a love of smoking. That was her theory, anyway. Because when you looked at a relationship closely, that was all some people had. A love of smoking in a world that increasingly marginalized smokers. Restaurants had smoking sections now, in the worst part of the building, usually next to the restroom. She wouldn't be surprised if they tried to stop smoking in bars. Ridiculous, since smoking and drinking went together.

But all the chicken eggs and strawberry jam couldn't make her like Minnesota. She'd finally admitted to herself that she hated it. She hadn't told Lyle yet, but she was hoping they could sell the farm and move the hub back to Oklahoma. But it wasn't going to be easy. Lyle seemed to like it here, and he would take some convincing. She didn't mind the contraband they smuggled from all over the country, but she was sick of the cold. And yet Lyle seemed to actually enjoy the life they had on their pretend farm that she was afraid wasn't really pretend anymore.

She spread the peanut butter, and he put the slices of bread together and stuck them back in the bread bag. "Gonna need water too," she said.

"Got it under control, hon. Checked the road report and everything's clear."

They'd talked about having a kid because she'd really like a little boy or girl of her own. But hell. Lyle was like a kid sometimes. She had to watch everything he did. What kind of partnership was that?

"I'm going to start the truck." At the back door, he stuffed his feet into a pair of boots that were supposed to be warm enough to wear when temperatures reached forty below zero. Forty freakin' below.

"Let's just move so we don't have to worry about this damn cold."
She wanted to see if he'd agree. He didn't.

He slapped on a pair of gloves and grabbed the bag of sandwiches.
"I'll put these and the water in the truck, then we'll load up." Frigid air
blasted her in the face, almost taking her breath away. A few minutes
later, he was back. He just stood there, wind blowing in.

"Shut the damn door." Distracted, she stubbed out her cigarette
and stuck her hands in the pockets of her sweatshirt.

He didn't move.

She started to yell at him about the cold and the door, but then she
noticed how white his face was. And was he shaking? Yes.

"What's wrong?"

He moved his mouth, but no sound came out. He pointed
behind him.

Something told her this was serious, this was bad.

The farmhouse addition had two entries. One for loading and unloading, and one just off the kitchen. She headed for the one off the kitchen.

"Don't open it! Go around, around!"

What the hell?

Without grabbing a hat or coat, she pushed past him and strode
out of the house. The wind was still blowing, and he hadn't shoveled
the freshly formed drifts. Some were maybe fifteen inches deep. He followed close on her heels as she trudged through the snow and skirted
the house to the addition. Concrete block walls that could be hosed
down, no windows, built to contain noise and odor. But the door, the
damn metal door, was standing wide open.

She ran for it, hampered by her boots and the drifts. She fell to
her knees, got back up, kept running. Lyle hurried after her, calling her
name as if he wanted to stop her from seeing what was inside. When
she reached the building, she hit the wall switch. The large lightbulbs
at the peak of the ceiling responded, illuminating rows of cots. And a
row of unmoving shoes and legs.

Boys, children, with duct-taped mouths.

And now she saw why the door was open. To air out the building. On the floor near the door was a portable propane heater. Off now, but what was it doing there at all? Not vented, something for outdoor use.

The next minutes were a blur as she searched the room for any sign of life, kicking and tugging and sobbing. Dead, all dead. Unable to take it anymore, she ran out, slammed the door.

Lyle, coward that he was, just stood there watching her, hands at his sides.

"What'd you do?" she screamed.

"You told me to put heaters in there."

The building had heat, but she'd been worried about the below-zero temperature. That's why she'd set the alarm. "Electric heaters! Not propane! *Electric.*" She beat him on the chest with her fists. "You idiot!" She started crying. Yes, they dealt in the trafficking of children, but those kids were her responsibility, her babies. She'd let them down.

She slugged Lyle in the face, maybe more than once. He put a hand to his bleeding nose, and he was crying now too. She wailed, thinking of the kids, thinking of the suppliers and buyers and how much damn trouble she and Lyle were going to be in.

He grabbed her by the arms and gave her a shake. "*Shh.* Be quiet."

He was right. They lived in an isolated area, but someone could be nearby. You never knew.

"Let's think," he said.

"What are we going to do? We can't bury them. The ground's frozen solid."

"I could haul them across the country. Dump them somewhere far away from here. Less chance of anybody being able to trace it to us."

"And what if you get pulled over? What if you break down? What if the delivery truck is inspected at a weigh station? And what about the smell?"

"We could burn them."

She marched back to the house. Pulled out a bottle of vodka and started drinking it straight from the bottle. Maybe they should just pack up and leave. That was it. In the bedroom, she dug through the closet and tugged out a suitcase. "We have to run. Get a plane to some other country. Any other country. Just get the hell out of here."

Lyle stood in the doorway, phone in his hand. "I called my brother."

Oh shit. "You shouldn't have told anybody."

"He has an idea. He owns an old food-delivery warehouse downtown. Says it's got a walk-in freezer. We put 'em in there and bury them later. But John's worried about one of the buyers. This person's not going to be happy and could cause some serious problems."

"What kind of problems?"

"Like turning on us, or worse."

She didn't want to ask what the *worse* might be.

"But we'll try to figure it out. Maybe we can substitute another boy for his."

"We don't have another."

"Maybe we can get one."

It wasn't that easy. They didn't do abductions. They were the middlemen for a reason.

Nan rode with Lyle to the meat locker. Thirty silent miles with a truck full of ten dead bodies. The vehicle was loud and the ride was rough, and she kept wondering if she smelled exhaust fumes, even cracking the window a few times to let in fresh air. Now she was paranoid about carbon monoxide poisoning.

She wished she could have stayed home, got drunker, but she didn't trust Lyle not to screw things up more than he already had. They rode in silence, Lyle occasionally making some weird sound with his throat, like he was having trouble swallowing. She'd tossed the bread bag on the front seat, and now she pulled out two sandwiches, offering one to him. He shook his head and put a fist against his mouth, like the thought of eating a sandwich meant for a dead kid made him sick. She put his sandwich back and ate hers. It didn't taste too bad. She still wanted to scream at Lyle some more, but what good would that do?

"I'm done with trafficking." He pounded his palms against the steering wheel. "Done."

She didn't know if it was the end for her, but she'd think about it. She wasn't surprised about Lyle. Even though it was his family business, started by his father and grandfather, his heart had never really been in it. But it was good, easy money when things went right. And she enjoyed her short time with the kids and felt like she'd helped them transition. A mother figure, even though she told them to call her Nan. The real question was whether she wanted to stay with Lyle. A guy who couldn't keep from screwing things up no matter what. But he'd never hit her, and he lit her cigarettes and poured her coffee. Sometimes he even fixed her breakfast.

Lyle's older brother John met them at the warehouse. He opened the big sliding door and they drove inside, John closing the door behind them.

The locker was located at the far end.

Unloading the truck was hard, gruesome work, the bodies limp as rag dolls and heavy. When they were done, the bodies stacked like firewood, his brother produced a length of heavy chain and ran it through the meat locker handles, the sound of metal against metal echoing in the empty warehouse. He secured the chain with an industrial padlock, then passed a leather fob with the outer door and padlock key to Lyle.

"Thanks," Lyle said, pocketing the keys. "Jesus, thanks."

His brother grabbed him by the throat and backed him to a wall, pinning him there, talking through gritted teeth.

Growing up, Nan used to wonder what was wrong with her, why she wasn't like other kids her age, why she didn't have the emotions others had, but then she met Lyle's brother. In comparison, he made her seem like a bag of love and warm fuzzies.

"You two blew the hell out of this," John said. "Our business was growing, but we might have to shut down thanks to you."

True about the growth. It was no longer a mom-and-pop operation, but that might be where they'd gone wrong. Too many people involved.

John released Lyle, who dropped to his knees, clutching his throat. John seemed to come to an abrupt decision and said, "I want you both out."

"What'll we do for money?" Lyle croaked.

"I don't give a shit. You should have thought of that before you destroyed our merch. Get this fixed and then go back to Oklahoma or grow your crops or whatever. Don't fucking talk to me again."

Back in the truck, Lyle threw up in the sandwich bag. Then he started crying.

"Scoot over." Nan waved him into the passenger seat. She half stood and he slid under her so she could take the steering wheel, grinding gears but finally hitting reverse.

He hopped out long enough to lock the warehouse door, and they were on their way home.

"You could have helped me back there," he said.

"I have to be honest: I get where your brother's coming from. You screwed things up for a lot of people, and you're lucky to still be alive. Knowing what a temper he has, I'm kinda surprised he didn't shoot both of us and stick us in that meat locker too."

Lyle wiped his nose with the back of his hand. "Would you have let him choke me to death?" He rolled down his window and tossed the bread bag.

Maybe. She reached across the seat and gave his knee a pat like you would a kid. "Of course not."

Back at the farm, she hung the warehouse keys on a hook next to the kitchen door. "Once spring comes, you can just pick the bodies up and put them in a deep hole on the farm. Easy peasy." And then they could move back to Oklahoma.

CHAPTER 20

Back at Homicide, Jude called Child Protection Services and offered to test the boy's reaction to the photo of Nanette Perkins she'd found online. Overworked, they were happy to let her step in. She caught up with Uriah in the break room and told him about her visit to the hospital. This time he reacted in the way she'd expected him to earlier.

"Maybe you should let them take it from here."

She appreciated that he didn't outright order her to step away even though their full focus should have been on the bodies from the lake. "I'm good at time management," she pointed out.

"That's not what I'm talking about." He poured a coffee, silently asking if she wanted one too.

She shook her head and filled her water bottle instead.

"Do you think you're becoming too attached?" he asked. They were alone, and he might have felt he could be more candid here rather than at their desks, where conversations could be overheard. "Is this because you want to see the boy again?"

"I'm concerned for him."

"Your loyalty to people is admirable. It's a good trait, but after all you've been through . . ." He paused as if considering whether he should continue. She got the idea he was working on something he'd wanted to say to her for a while now. "You're drawn to people who need your help," he said.

She wouldn't disagree. "Is that a bad thing?"

"Sometimes. I seem to recall a dead body in your apartment not that long ago."

"I don't think my attention and concern was misplaced. She needed help. And she was someone who could have broken the case. Either way, it was a logical approach. You're talking emotion." She didn't have emotion anymore.

He set his mug aside. "Just think about trying to keep a little more distance. That's all I'm saying. I've seen you. You feel for these people. Not just the victims and the dead, but the criminals."

His words reminded her of what Elliot had said about sympathetic resonance. She just didn't see it. "That child is not a criminal."

"I never said he was. I'm just laying out why I'm concerned. Your experience has changed you in ways I can't begin to imagine or really understand. You're an empath. You soak up the people around you. You feel their emotions."

"I didn't know you were into science fiction."

"I've seen it, Jude. I doubt you're even aware of it, which is why I'm bringing it up. I think you should be conscious of it and try to protect yourself."

"This conversation has gotten ridiculous." She wasn't angry, just baffled and annoyed. "I'm going to see the boy, and I'm going to find out if he recognizes the woman I saw at the hospital. How much more straightforward can that be?"

Back at her desk, she picked up a stack of papers still warm from the copy machine, tapped them together, and tucked them into the side pocket of her messenger bag along with the photos of the boy.

The distance from the Minneapolis Police Department to the foster home was under ten miles. Due to side streets that still weren't optimal, it took Jude thirty minutes to reach the Richfield address given to her by CPS.

The south Minneapolis neighborhood was composed of streets laid out in a grid—a logical design—with similar small houses interspersed with larger apartment buildings. Stucco had always been a popular building product in the Twin Cities, and this area of town reflected that aesthetic.

The heater in her car spit out tepid air as the GPS on her phone told her to stop at a two-story foursquare with a chain-link fence and narrow sidewalk. Three snowmen in the yard. Through the narrow space between the houses, she caught a glimpse of a swing set and snow-covered garage in the backyard.

The foster mom, a woman named Lori, was expecting her. She answered the door and invited Jude inside. As was typical of many Twin Cities homes, the space had been remodeled at some point; walls didn't quite meet, and there was evidence of patched floors where built-ins had once stood. Directly in front of the entry was a kitchen, to the right a living area. Wooden and tile floors, paint of soothing shades. A wall-mounted wooden rack packed with children's coats, the boy's included, with boots lined up below. From beyond the open pocket doors came the sound of a television and cartoons.

"We're calling him Michael," Lori said. She held out her hand to take Jude's jacket. Jude shook her head but unzipped. "I know it's not his name, but we had to call him something. It just didn't seem right otherwise."

Jude picked up on how tense the woman was, and she thought about Uriah calling her an empath. "Michael's a nice name." He did not look like a Michael.

Lori was one of those earth mothers, probably good at hugs and giving comfort. She wore a heavy floral skirt, clogs, and wool socks; medium-brown hair skewered to the top of her head with two decorative sticks; fresh face, no makeup. She smelled like dish soap and coffee, and maybe a bit of the Goodwill store. Her agitation might have been caused by having a cop dropping in with very little warning. Or it could have been because of the boy.

"He's sweet," the foster mother confided as if trying to convince herself as she glanced over her shoulder into the living room, where two children were lying on the floor, watching cartoons. The third, the child with the temporary name of Michael, sat cross-legged on the puffy brown couch. He wasn't watching the TV. Instead, he was watching the children watch TV.

"I don't think he's ever been around other kids," Lori said. "He doesn't play or interact. He just . . . observes." She leaned closer, her voice dropping, lines of worry around her eyes. "Do you think it's safe for my girl and boy? To have him here?"

Good question. Jude had been surprised to hear he'd been put in a house with other children. She would have avoided kids until they could be sure he wasn't a danger to anyone.

Violence instilled violence. That was a fact. It didn't mean every child who grew up around violence would become violent, but kids learned from adults. Even a child with no natural violent tendencies would pick them up if that's all they were exposed to. Children mimicked adults. But the good news was those kids could sometimes unlearn the behavior with the right guidance and role models.

"I honestly can't answer that question," Jude said. "It's obvious he's experienced some bad things in his short life. Add that to his lack of socialization, and I don't blame you for being concerned. I would advise you not to leave the children alone together, and if you have any pets, take the same precautions."

The woman put a trembling hand to a red cheek. "I don't like this. I don't like this at all. They called and were desperate for a home, and I'm a softie. This month has been a busy one for them. I'm not sure why. Maybe it's the cold weather. Everybody has cabin fever and they're taking it out on the kids."

"I can't really give you advice other than to take precautions. Call your contact person if you have any concerns. Call me, for that matter." She pulled out a business card and handed it to the woman. "Day or night."

Lori glanced into the living room. "He's been through so much." Her eyes teared up. "Poor little soul."

"I know. But don't put your own family at risk. Never do that. Trust your instincts." It was what she told everyone. And it was probably a much more realistic warning than the one the woman had gotten from CPS, if she'd gotten a warning at all. "Listen to that nagging voice."

"It's talking to me now, honestly, but I don't think it's directly related to anything he's done. I think it's just his odd behavior." She dropped her voice again. "It's kind of creepy."

Jude thought about conversations she'd overheard about herself since her escape from captivity. Almost everybody at work was uncomfortable around her except for Uriah. "I'd like to talk to him privately," she said. "If that's okay."

The mother seemed relieved to pass the responsibility of him to someone else, even for a few minutes. She called into the living room. "Kids! Come help me fix a snack."

"Michael" didn't respond. The two other children jumped up from the floor and scrambled to the kitchen, jockeying for position, one opening the refrigerator and the other grabbing a bag of sliced carrots. One of them said something about cookies.

Jude nodded to the mother and slipped into the living room. When "Michael" saw her, he let out a gasp and jumped off the couch. "Hey!"

"Hey, you too."

"Are we going back to your house? So my Nana can pick me up?"

"Not today." Jude sat down on the sofa and grasped him by both hands, holding on gently, giving him the option to pull away if he wanted to, as she looked into his serious face. She didn't even care that his palms were slightly sticky. "I just came to see you. And talk to you."

She smiled, and she didn't have to force it. She was glad to see him again. That was followed by a drop of her stomach as she thought about what Uriah had said. Maybe he was right. Maybe she was getting too attached. "Do you like it here?"

He nodded.

"What about the other children? That must be nice. To be around children close to your age."

He shrugged. "I guess."

They talked a little more. She asked about the snowmen outside. No, he hadn't helped make any of them. They were there when he'd gotten to the house. But he liked them.

Despite the sticky fingers, she noted that his face was clean and his hair had been brushed. His foster mother seemed like a good person. Jude was reassured by everything she saw. Her concern had undergone a shift in the last ten minutes, and she was no longer worried about the boy as much as she was worried about the foster family. They knew nothing about him. Nobody did.

"I want to show you something." Jude let go to reach into her messenger bag. She extracted the pile of papers she'd tucked inside earlier, most of them photos she'd printed from the internet. "I have some pictures for you to look at."

He slid off the couch to stand next to her, pressed the palms of his hands together in a paused clap, and waited, shaking a little in excitement and expectation.

Like in a police lineup, Jude deliberately included several different images and faces in hopes of getting a truer response. "What's this a picture of?" She showed him the first one and waited.

"Lady," he said, pointing.

"That's right."

She pulled another from the stack.

"Dog!"

Another image of another woman.

"Lady."

From the kitchen came sounds of cupboards slamming. The boy looked away from Jude, distracted.

"And another," she said, pulling out a fourth photo. He was watching the kitchen, probably thinking about food and maybe the chance to eat a cookie. "Boy?" She'd never called him that before.

He reluctantly looked back at the paper in Jude's hand. And his face changed. "Nana! Nana!" he shouted. He jumped up and down, knees and elbows bent. "Nana!"

His reaction left no doubt that Nanette Perkins was his "Nana." It was heartbreaking to see how much he'd come to life upon seeing the face of the woman who'd abandoned him to die in a blizzard, the woman who was indirectly or even directly responsible for his abuse. He was a child and Jude was an adult, but she recognized the bond that formed between a victim and the person who inflicted the pain and suffering. On the surface, even for her, it was impossible to understand that pull. She knew only that it was real.

She started to put the photos away, then paused. "Would you like to keep this one?" she asked, indicating the image of Perkins. He nodded and jumped from one foot to the other.

She handed the photo to him, and he pressed his face against it, giving it a kiss.

"Let's go get a cookie."

In the kitchen, the boy waved the photo in the air. "Nana! My Nana!" he said in excitement and what might have been his first real interaction with the other children.

Jude's mobile buzzed. She checked the screen. Uriah, telling her to unsilence her phone. He was following a lead and might be calling soon.

"I'm going to have to go," she told the foster mom. Then she picked up a homemade oatmeal cookie from a plate, crouched down in front of the boy, and handed it to him. "I'll see you later," she said, even though there was a chance she might never see him, and she might have been saying the same thing Perkins had told him a few days earlier. She straightened, feeling a tightness in her throat, anxious to get away from the child munching on the cookie, watching her.

"You should take a treat for yourself." Lori held out the plate. Jude grabbed one, mumbled a quick thanks, and left. Outside, cookie in her mouth, she started the car, turned on the heat, felt the same cool air she'd felt earlier, and headed for the hospital to visit Nanette Perkins again.

CHAPTER 21

Five years earlier...

Doctors said it was the cigarettes and heavy drinking that caused Lyle's cancer. Funny, the thing they'd bonded over was the thing that was now breaking them up forever. Lyle had just been given a week to live, and Nan wasn't ready to tell him good-bye. Their life together hadn't been all puppies and kittens, but they'd quit child trafficking after the fiasco of that night fifteen years ago. He'd convinced her to stay in Minnesota, and she'd almost gotten used to the winters. They went to church on Sundays, and they'd made a few friends. Not close friends, because they could never have that, not with their secrets. The friends were farming, salt-of-the-earth people who'd even helped with the harvest when Lyle was in Rochester having surgery and radiation. But the cancer had come back, leaving him unable to speak and ready to go.

Their secret had become another kind of bond.

Right now they were lying in bed together, watching the small television on the dresser. Nan was drinking a beer and eating chips; Lyle was clicking through channels, stopping on anything that looked a bit religious.

Funny how that happened too. How he used to cuss and never go to church, but suddenly, once the cancer hit, he was all God this and

God that. So together they watched some woman with big blond hair tell them they needed to repent, needed to ask for forgiveness.

Lyle tapped a pen against the tablet in his hand, and Nan read what he'd written.

Maybe I should go to confession.

"But you aren't Catholic."

I want to confess my sins.

They'd never talked about the night they lost the kids, and they'd been good people since then. Wasn't that enough?

I want to confess. I want to tell somebody.

"You mean the police?"

Maybe.

She shook her head. "Don't you dare do anything like that. It's fine for you, because you'll be dead anyway, but I have to live and I'll have to go to prison for the rest of my life."

I can't die without telling somebody.

"How 'bout this? You write it all down, and I'll get it to the police somehow so they won't know where it came from or who it came from."

That seemed to satisfy him a little, but not completely. Hopefully he'd forget about it because he was on a lot of morphine. He'd forgotten things before. But the next day he started in on his confession again, so she turned the tablet to a fresh page and handed it to him so he could write everything down. When she read it, she had to reach for a chair.

They'd done bad things. Really bad.

Later, she folded the paper and stuck it in an envelope she addressed to the Hennepin County Sheriff's Office. She wasn't sure why she chose them rather than the FBI or some such. It just seemed kinda local and more important somehow. And she hoped it would get Lyle to quit going on about confessing. It made her mad that he thought he could confess and leave her with all the damage.

She showed him the stamped, addressed envelope. "I'm going to drive into the city to mail it," she said. "So it won't be postmarked from here. But I'll be back in an hour and a half."

He nodded from the bed and picked up the remote.

It was nice to get away and not be a caretaker for a while. While she was gone, she stopped in an antiques shop and just browsed, and she went to a café that overlooked a river. She had tea and a sandwich and a scone. For some reason it felt perfect, like something her soul needed. Back at the farm, she parked the car, and as she headed up the sidewalk, she braced herself for everything.

Cancer had an odor. That had surprised her, but now she got how those cancer-sniffing dogs could identify it. Hell, she'd be able to sniff it out after this.

She stepped inside to the sound of the television coming from the bedroom. Shades were pulled down tight, and the place was dark and sad. Lyle was in bed where she'd left him. He appeared to be sleeping, but something about him said otherwise. She dropped her purse with the confession she'd never really mailed and ran to the bedside. With fingers on his jaw, she shook his face and waited for his eyes to open, waited for him to smile up at her. But his skin was already cold, and his eyes never opened. He must have been hanging on for that confession.

They'd said a week.

Her legs buckled, and she collapsed to the floor and cried until she didn't have any more tears left in her. When she was done, she pushed herself to her feet and crawled into bed beside him. It was then she noticed writing on the tablet lying across his stomach. Another confession, this one just for her.

I lied to you. I never buried the bodies. They're still in the locker.

CHAPTER 22

When Jude arrived back at the hospital, Ms. Perkins's leg hammock and IV pump were gone, a sign that she'd be going home soon. At the very least, they liked to leave a plugged IV port until release. It was gone too. On the wheeled table in front of the woman was an empty medicine cup and a glass of water with a bent straw. The curtains had been reopened. Was that a rule nurses were required to follow? Lights on, curtains open? Jude crossed the room and reclosed them, blocking all sunlight except for a sliver that fell across the floor and foot of the bed.

"The child has identified you as the person he's been living with," she told Ms. Perkins. *Ms. Perkins.* The name now seemed awkward. Jude was used to thinking of her as Nana. "Which means you're the one who left him at my door."

Without waiting a beat, the woman let out a wail, like some bad actress executing her reaction too soon. Or had she been lying there, emotions smoldering?

Jude closed the door, grabbed a box of tissues, and placed them on the hospital table. "I'm going to have to ask you some questions. The first: Are you the child's mother?"

"Yes. God, yes." Perkins pulled a tissue from the tiny box and dabbed at her eyes as if afraid to smear makeup she wasn't wearing. "My husband died and I couldn't take care of him anymore, so I left the boy at your house because I knew you protected young people, and I knew he'd be safe and you'd do what you needed to do." She looked at Jude with red-rimmed eyes and what appeared to be real tears. "He was supposed to go inside. I don't know why he didn't. He was supposed to."

"You have to be buzzed in."

"I didn't think about that. A car was coming. I panicked and pulled away. I didn't know he couldn't get in the building. I would never have left him to freeze. I brought him there to give him a better life. When I think of what could have happened to him . . ."

"You could have put him up for adoption."

"Kids that age aren't picked. And I didn't know what I was doing, wasn't thinking straight. I was overwhelmed. I thought maybe he would get more attention if you found him. Like those dogs with tragic stories that everybody wants to adopt."

"Where was he born? Child Protection Services will be following up, but they'll be looking into his birth records."

"There aren't any."

Not totally unexpected.

"He was a surprise. I sure didn't expect to get pregnant at thirty-nine. It was a home birth. I never reported it."

Hmm. Could be true.

"I don't think it's anybody's concern when or where or how my kid was born," Perkins said. "That's nobody's business but mine."

"You didn't file a birth certificate?"

"Nope."

Jude watched as she tossed the tissue on the floor and pulled out a fresh one. There were thousands of undocumented American citizens in the country. "If you're his mother, then I'm sure you won't mind taking a DNA test to prove it."

Perkins shrugged. "Bring it on."

"That's something else Child Protection Services will want to be in charge of and follow up on once I report this new information to them. We'll need to make sure he's who you say he is. And when the results come back, we'll have another issue on our hands. What to do with him."

"I want him back."

Jude blinked in surprise. "That's not up to me, but personally I'd rather he never live with you again. CPS might also be sending someone here to serve papers on you for child endangerment. You'd have to appear before a judge."

"I deserve it. It was a stupid thing to do."

"What's his name?"

"I never named him."

Jude wasn't surprised about that either, and his lack of a name underscored a disconcerting level of neglect.

"It's not what you might think. I'd read about how some cultures let their kids name themselves when they get old enough. It seemed like a cool idea at the time, but then I just let it slide. He became Boy. We tried a few different names, but nothing worked."

Jude's phone rang. The call Uriah had promised. She had to take it. Without further conversation with Perkins or an explanation of her departure, she answered as she stepped from the room.

"We might have an ID on the first body from the lake," Uriah said. "Someone who worked the case years ago was following a conversation about it on Reddit, where all the armchair detectives hang out. Name's Paul Savoy. Kid's name, Billy Nelson. Savoy recognized some of the details, saw the police sketch we submitted to the press, and thought it might be his old case."

She tried to mentally shift gears from the child with no real name, to another child, a dead child.

"These retired detectives just can't stop following the stories and trying to solve them, even from the comfort of their own homes," Uriah continued.

"I'll be right there. Let's go talk to him."

"That could be a little tough. He lives in California."

"Oh, okay. Guess I don't blame him for wanting to get out of here if he lived through any winters like this."

"That's where the crime took place. California. And where he lives. Orange County. And get this. The case is twenty years old."

She let that sink in.

A body from Orange County, California, turning up in Minneapolis twenty years later. "How reliable is our source?"

"He's legit. He called, hooked me up with someone working on updating and streamlining some of Los Angeles County's antiquated databases."

Accessing crime data was still a problem due to databases around the country that weren't linked, and the need for much of the information to be entered manually into the new systems. County level, state level, federal, all had issues. They were getting there, transitioning, but there still wasn't one database to plug into that would pull up everything you were looking for, especially when dealing with cold cases. Or a way to just magically sync everything. So the backlog of cold cases was pushed aside as a lesser priority.

"They didn't have any DNA on file," Uriah continued, "but they had fingerprints taken of the missing kid when he was still in school. A fifteen-point match."

Some departments in the US required a twelve-point match, but Jude tended to agree with the UK and preferred something closer to sixteen or seventeen. "That's fairly indisputable." Her adrenaline pumping from the news, she moved quickly down the hallway, updating Uriah on the child found in her apartment, avoiding carts and nurses and the occasional person shuffling past with an IV rack.

"You believe her about being his mother?"

"I don't know." She pushed the elevator button. "She didn't balk at taking a DNA test." Back to the cold case. "I think we should Skype with this detective."

"No need. He's on a plane right now and should be here shortly. I'm sorry to dump this on you, but Valentine is working a case, and we got a report of a shoot-out in North Minneapolis. One dead. McIntosh is at the scene, but I need to be on the ground too. I want you to swing by and pick up the detective from the airport. I'll follow up this call with a text. His flight, cell phone. I know you probably aren't crazy about collecting a stranger and giving him a ride."

"I can handle it." But it wouldn't be pleasant.

CHAPTER 23

At the Minneapolis–Saint Paul International Airport, Jude parked in the short-term ramp and went inside the terminal. Meeting Paul Savoy face-to-face seemed the polite thing to do. Awkward, but not as awkward as simply inviting a stranger into her car before even saying hello. And he was flying halfway across the country to help them.

Before heading to the airport, she'd called Kim Tharp at Child Protection Services to give her the information about Perkins.

"Good. We have a parent," was the reaction. Not *Let's make sure to keep that monster away from him.* Jude hadn't liked that. She'd strongly suggested they run a DNA test, and Kim had agreed.

Checking the arrival board, she noted that Savoy's flight had just landed. She could have used her badge to gain access beyond the security checkpoint. Instead, she sent a text to his mobile to let him know she'd meet him at the bottom of the escalators, near the luggage carousels and Starbucks.

While waiting, she Googled him, pulling up headshots that covered a large span of time. Paul Savoy with brown hair, Paul Savoy with a beard, Paul Savoy with a mustache, Paul Savoy with salt-and-pepper hair, even though she'd determined he was only fifty-seven.

Along with headshots were articles on cold-case interviews with Savoy, conducted after his retirement. Curious to think he would have been about Jude's current age when the child went missing, and Jude would have been about sixteen at the time of the abduction. Back before the internet and social media and all the multitude of news outlets available today.

She recognized him immediately through the glass doors that separated travelers from nontravelers as he rode the steep escalator to street level. Tall, fit. Beige jacket over one arm, maroon tie, briefcase, small carry-on bag. He had that old-school California detective vibe about him. Confident. Tan. Very tan. Maybe he golfed.

He spotted her and lifted his hand in recognition, but not a full-blown wave. The automatic doors opened, a gust of diesel-tainted air entering with him as he approached.

"Thanks for coming," Jude said. They shook hands.

"I wouldn't have missed this."

"Do you have a hat and gloves?"

"I didn't bring winter clothing. Don't own any and I'm only going to be here until tomorrow. I've got an event to get back to in California."

"That's a quick turnaround."

"A wedding. My daughter." He continued with details he didn't need to share and were none of her business. "Second marriage."

"You might want to put that on." She indicated the jacket over his arm. It was a suit jacket, nothing that would do much to keep him warm, but better than nothing.

They started walking, and she pointed wordlessly in the direction they should go, taking another set of escalators down, past the boarding area for the light rail, and up another escalator to the parking area.

At her car, he tossed his carry-on and briefcase in the back seat. "How do you stand this cold? It's insane. How does anybody live here? *Why* does anybody live here?"

"I don't usually mind it, but this winter's been a challenge. First time to Minneapolis?"

"No, but first time for these temperatures."

Inside the car, Jude turned the ignition key as they both fastened seat belts.

"Is that accurate?" He pointed to the dashboard digital readout.

Ten degrees. Balmy. "Yep." She guided the car down the narrow ramp to the row of pay booths. "They say the Twin Cities would be as big as New York City or LA if not for the winters. Because summers are nice. Almost perfect. But they don't last long."

"So you cram a lot of living into a few months?"

She gave the word *living* consideration. He wasn't the most astute detective if he thought someone who'd been through what she'd been through was doing any living. But maybe he was a glass-half-full kind of guy. Or better, maybe he'd never heard of her before today. Doubtful.

"Most people try to embrace winter here," she said. "It's about the only way to do it. And the ones who don't, eventually leave. Many expats end up in California." She stopped at the pay booth, swiped her credit card, and then they were heading away from the airport. "We can sometimes be colder than Antarctica."

"Not sure I'd brag about that." He sniffed. "Do I smell mothballs?"

"Probably."

He lowered his window. Frigid air filled the vehicle, and he quickly hit the up button.

"You get used to it after a while." She didn't even notice it anymore. "It isn't my vehicle of choice. I had to park my motorcycle for the winter. This car was stored in a garage for years, and the owner used mothballs to keep the mice away. So they wouldn't eat the seats," she added, in case he didn't understand the purpose.

She took Highway 62 to I-35 north.

It was midafternoon, and Uriah had reserved a private room in a restaurant near Headquarters. A nice gesture. Savoy could probably use a meal, and Jude hadn't eaten since wolfing down a bowl of instant oatmeal that morning. And anything was preferable to the bright lights of one of their meeting rooms.

Like many businesses in the Twin Cities, the restaurant was a throwback, mimicking the past or preserving it. The lounge was dark and not very busy. It had a back room with bookcases and real books and a gas fireplace they had to themselves. A tin ceiling and hardwood floors. Like some gentleman's private smoking room. No wonder Uriah liked it. It kind of reminded Jude of his apartment, especially the old books.

They perused red menus with gold tassels. She was uncomfortable but tried not to show it. She decided that she actually would have preferred the bright lights of a meeting room because this had the feel of something you might do with a friend or even a date.

Savoy ordered a gin and tonic, not a manly or trendy drink but one typically employed to get the job done. Jude made do with hot tea. They both ordered sandwiches. After the food arrived, they discussed the case.

"As soon as I saw the police sketch on Reddit, I knew it was Billy Nelson," Savoy said. "So I had the prints faxed to your office. We've also got mitochondrial DNA on file. But when you've been looking for so long, you just know when you finally have it. I was sure it would be a match."

"The question is, how did Nelson wind up in Minneapolis?" Jude poured ketchup on one corner of her plate and picked up a thick fry. "The fact that we have two boys about the same age who look very much alike . . . One of my theories is sex trafficking."

He didn't seem particularly interested in that theory. "The similarity could just be a coincidence."

"True. And it doesn't explain how he ended up in the lake twenty years after he went missing. And we still don't have an ID on the other boy. Did he die around the same time? Twenty years ago?"

"Billy Nelson should have been an FBI major case," Savoy said. "But back then, info wasn't shared, not even with the public, like it is now. Everybody was afraid of putting too much information out there. But now, with social media, it's leaked before the first press conference."

Sandwich abandoned, Savoy ordered another drink. When it came and the waiter left, he said, "I'm not going to lie and put on a macho act. This case has haunted me. I started out as a beat cop, moved up to detective, and this was one of my first disturbing crimes. I always worried that I didn't do enough in those first few days. And even today, I'm still trying to get legislation passed that would require DNA collection in the first twenty hours of a child's or even an adult's disappearance. Wouldn't have to be tested—that's expensive—but just collected and stored. There's no protocol anywhere in the country for missing persons DNA collection."

"Typically it falls on mitochondrial DNA," Jude said. "Which isn't ideal."

"Yep." He swallowed half the drink and shook the glass until the ice rattled.

Once they were done eating and their plates were gone, he opened a leather briefcase and pulled out a stack of files. "I made copies of everything before I retired. I'll often go over things, looking for any clue I might have missed. I conduct fresh interviews, dig a little deeper, but many of the people are dead, and the ones who were alive back then . . . Well, you know memory changes over time. It's unreliable days later, and now we're talking about twenty years. Nelson's mother and father are both dead. I think stress played a role in that because they died fairly young. He has a sister who's still alive. We've been in touch over the years, and I'll give her a call tonight. I'm glad she'll finally have some closure. She might want to come and maybe even take the body back to California."

He ordered another drink, and Jude now questioned the wisdom in coming to a restaurant where they served liquor. They talked a little more. She picked up the bill and left a generous tip. "What time does your flight leave tomorrow?" She wondered how the boy was doing. Had someone from CPS gone to the hospital to take a DNA sample from Nanette Perkins, hopefully before she was released?

"Early." He finished his drink, slammed the glass down, and said, "I'd like to see Billy." He nodded to himself, maybe only just realizing the true reason for his visit when they could have easily Skyped. "I have to see him."

"For your own closure."

He didn't look surprised by her words. Impressed, yes. "I heard you were good at figuring people out. In fact, I was a little worried about meeting you because of that. You're right," he said. "It broke me, at least for a while. It ruined my marriage, and it almost destroyed my relationship with my daughters. Those have been repaired, and I have two grandkids. And I'm thinking about getting a dog."

"I have a cat."

"Pets are good."

"That's what Detective Ashby keeps telling me." She pulled out her phone and called the medical examiner's office to let them know they were coming.

CHAPTER 24

Jude pulled into the back lot of the Hennepin County Medical Examiner's Office. The sun was just right, the building darkened by the shadow of the US Bank Stadium. People said it was creepy; Jude thought it was cool. Didn't matter. Ground would be broken soon on a new facility in the suburb of Minnetonka, fifteen miles away. Jude heard it would have woods and walking trails, which would be a nice respite from the solemn and serious work taking place inside. Employees in the facility liked their jobs, and most people who conducted autopsies had gone into the field because they enjoyed solving puzzles, but some cases were especially tough and few could go untouched by the innocent victims. Being able to step outside into nature might be mentally beneficial. But even though it was past time to move to a new location, Jude was fond of the old place. It was a part of the city's history; plus, it was close to the police department.

They headed for the concrete building, Savoy walking fast, maybe because of the cold, maybe because he was anxious to finally see the child he'd spent so much time searching for. Jude had to lengthen her stride. Normally she was the one people tried to keep up with. Inside, she explained their mission to the woman at the front desk.

"We're expecting you." The receptionist clicked some keys, checked her monitor, then Savoy's ID, and said, "I'll buzz you in." Security was important. They'd had a few instances of gang members showing up, trying to retrieve dead enemies or friends. "The body is in room three, drawer four."

Jude blinked and opened her eyes wide. "He's no longer in the big cooler?"

"Nope. Moved just a couple of hours ago."

Which meant the autopsy could be performed. She'd contact Uriah, and he could get in touch with Ingrid.

"Do you need an escort?" the receptionist asked.

"I know the way."

Down a familiar hall of blinding lights and white polished floors and walls lined with photos of magazine articles and retired staff, past the large walk-in unit where the boys had initially been taken to thaw. The steady drip of the melting ice was something that would probably be forever embedded in Jude's brain.

In the morgue, the lights automatically reacted to their presence, room 3 slowly coming to life. A wall of twelve stainless-steel drawers, three high. The refrigeration fans were a roar of white noise—loud, but not loud enough. Jude released the latch, stainless steel meeting stainless steel, the sound traveling into the drawer and throughout the cavernous space of the room, creating two echoes, one sharp and one deep. Along with the drawer sliding open came the thick odor of putrid flesh. She and Savoy recoiled, then waited a moment for the smell to disperse.

Jude checked the toe tag to make sure they had the right body. No longer John Doe, but Billy Stewart Nelson. Savoy made no move to assist; he seemed in something close to shock as Jude eased the tray halfway out. Even though the body was light, it took some effort. New coolers were on order too.

Savoy was breathing hard. Despite the stench, she caught a faint whiff of the telltale evergreen scent from the gin he'd put away. She waited for him to engage—he was the only one who could know when he was ready. Savoy finally drew down the sheet, slowly, as if the child could feel it, past the shoulders until the entire face was revealed, along with half the belly.

In some cases, bodies didn't look a lot different dead than they would have looked in life. This child looked very dead. Now that he was thawed and no longer under ice, it was easy to see that the tips of his ears were black. His fingers were black too, eyes sunken, lips blue, reminding her a little of the photos of people who'd frozen to death in places like Mount Everest.

Sometimes bodies spoke to her, emoting what they'd gone through in those last moments of life. It could be anything from fear to surprise. It was slight; it was in the muscles, a hint of expression that she picked up on. This poor child was too far gone to emote anything.

"Oh my God." Savoy put a fist to his mouth. "I didn't know he'd look so bad. But he's been dead twenty years. I think maybe the ice had me expecting something else." He pointed. "Is that freezer burn?"

"I think so."

"I hoped this might tie up loose ends, mental loose ends, but I don't know. I think it might cause more nightmares."

"I'm sorry. Do you want to leave?" She moved to cover the body, and Savoy put out a hand, stopping her.

"Wait." A full minute passed before he sucked in a long and shaky breath.

"I think we should go." She reached for the sheet again.

"Don't."

Instead of covering the child, she stepped to the corner of the room to give the detective a semblance of privacy. Maybe he wanted to say a prayer, if he did that kind of thing.

He leaned closer, then he held his hand near the child's face, his fingers hovering very near but not touching, the detective in him knowing better than that. "I'm sorry," he whispered.

Oh, he was a very damaged man.

"I'm sorry I didn't find you. I'm sorry your parents are dead now. I'm sorry this happened to you."

The hum of the units seemed to overpower the room, like an oddly ill-suited soundtrack. Just this unfeeling and insensitive roar. People didn't often think about how crimes impacted detectives. And that was right and understandable. The spotlight wasn't supposed to be on them, but this was twenty years later. Savoy's wrenching response was similar to that of a parent. And when she thought it couldn't get any worse, when she thought she could finally step forward and put the child away, Savoy let out a wail and staggered back, leaned against the wall, and sobbed, one hand pressed to his face. He eventually dropped to silence, shoulders shaking. But once he pulled himself together, he didn't seem self-conscious of his outburst. No apology. No awkwardness.

Jude finally covered the body and closed the drawer. Without looking at each other, they left. Outside, they pulled in deep breaths, trying to clear their lungs of the smell of rotten flesh. It was a minute before she noticed the sun was dropping fast, the way it did in deep winter. That time of day when the world became muted and seemed to merge with its surroundings. Along with the dimming light, the temperature was plummeting.

"Sunset always makes me feel a good kind of melancholy." She didn't know why she said that. Maybe hoping it would give him a little comfort without offering any real words of sympathy. They might both be detectives, but she didn't know him, didn't know what he might or might not want from another human.

"You don't happen to have a cigarette, do you? I quit six months ago, but times like these . . ."

"No, sorry."

Back in the car, Savoy gave her the name of his hotel as he fixated on the digital readout on the dash. It was zero now. He pointed wordlessly.

"Since you'll be here overnight, you might be able to experience what ten below zero feels like," Jude said. "Something to tell your grandkids."

"I think I could have lived without that."

She pulled up to the entry of the downtown hotel. Doormen, revolving door, gold luggage cart. Pretty fancy for a retired detective's income.

"I've always wondered why they cover the body with sheets," he said. "Not everybody does it. I like when I see a sheet and not just a naked body lying there on the cold metal."

She made a sound of agreement because she had no answer for him.

"Call me anytime." He unfastened his seat belt. "If you have any questions, anything to tell me—I'll be around." He opened his brief-case, pulled out the folders he'd produced earlier at the restaurant, and handed them to her. "I'm done. I've gotten what bit of closure I could. These might or might not be of any help to you. This chapter of my life is finally over. It will haunt me until I die or until I forget why I'm living, but at least I'm done looking for a child with blond hair and blue eyes."

She took the folders. "I think the sheets are to make us feel better."

He ducked out of the car, bent at the waist, and put his hand on the roof. "A sign of respect." He closed the door firmly and walked away, soon to return to California and sunshine.

CHAPTER 25

Someone rapped on Nan's hospital door, and a man in a heavy coat, insulated hat with side flaps down, and dark glasses stepped inside. It took a few moments for Nan to recognize him. When she did, she let out a gasp and her heart began to slam.

Her visitor pulled off the glasses that were part of his disguise and took in her broken leg, now resting on a pillow, and shook his head at her like he couldn't believe the mess she'd gotten herself into.

What was he doing here?

She'd always been afraid of him. Lyle had feared him too, even though he'd never admitted it, but Nan could tell. After Lyle's death, he'd started coming around, and she'd let him stay in her life too long. Maybe he'd reminded her of Lyle and the good days. He could be so charming, but it was a psychopathic charm. Even before he was gone, she'd started keeping a loaded handgun and a knife next to her bed.

He closed the door.

"You can leave that open."

He shook his head and smiled.

Her plan to let him lead the conversation was abandoned. "I never mentioned your name," she said. "And I never will. You know that."

He moved closer, grabbed the remote, and turned the TV up a few notches, probably to mask their conversation if anybody happened by.

"Why do you exist?" he asked. "Why are you even alive? Can you tell me that?"

That made her mad. Scared mad. "I almost died in that car wreck. You could ask how I'm doing."

"You screwed up again."

She would never outrun the past. "Those kids. They were *Lyle's* fault." She hated to say it, but the truth was the truth. Although she was the one who'd told him to get the heaters. And she hadn't specified which heaters. So . . .

"Blame it on a dead guy who can't defend himself. And whose fault are the bodies in the lake? Not mine. And who dumped that boy on the detective's doorstep? Not Lyle. And not me. I could have found some-body to dispose of him easily," he said. "Nobody would have known, and nobody would have missed him."

He still smelled the same. Like expensive cologne and alcohol. He loved his alcohol. She didn't remember a time when he didn't have a fancy flask with him. He couldn't even get out of bed in the morning without drinking. "Just to get going."

He poked at Nan's face with a hard finger. It seemed like he wanted to drill it into her brain. "What was in that head of yours?"

Somehow, even with all the drinking, he was still good-looking.

Nan had a line she wouldn't cross, and she was still capable of caring for a few people. She had no problem selling kidnapped boys, but she did have a problem killing them. She wasn't sure about him.

"I gotta have a drink of water." Nan reached for the button that operated the TV so she could call the nurse. Her visitor's hand closed over hers.

"Let go." He squeezed hard.

Nan let go.

He unclipped the remote from the bed and pulled it out of her reach, placing it quietly on the floor. "It's nice they gave you a private room. I was a little concerned about that."

Her mouth went dry and she began talking fast. "You're right. It was stupid. I don't know what I was thinking. I liked the kid. I guess that's it. But I don't know what you're worried about. He had nothing to do with the business." A business they'd closed down after the kids died.

"He draws attention to you. And you'll draw attention to me. He can lead people right to your place."

"He can't. He never went outside. He wouldn't be able to describe where he was living." Not quite the truth. Nan didn't mention the few times she'd taken the boy out at night. "He never saw anybody. There's no way he can tell them anything important."

"He can identify me."

True. The child wouldn't forget the man who'd burned and broken his little body.

"I'm sorry," Nan whispered. It would have all been okay if she hadn't blown it by saying the boy's name while she was in a morphine haze. "There was no more money. I needed to get out of here, out of Minnesota, and I couldn't bring the kid with me." Everything would have been fine if Lyle had disposed of the bodies years ago the way he was supposed to. Even after death, he was still screwing up. She wouldn't mention the six bodies still in the warehouse. She'd never gone back for them. After having the van towed to a shop and discovering the engine was shot, she sold it to a junk dealer. But she wasn't sure she could have made herself return to the warehouse anyway, after the close call with the cop.

"Where's the boy now?" he asked.

"I don't know. With someone in Child Protection Services." Nan started crying. "Don't hurt him. Please."

"That's where you screwed up to begin with. You started caring about these kids. Even years ago, mothering them, baking them cookies, talking to them when they were scared and crying. You should never have been in the business in the first place."

"I helped them. I helped them transition. I wasn't just doing it for them. I was doing it for all of us. So they'd cooperate. I made it easier for you. You're just too much of an ass to see it."

Calling him an ass was a mistake.

She knew it before his fist hit her face. Her sight blinded by pain, her nose bleeding, she reached for the call button but remembered he'd pulled it off the bed. And really, how many times had she pressed it only to have no one come?

His knee pushed down hard against her wrist. Nan opened her mouth to scream. Not fast enough. The pillow was jerked from behind her head and shoved against her face. She waved her free hand, trying to find a pair of eyes to poke or hair to grab.

It was true your life flashed before you moments before you died. She wished she could tell someone, Lyle maybe. She saw them together that morning on the farm when their lives had changed. Young, healthy, making sandwiches, Lyle's return to the house with his ashen face, her opening the door of the addition to see the bodies belonging to ten beautiful boys.

Suddenly the pressure was gone and she was gasping for air. She knocked the pillow away as the darkness at the edges of her vision cleared. Nobody in the room. Had he come to threaten but not kill her? Had someone scared him away? Like Jenny Hill from CPS, who'd been by earlier. She'd been surprisingly understanding as she'd taken saliva for a DNA test, saying the results could take days or weeks.

Nan knew what she had to do. Get the boy back. Hide him. Run away with him. Or if it came down to it—kill him.

CHAPTER 26

F our thirty and already dark when Jude got a text from Uriah asking how the meeting had gone, letting her know he was back at Homicide. She was tired, but she wanted to catch him up before heading home. She especially wanted to let him know Billy Nelson was ready for autopsy.

Rush hour was bad. A drive that should have taken twenty minutes stretched to forty. Traffic on I-35 was at a standstill, red taillights snaking to a vanishing point in the distance. It was so cold in her car that frost had built up on the inside of the windows. She fiddled with the heat settings, directing all the air to the upper vents even though her toes were aching. Traffic inched forward. She removed her gloves and scraped at the frost with her fingernails.

Finally in the underground parking ramp, she shut off the ignition, anxious to get inside the building to warm up. A car horn echoed in the distance, and someone hit a lock button on a vehicle, the sounds distorted in the enclosed area. Tucking the file Savoy had given her into her messenger bag, she headed for the stairwell.

Normally she was vigilant in garages, any garage, even a restricted one like this, but she was thinking about the case and Savoy's behavior. On top of that, she couldn't stop rerunning her visit with the boy. Crouching down, giving him a cookie. How glad he'd been to see her.

Despite the warnings she'd given the foster mom, Jude sensed he was good at his core. Hopefully it wasn't too late for him.

She was almost to the elevator entry when her brain tripped, causing her to come to an abrupt halt. She'd passed an unmarked car, the only one in the designated area. Someone had been sitting inside. *Not normal.*

She retraced her steps. The vehicle wasn't running. No sound, no radio, no conversation coming from the interior. Approaching it from behind, moving along the driver's side, she noted that the back seat was empty. Then she spotted Uriah sitting behind the wheel, eyes closed, head back. Cops were known to exhaust themselves and fall asleep in odd places. Desks, toilets, standing against a wall. This felt different.

The parking area was dark, and the poor lighting gave his skin a green cast, but there was a pallor to it that seemed true. He was so washed out, his face almost glowed. Normally he was clean-shaven, but it looked like he might have forgotten to shave that morning. The curly hair on his forehead was damp or recently damp, and his tie had been tossed to the seat beside him, the throat of his white dress shirt open a couple of buttons as if he'd tugged it in a need to cool off in a hurry.

She tapped lightly on the window. No response, so she tried again, a little harder this time. He jerked awake, sat up straight, then tried to act alert as he lowered the window. He *was* pale. And he'd been sweating.

"Just a little cat nap." He rubbed his face. "Thanks for waking me."

He fumbled about, found his tie, slipped it around his neck, and got out of the car, locking the door with the fob and pocketing the keys. Then he buttoned his shirt and slung one end of the tie over his hand to begin the knot. "Even though we had a good match, I wanted to run the DNA profile of our first body," he said. "You know how it is with prints. I'm okay with twelve, especially in a case like this where we have other clues, but some people might balk at that number."

"And?"

"It matched the mother's and sister's mitochondrial DNA."

She told him about the Nelson body being ready for autopsy, then asked, "What's going on?"

He began walking, strides long as he tightened the knot at his throat. "You mean back there? I fell asleep." At the elevator, he pushed the button for their floor and rolled his shoulders, obviously still trying to wake up. The door opened with a ding.

"Don't keep secrets from me," she said as they stepped inside.

"Not sure what you're talking about."

She noted a breathy weakness in his voice.

"I just need some coffee."

The elevator stopped, the doors opened, he exited and walked straight for the break room. Jude followed, glad to see it was empty. She closed the door behind them. If she'd been able to lock it, she would have.

She picked up a mug and filled it with coffee, replacing the carafe with a clatter. Handed him the cup. "Are you drinking?" She almost hoped that was it. "I'm not making accusations. I just want to know what's going on."

He lifted the mug, poised to take a sip. His face went pale again, and he set the drink aside and moved to the corner of the room to drop down on a couch. "I've just been a little off lately."

"I'm fine with keeping my distance from everybody else in the building and beyond," Jude said. "I prefer it because, let's face it, people have a way of being less than I want them to be. But we're partners. So anything that's going on with you affects me and could even put my life in danger."

Neither of them needed to point out that she didn't seem to have much interest in her safety, but the statement drove her point home. Something was going on that he didn't want her or anybody else to know.

He got up, dumped the coffee, rinsed the mug in the sink, and filled it with water. He took a cautious sip, then another. She considered pulling out a chair to sit down but changed her mind.

Leaning against the counter, he said, "Remember a few months back when I passed out at that crime scene?"

"Not easily forgotten." She'd called 911 and had ridden to the hospital in an ambulance with him.

"And I had some tests run?"

She remembered that too.

"And I told you everything was fine?"

Her heart began to pound. "Yes."

"I lied."

She wished she'd sat down. To do so now would underscore her shock at his revelation, and she didn't want him to see any response at all.

He took another small sip of water. "The MRI revealed a tumor."

For someone who'd been denying any and all feelings ever since her escape from captivity, today had been a challenge. First the boy, and now Uriah. She gave up and pulled out the nearest chair, dropping down hard. "I suspected something the day you told me the tests were fine." But she'd moved past her suspicion. She'd wanted him to be okay. She'd needed him to be okay, and so she'd believed him, even when deep down she'd known something wasn't right.

His cancer must have returned. His father had told her about Uriah's childhood leukemia. "You shouldn't even be here," she said. "You should be resting. You should be home in bed. You should be vacationing in Florida. You should be . . . What are they doing about it? Surgery? Chemo? Radiation?"

"Maybe all of those things. The good news is that it's benign. But it's growing, and it's not in an optimal area for surgery."

"You should go somewhere else. Get a second opinion. That's always good. Go to Mayo Clinic, a research hospital." She was talking fast, but she couldn't slow down. "I can start working on that. Find the best place."

"Whoa. Stop right there. This is exactly the reason I didn't tell anybody."

"Do your parents know?" Of course not. They'd seemed too happy the couple of times she'd seen them recently.

"I don't want people fussing over me. You're fussing over me. They would fuss over me. I'm doing everything I'm supposed to do."

She got to her feet. "What is that? Working late? Not getting enough sleep? Probably eating poorly."

"I'm getting chemo. They're hoping to shrink the tumor enough to operate on it." He let out a breath, seeming relieved to have gotten rid of his secret. "I'd been told the chemo might not cause side effects. It's a limited dose that only seems to negatively impact about twenty percent of patients. I was hoping to be in the eighty percent. Well, that didn't work out, but I'm taking something that helps with the nausea and fatigue. I had the third and final treatment this morning—that's why I missed the press conference—so I've been a little off today."

Holy hell. "Tired?"

"Yeah. And unable to be around food sometimes, especially hot food, just cooked, with a strong odor."

Another reason for not meeting Savoy. He started looking queasy just talking about it.

"You should be home."

"I don't want to be home."

"You could work from there."

"I don't want anybody to know."

"Why?"

"You're going to have to keep my secret. You're going to have to help me with it, cover for me when I need you to."

"Did you hear me? Why? Do you think you're too tough?" Tough. That was so far from who Uriah was. No, that wasn't it.

He laughed. "If you think that, then you don't know me very well."

"Sorry. Okay, I'll take a shot at it. You've been through this before, and you want to keep things normal. You don't like the attention, and you don't like people treating you any differently. And this—this is the most important part: you don't want it to interfere with your job."

"You got it. Especially the last bit. Once people know, they'll go easy on me, maybe not fill me in on important information, not call when we have a crime scene I need to see. There might be a time when all of that behavior will be necessary, but until then, I want to keep things the way they are. And I want you to help me do that."

She picked up an orange from a bowl, considered peeling it, not because she wanted to eat it, but because it would give her something deliberate to do. The smell might bother him. She put the orange down. "Are you in danger from it? Right now?"

"It's possible. A blood vessel in my brain could break without any warning, and I could bleed out."

"And stress could cause that."

"Maybe. Maybe not. There's no way of knowing. I should probably tell somebody this, but I had a will drawn up last week. It's in my apartment. You know. Just in case."

She turned her back to him and pressed shaking fingers to her lips in a *there, there* patting motion. She squeezed her eyes closed, opened them, blinked fast.

"Think of it this way," he said, sounding way too calm for the heaviness of the situation. "We see death all the time. You and I. And our lives are in danger more than the average person. This is just another thing." *He* was the one with a damn tumor, yet he was comforting her.

She heard footsteps behind her, and then his hands were on her arms turning her around. They were almost the same height, and she couldn't avoid looking into his eyes. "I don't want you to die." Her mouth shook.

He pulled her close and held her.

She knew his scent—the shampoo he used, the deodorant. She knew his gestures, large and small, the eyebrow lifts, the twists of his mouth that could mean many different things depending upon the situation, but the sensation of being so physically close to him was new, chest to chest, his arms around her. She would have expected it to be unpleasant, maybe even have expected to flip out because she didn't think she liked to be touched. But even though it felt foreign, it also felt okay. Tolerable.

"I'm going to try not to die," he said. He didn't tell her everything would be okay. He didn't promise her things he couldn't promise.

"Good."

He stepped back. "I want to hear about your meeting with Savoy. Then let's get a press release written for tomorrow morning. This will go global, so be prepared for cameras in your face again."

"We need the press involved," she said. "We've been focusing on missing children from Minnesota and nearby states when we should be focusing on the entire nation." That took her back to what she'd proposed to Savoy, that this was bigger than they'd first thought. He'd dismissed the idea, but she wasn't convinced they weren't dealing with something organized.

CHAPTER 27

Alan Reed, along with everybody else in the dark Oklahoma bar, was watching the flat-screen television high on the wall. National news, and a woman with a logo attached to her mic stood in the middle of a frozen lake, wind howling. She wore a giant hat, probably fake fur, and she was talking about two bodies that had been found in the ice. Hard to imagine a place so cold somebody could freeze like that.

"One of the bodies has been identified using fingerprints and DNA. The victim? A boy named Billy Nelson who disappeared *twenty years ago*."

A murmur of surprise passed through the bar patrons as an old photo appeared at the bottom corner of the TV screen. A blond kid in a red shirt looking straight at the camera. One of those school photos they made you take. Did they do that anymore? Seemed outdated with digital phones and all.

The reporter was still talking. "The other body remains a John Doe."

Cut to a woman at a news desk, the frame of the exterior shot shrinking to a small square. "Do police think there's any connection between the two bodies?" the woman at the desk asked.

"It's too early to speculate," said the on-site reporter, "but the unidentified child's clothing appears to be from the same time period. Unfortunately, due to details too disturbing to delve into here, an approximate year might be impossible to determine from the autopsy.

We can't show you an image of the John Doe's face; that would be too upsetting for some viewers, but the Minneapolis Police Department has supplied us with a sketch."

Another face appeared at the side of the screen. "If you have any information about this case, or if the person in the artist's rendering looks familiar, please give the number on the screen a call."

They broke away from the live shot to recorded footage. Suddenly Alan was looking at a view taken from a helicopter or drone. The clip moved fast, the camera sweeping across the landscape of the Twin Cities, flying low over lakes dotted with people. The woman's voice continued even though she was no longer on-screen. "In the meantime, the entire city of Minneapolis is on high alert. Typically, at this time of year, the lakes are full of colorful fishing shacks. Now they're packed with people hoping to find more bodies. Like a sick sport, some people come out every day to search."

The frame went full-screen again as they cut back to the reporter in the fur hat. "We're here with someone who's been at the lake daily since the first body was found. That's quite an accomplishment because the temperature is almost zero right now. What drives you?" Her mic and the camera shifted to the guy on her left, a bearded man in brown canvas overalls. "Are you looking for someone you lost?"

"Just tryin' to help."

"What do you say to those people who call you morbid?"

He shrugged. "Don't matter to me. I'm retired, and it gives me somethin' to do. It's kinda fun."

People in the bar laughed. Alan laughed too, but his heart wasn't in it.

The camera returned to the woman with the mic and her uneasy expression. Not the interview she was hoping for.

He had to get some air.

He pushed himself off his stool and grabbed his cigarettes. Outside, he lit up with shaky hands, exhaled, and looked at the Oklahoma sky.

His childhood, for the most part, was a blank. But occasionally something would pass by—an image, an odor—that nagged at his brain and tried to get him to remember things too painful to recall. Yet most of the time the past was the past. Nothing he could do about anything except forget and move forward, no looking back, no going back. And he really *couldn't*, not after all he'd done and all that had been done to him. A person couldn't go back from that.

He jumped, realizing his cigarette was a long hot ash, so hot it burned his fingers. He'd been sucking on it like a fiend and hadn't even noticed. He shook it to the ground and went inside.

The damn news. It was still on. Why didn't somebody change the channel? He was about to suggest just that or find the remote and do it himself, when a new interview launched.

This one was with a woman with brown hair, some gray strands in it, looked about sixty, maybe a little older. Her name was Gail Ford.

"Want another beer?" someone shouted to him.

Transfixed, he waved the words away with one hand as he stared at the screen. She talked about how her son had vanished one day.

"He just never came home from school."

His head roared, and he felt like he might throw up. It took a lot for him to focus on the rest of her words. He didn't catch them all, but she talked about how she'd searched, and it wasn't until hours later that she'd started to worry something had really happened to him. And it wasn't until then she got the police involved.

"If I'd called them sooner, maybe we could have found him."

"Hey, bud." An arm went around his shoulder. Alan looked up with confusion, like waking from a bad dream. "You ready to go?"

Near the door, two others waited.

This was his tribe. These were his people now. A pack of criminals, bound by the things they'd done. But no matter how bad those things were, they would never compare to what he'd lived through before meeting them.

"I've scoped out a job," his friend said. "A house with an alarm system but no cameras. We get in, we get out before the cops even know we've been there."

As far as he knew, he was the only one of the bunch who'd never killed anybody. But it was just a matter of time. If the right circumstances came up and it was him or someone else, he'd kill.

He glanced at the screen again. The woman was still talking, crying now, thinking about an innocent eleven-year-old boy, not the man he'd be today.

"And since we've got a crew here in Minneapolis, we thought we'd break new information in another strange case," the reporter said. "We've been following the story of the young boy found on a doorstep. Well today, just hours ago, we got word that his mother has been found. Her name is Nanette Perkins."

Another face filled the screen. He must have been losing his mind, because damn if she didn't look familiar too.

Call me Nan.

"She's a little old for you, isn't she?" one of his friends said with a laugh.

A tug on his arm, and Alan began walking backward toward the door, unable to tear his eyes from the photo on the screen.

CHAPTER 28

Four years earlier . . .

After Lyle died and left his shocking deathbed revelation, Nan fell into a deep depression. She had trouble doing anything but sleeping, even though sleep brought dreams of bodies stacked in a meat locker like firewood. She started drinking more, hanging out with the wrong people, Lyle's brother for one, and the months just became a sleep- and drug- and alcohol-induced blur until a contact in their old trafficking business called and asked if she'd be interested in taking in an infant, a boy, from a past client.

"We'll pay you," her contact said. "A clearinghouse job, like the stuff you used to do, but this is a baby, two weeks old. You can take care of a baby, can't you?"

Nan didn't know anything about babies. "Sure I can."

She was to ask no questions and keep him hidden until someone came for him.

"We'll give you a heads-up."

So easy. They delivered him to her house. They would eventually take him away. She needed the money.

The arrival was romantic, really. Like a fairy tale. A baby, delivered to her around two a.m. one summer night, arriving in a black SUV, her contact scurrying to the door with the bundled child in her arms.

Leaving diapers and formula on the kitchen counter. Inside, under the dangling table lamp, Nan signed a nondisclosure agreement, only slightly alarmed at some of the wording, like, *at risk of death*. She'd seen forms like this before.

They'd chosen her because of her past child-trafficking experience. They knew she would feel no moral outrage at the idea of holding a mysterious baby for a few days. And they knew she could keep her mouth shut. It was probably a kidnapped child, probably being sold on the black market to a couple desperate for a little one of their own. He would make somebody happy.

Even though she wasn't supposed to ask questions or have any knowledge of where the baby had come from, she couldn't help but peek through a slit in the curtains once the kitchen door was closed and her contact had stepped outside. Nan squinted, watching as the woman opened the car door, the dome illuminating a passenger in the back seat. Nan caught a glimpse of a well-groomed man she thought she recognized. But it was so fast. Before her brain could sort the features and confirm, the door closed and the light faded.

◆ ◆ ◆

She waited for them to pick up the kid. She waited months, then years. By that time, she'd been calling him Boy so long it was too late to change it, to give him a real name. But the money kept coming, like clockwork, the first of every month, deposited into her bank account.

Enough to live on.

But then one day it stopped. Her contact person didn't return her calls. And she began to worry about everything. The bodies still in the locker. The boy who wasn't hers.

Her contact finally reached out from a number Nan didn't recognize, probably a burner phone. "This is just a courtesy call to let you know there'll be no more money coming from my employer for the kid." There was more to the conversation. Quick alarming words, spoken in a whisper, filling Nan in on things she'd suspected, like the identity of the man in the car.

"What am I supposed to do with him?"

"Kill him." A pause. "You're pretty good at killing kids, right?"

Nan disconnected and tossed the phone.

Kill him. You're pretty good at killing kids, right?

Bitch.

It took her a while, but money got alarmingly low, and she finally made the decision to run. She had to tie up loose ends first. Getting rid of the bodies, then getting rid of the kid. Even though temps were dropping, it was still early in the season and the ground wasn't frozen deep. She could drive a tractor with a front-end loader. No reason why she couldn't carry out their original plan.

Bury them.

If you want a job done right, do it yourself.

She left the boy home alone, locking him in the dog kennel, where he'd be safe, giving him snacks and telling him he had to play the quiet game. "I'll be back in a little while."

He was a good kid, and he nodded without even glancing up. Sitting cross-legged in the dog kennel, he was looking at his favorite volume of the encyclopedia. He particularly loved the pages with the transparencies of the human body. Maybe he could have been a doctor in another life. But knowing who his dad was, probably more like a murderer. She sort of wished he could run away with her, but questions would be asked that could lead people back to the farm. And it was time for them to go their own ways, time for her to be free of him and start over somewhere else, without a kid.

In the kitchen next to the door were the keys she'd hung almost twenty years ago. Two of them, one smaller, for a padlock, both on a chain attached to a worn leather fob.

"For summer," Lyle had said.

Had he really planned to go back? Or had leaving the bodies always been his intention? Knowing Lyle, she was going to guess he'd left them out of laziness. Out of sight, out of mind.

The delivery truck they'd used that day was long gone, probably passed through several hands over the years, maybe crushed in some junkyard by now. Funny to think someone had driven it around, never knowing it had hauled the bodies of ten boys. She and Lyle had gotten a good laugh out of that.

They'd traded the truck in on something more suitable for farming, a bare-bones cargo van, a rattling tin can with 150,000 miles on it. Inside, there were two torn seats, the back unfinished, just a metal floor and metal walls. The interior smelled like fertilizer, the odor forcing her to roll down her window even though it was close to zero out.

She'd driven past the Minneapolis warehouse where the bodies were many times over the years. Never much activity at the building even as the structures around it had changed: some were torn down while newer, taller ones went up. Maybe the warehouse would be next. It looked old next to the new.

The key worked.

That surprised her.

She slid a giant metal door until it was open wide enough to drive through, closing it behind her. In the cavernous space, she backed up to the locker located in the far corner and opened the padlock with the other key.

They were still there. That surprised her too.

She'd really expected them to be gone. Gone where, she didn't know, but twenty years was a long time. And they were still frozen. The motor for the unit was external. Someone, a maintenance person, must have kept it running. Lyle's brother had probably made sure of that.

Four bodies to start with. That was her plan. She could easily drive four bodies back to the farm and bury them. Once the boy had arrived in her life, there was no more allowing anyone to help out. The few friends she'd made at church were no longer invited to her house, but going it alone had made her physically stronger and more independent.

She could do this.

Luckily, frozen bodies were easier to move than fresh ones because they could be levered and didn't feel as much like dead weight. Put one on a plastic tarp and drag it across the cement to the back of the van, prop it against the bumper designed specifically for loading and unloading. Breathing hard, she clambered into the cargo area and tugged the frozen carcass the rest of the way in, rolled it off the tarp, and returned to the locker for the next one. Hard, but not as hard as she'd expected.

Bodies loaded, she slid into the driver's seat, turned the ignition key—and heard nothing but a terrifying click.

CHAPTER 29

Something woke her. Out of habit, Lori checked the digital clock by the bed. The illuminated numbers read four a.m. Some people said four a.m. was the time spirits were most active. Ridiculous, but now that she was fully awake, she heard someone talking in a strange and throaty voice. Not her husband, who was asleep beside her. This was coming from down the hall.

Their house was a three-bedroom, all on the second floor. It was a layout that worked well for fostering. Her two children were in one room, and Michael in another by himself. She'd struggled with that decision. Sometimes she put boys with her son and girls with her daughter, but when they knew so little about this child, and whether he might be violent, putting him by himself had seemed the wise choice. And she'd felt backed up by that decision after talking to Detective Fontaine.

She checked on her children first. Quiet, sound asleep. The voices were coming from Michael's room. Low, growly, conversational. Without stepping inside, she peered around the corner. In the glow of the hallway night-light, she made out the silhouette of the boy. He was sitting on the floor, holding the two stuffed animals he'd arrived with: a panda and a striped cat. He was playing with them, making them talk to each other.

She relaxed. Normal child's play, although unsettling that it was taking place in the middle of the night, and yet he was dealing with a lot of change. He might have lived with no kind of schedule, and he and his mother might have been active at night. Maybe darkness was more familiar to him. His drawings would certainly indicate that. She was about to enter the room and suggest he get back into bed when his next words and actions stopped her cold.

CHAPTER 30

Jude's phone rang.

She used to hate sleep because it brought nightmares she couldn't remember after she was awake. But the nightmares hadn't visited for a while, maybe months, and Elliot hadn't had to knock a broom handle against his ceiling to get her to stop screaming. Both pluses. Neither of them had ever mentioned the screams, and Jude felt it was best that way. But she wondered why they were gone. It seemed to have coincided with the demolition of the house where she'd been tortured. Like an exorcism.

In the dark, she squinted against the brightness of her cell phone. A number she didn't recognize. She gave out her card to a lot of people, telling them to call her day or night. It was her thing, and Uriah nagged her about it, saying it was a bad idea. The call could be from anybody. Someone in need, someone with information.

She answered.

It was Lori, the foster mother. She should have been informed about Ms. Perkins by now, hopefully before it had hit the news outlets.

"You told me to call you anytime," the woman said as a way of apologizing for the late hour. "I tried my contact at Child Protection Services, and she said no one could come until morning since this is not really an emergency."

Jude sat up straighter in bed. "What's going on?"

"I'm in the kitchen," the woman whispered, "because I don't want to wake anybody, and I don't want the boy to hear me. Sorry for whispering."

He was "the boy" now. Not Michael.

"I heard someone talking. Just a low conversational but creepy voice. So I walked down the hall and saw the boy sitting on the floor in the corner of the bedroom. He was holding two stuffed animals. The other kids, they sleep in another room." Unspoken was that she didn't trust the child alone with her children while they slept.

"Understandable."

"He was just sitting in the dark. And if you know kids, they don't like to be in the dark. It was a long time before my kids were okay with no light in their room. But anyway, he was making the stuffed animals talk, the way kids do, playing both parts." She pulled in a shaky breath. "The animals were fighting. One was scolding the other, calling him bad. And Detective, the panda was holding the cat down, threatening to smother it with a pillow."

Jude made a sound of dismay and thought about the boy's reaction to the tub. He might have been displaying murderous tendencies, but he could also have been reenacting a trauma from his own past. "That would have been disturbing to witness."

"I can't have him here. What if he did that to one of my children? While they were sleeping? He has to go. Now. Tonight. And you said to give you a call if I needed you. Well, I do."

Jude checked the time. Four-fifteen a.m. "I'll be there in thirty minutes."

She got dressed and bundled up. Heavy wool socks, a hooded sweatshirt under her down jacket. As she headed for the underground garage, she wondered how low the temperature had dipped and how unresponsive her heater would be. At least her car wasn't sitting outside in below-zero weather. When she got in, the windshield was clear. But a few minutes after pulling from the garage, the glass started to frost

over again on the inside. As she drove, she swiped at the buildup with
her gloves and tried to redirect her breath. Not that easy.

At the house, Lori was waiting for her.

Porch light on, the door opening before Jude knocked, the foster
mom standing with her hands on the boy's shoulders. He was ready to go,
his coat zipped, mittens and knit cap on. The whole family was up, clus-
tered behind Lori like they'd been arranged for a portrait, the kids sleepy
and confused, the dad looking sheepish and awkward in his pajamas.

Jude crouched to pick up the boy, lifting him into her arms. He
was tired, his body weighted and heavy rather than wiry. Funny how
limp bodies always seemed to weigh more. But he was alert enough to
pat her cheek with a mitten. Lori's eyes welled up.

Sorry, she mouthed, handing Jude his backpack of belongings, the
two stuffed animals, perpetrator and victim, sticking out of the top.

"Not a problem," Jude said. "Better that you listened to your gut.
Better that you called."

"I don't know." Lori was having second thoughts. Jude could see it.
Before she could voice a change of mind, Jude turned and carried the
boy down the front steps, pausing long enough to say good-bye. Then
he was in her vehicle. She didn't have a car seat. At what age did kids
stop using car seats? She had no idea.

She tucked him in on the passenger side and fastened the safety
belt. "I know it's cold in here."

He didn't seem to mind and was asleep before she pulled from the
curb. Twenty minutes later, they were in the parking garage of her apartment building, where the canned air was warmer than the air in her car.

She packed him up.

With the boy balanced on her arm, his head against her shoulder,
she climbed the metal stairs from the parking area to the first floor.
Jude winced as the thick metal fire door slammed behind them. Elliot
must have heard the noise. As she passed his apartment, he peeked his
head out.

"Sorry about the door," she whispered.

"Oh wow." His eyes widened when he saw the bundle in her arms. "What's going on?"

"He'll be staying with me the rest of the night. Maybe longer."

The boy tried to perk up and lift his head from Jude's shoulder. He failed.

"Poor little dude." Elliot pushed the child's knit cap back off his eyes. "Can I help?"

"I have to be at work in a couple of hours. Could you watch him?"

"No problem."

In her living room, she tugged off the boy's mittens, cap, boots, and jacket. He grabbed the stuffed animals, hugged them to his neck and face, inhaled, and headed straight for the bedroom and the cushion and blanket that were still on the floor in the corner. Jude made a mental note to tell Elliot not to let him near either of the cats.

Once the boy was settled, knowing she wouldn't be getting any more sleep, she pulled out the files Savoy had given her. Next to them on the coffee table was the letter from her lawyer that had arrived a week ago. She wasn't one to ignore paperwork in her job, but in real life? She didn't want to deal with it now. Instead, she opened the first folder in Savoy's bundle. With Roof Cat beside her, Jude went through the case files for Billy Nelson. They were thick, and they covered a long period of time and various theories and suspects. Followed trails that came to abrupt dead ends.

A whole career could pass with nothing solved. Detectives retired; new people took over. Sometimes a fresh pair of eyes helped, but after two hours, she didn't feel she'd learned anything new. Savoy's visit had probably been more about putting a strong period on this part of his life and what might have been an unhealthy obsession with an unsolved crime than about sharing information.

But the letter from the lawyer was still taunting her. She picked it up, considered opening it, then walked to the kitchen and stuck it in a cupboard out of sight.

CHAPTER 31

B oth bodies appear to have been through thawing and refreezing," Ingrid Stevenson said. It was early afternoon, and Jude's interrupted sleep was catching up with her. The ME had called the homicide partners to the morgue, surprising them with the presentation of two bodies in the autopsy suite, Billy Nelson, with a Y incision and full autopsy, and John Doe, not fully thawed but present for some reason Jude and Uriah had yet to learn.

"Look at the fingers and nose and ears," Ingrid said. "They show signs of decay. The rest of the body shows signs of freezer burn. If you've ever left something in a freezer too long, you know what I'm talking about."

"Could they have been moved from one location to another?" Jude wondered aloud. "And can you determine whether this was a onetime thaw or something that happened more than once over a period of years?"

"I think it's happened over a period of years."

Uriah straightened away from the body of Billy Nelson. Her partner looked better today. Not as pale, but Jude worried that the odors in the autopsy suite might reawaken yesterday's nausea.

"So, wherever these bodies were stored," Jude said, "it most likely was an industrial freezer. And they were both frozen without bending limbs." She'd seen bodies put in freezers, and they were usually folded. But if a freezer was big enough . . .

"The low temperature required, along with the span of time, is mind-boggling," Uriah said. "How low are we talking about?"

"Zero?" Ingrid said. "I've seen bodies that were found frozen after ten years, and they looked like they'd died recently. So anything is possible. And if you're trying to pinpoint dates, that's going to be tough because we don't have the data needed to do that."

"What about sexual assault?" Jude asked.

"I wanted to talk to you about that. No overt signs of sexual trauma, but I can't a hundred percent confirm that due to the condition of the body. But, as you know, I like to save the best for last." She turned off an overhead swing-arm light. "I now have a solid cause of death, and it was surprisingly easy to determine. I have to admit, I'm almost disappointed. I haven't even sliced our John Doe open yet."

"And?" Uriah said.

"Carbon monoxide poisoning. Both of them. In this situation, the freezing actually helped. I ran a couple different tests just to be sure. The pink cheeks were a clue. So I dissected an artery and ran a blood sample through our analyzer to test for carboxyhemoglobin. Carbon monoxide binds to hemoglobin. And it doesn't go anywhere in a frozen body, even one that's been frozen for years. The normal range for an adult is less than 2.3 percent. Unless you're a smoker, then it can go up as high as eight or nine, depending upon how many cigarettes are smoked a day. Both of these bodies had extremely high levels. Ten to thirty percent, and we see the symptoms we all know about. Thirty to fifty will result in death. Nelson had a reading of sixty. And being young with smaller lungs, he probably died fairly quickly, although it's not a pleasant death."

She crossed her arms. "Once I had the cause of death for Billy Nelson, I decided to see if John Doe was thawed enough for me to grab an arterial sample. Same results. Sixty percent. I'll of course do a full autopsy once he's completely thawed."

"Excellent work," Uriah said.

Jude added, "And that leads to the theory that these two bodies died together."

Ingrid nodded. "It's highly probable, but of course unproven."

"You ever smoke?" Uriah asked once he and Jude were back in the prep room stripping off gowns.

"A little bit when I was a teenager. I never went pro. You?"

"No. But I can tell you that if I were smoking today, I'd stop right now."

Outside, they spotted Ingrid Stevenson leaning against the building, puffing away on a cigarette.

CHAPTER 32

The next day, after another evening of heavy snow, an unmoving man amid a crowd of people coming and going on the shoveled sidewalk in front of the police department caught Jude's attention. She paused near a lamppost and pretended to focus on something in her hand while furtively eyeing him as he stood near the corner of the building looking her direction.

City street. Light-rail train clanging, announcing its arrival at a nearby station. Midday sun shining bright as exhaust from idling cars hit the cold street and immediately froze, exacerbating the number of slow-motion pileups and fender benders. In her pretense of not noticing him, she was unable to glance up long enough to get a strong take, but she put him around thirty, white, light-brown beard and mustache, not dressed for the snow or the cold. No hat, no gloves, flimsy green jacket with a narrow white stripe down the sleeve. When he didn't move or leave, she turned her head and looked at him directly. Like a black widow spider hit by sunlight, he scurried away, hands in his high jacket pockets, shoulders up as if to hide his face. The soles of his shoes were white. Sneakers.

Everything about him was suspicious. He wasn't doing anything illegal, and people—paparazzi, even Elliot, damn him—often tried to snap secret photos of her. But this felt different. She walked quickly, weaving through sidewalk traffic, increasing her speed until she was running, her technique awkward and hampered by her heavy coat and insulated boots.

He cut down an alley. She followed. A half block between them, she unzipped her coat, giving herself access to the weapon at her waist. Just a precaution.

She paused and shouted hello.

He skidded to a stop. She could see he was considering two things: a conversation or running again.

"I saw you watching me," she said. God, that sounded like some creepy pickup line or a Taylor Swift song.

His shoulders relaxed, but he stayed where he was, still nervous. She was near enough to see his features now. Thin face, slightly hooked nose, bristly collar-length hair, black tattoo on one side of his neck, tattoos on the fingers that he kept curling and shoving in and out of his pocket. She kept a close eye on those hands while also observing his face, especially his eyes, which could give him away if he decided to do something like pull a weapon.

"I kinda wanted to talk to you," he finally said. If somebody had been listening to their conversation, they'd have thought they were witnessing some Tinder meet-up.

"Okay." Her breath was a cloud in front of her face. "Let's get out of the cold. We can go to my office. It's just around the corner."

"No."

It wasn't unusual for witnesses of crimes to be reluctant to come forward. Sometimes they made a few false starts before contact. Something told her this guy might fall into the reluctant witness category. Could be he knew something about a case, old or new, or about something she had yet to know. She didn't want to scare him off.

He looked lower middle class, judging from his clothing, and he had a tan. Too tan for the middle of winter in Minnesota. And he had a southern accent. More like Texas than Georgia. She wanted him to talk again so she could zero in on the state. Whatever was going on, he wasn't from the area, and he was new to cold weather. Like Paul Savoy, most everybody came to Minnesota unprepared, especially people from the South. They just couldn't imagine weather so cold it could freeze your skin in seconds.

She got the idea he was here on a mission.

"Maybe we could go somewhere else," she suggested. "Not my office. A café." It wasn't that cold today. About ten above zero, but dropping. He was shivering, and his nose was red, his lips pale. Nerves could also constrict the blood vessels and lower the body temperature. "There's a café around the corner," she said. "They have great scones and even better coffee. My treat. I was heading there anyway."

He was so damn nervous, though. She tried not to let it rub off on her. It was the kind of nervous that people who broke the law had around cops. And even people who didn't. She was afraid he was ready to bolt.

"I'd suggest a food truck and the park just down the street, but it's a little too chilly for that." She smiled at the shared absurdity of such an idea, sniffled, and resisted zipping her coat, keeping her hand near but not on her weapon.

He was half a block away. It was beginning to feel like a high-noon confrontation from some Western. Somebody needed to make a move or call it off.

"I might be that kid."

Texas. Or maybe Oklahoma. The word *kid* had been drawn out, with a bit of an *e* sound. The words themselves had come hard, like he'd rarely spoken them aloud to anyone. Painful, torn from him, his voice hinting of shame and awkward emotion. It took her a moment to grasp who he might be talking about.

"Shaun Ford?"

"Yeah."

Her heart began to pound. She forced herself not to appear that interested. He was still ready to bolt.

He could be wrong. Could be a mistake. Good chance of that. Someone looking to make sense of his life and past. But he was about the right age. Hair similar to Gail Ford's. Straight light-brown strands that could've darkened over the years. But hair was known to change color and even texture, especially when males reached puberty, so it wasn't the best indicator of identity.

"I saw the stuff on the news." He shifted his weight, his eyes wet with emotion. "About the bodies and how at first they thought it was Shaun Ford, but it wasn't."

She let her coat fall closed. "Come on." Enough of this. "Let's go somewhere and talk."

"I saw the mother on TV."

"That had to be tough."

"I'm probably wrong. This is probably stupid."

Maybe. "Never stupid," she said. "There's an easy way to prove it. We have Gail Ford's DNA. If we had yours, we could see if they match."

She began walking slowly toward him. As she came closer, he took a few steps back, distrustful. She was going to lose him, and right now she didn't even know his current name. "It can be done anonymously," she assured him. "Come to a private room at the police department. I'll take a mouth swab, label it *Joe Smith*, followed by a number. I'll seal it and send it in. Nobody will have to know."

"I don't like the idea of my DNA being on file."

Ah. He *did* have the jitteriness of a criminal. Maybe small-time, maybe more. "If there's any chance you're Shaun Ford, wouldn't you want to know?"

"Not sure it'd make any difference. I have my life already. I got a girlfriend."

He didn't seem sure about the last part. Having problems, she'd guess. "Your mother's been waiting for you for twenty years."

"She wouldn't like the person I've become."

"Give her the chance to make that decision."

"You're talking like I'm that kid. I don't know if I am." He frowned, looked confused. "I have these memories . . . But I don't trust you about the DNA. I don't want it in your system."

"We can circumvent that. Sign a contract. It's called a Provision of Exculpatory DNA. We'll promise not to share your sample for any purpose other than to determine your relationship to Gail Ford. The physical sample will be destroyed, and all data in the genetic profile pulled from that sample will be deleted and in no circumstances held any longer than thirty days."

If he passed on her offer, he might return after some thought, but more likely she'd never see him again. He'd vanish, go back to Texas or Oklahoma, or wherever he was from. But she couldn't force him to do anything he didn't want to do.

"I don't know . . ."

He needed a push to make up his mind one way or the other. "I can't help you, then." She turned and began walking away.

"Wait!"

She swiveled.

He was striding toward her, slipped, caught himself, hardly missing a beat. "I'll do it."

CHAPTER 33

J ude got the man from the alley into the police department building, through the metal detector, and to a private room, all with little or no attention drawn. She left him by himself long enough to print out the contract she'd promised and grab a DNA kit. Minutes later she was back, glad to see he was still there as she placed a bottle of water in front of him, telling him to refrain from drinking until she took the sample. The room was bright and hot, the smothering heat a typical problem in cold climates. You froze outdoors and melted inside. They both removed their coats.

He was wearing a blue plaid shirt, white T-shirt underneath. His short beard was clean and trimmed. He smelled like cigarettes and maybe the alcohol he'd put away last night. Interesting, but he seemed less of a threat here, sitting close, in a private room, than he had outside.

They both signed the contract. She'd hoped he'd use his real name. He didn't, just signed it *the man who might be Shaun Ford*. A good idea, actually, and just as binding as his name.

Taking the DNA sample put Jude physically closer to him than she wanted to be, but it also gave her a chance to gather more information. The scar on his wrist, for example, possibly a suicide attempt, but it could have been from a fight. She'd also seen similar scarring on someone who'd been kept in restraints. It didn't look fresh, could have been years old.

With both of them sitting at one end of the conference table, she snapped on a pair of gloves, opened the DNA sample tube, and swabbed the inside of his cheek.

He gagged and his eyes watered.

"Sorry." She stuck the swab back in the vial and twisted the cap. She labeled the container with her contact information, the name *Joe Smith* with a number attached, and stuck it in a ziplock bag. She would personally deliver it to the crime lab.

He was sweating. The kind of nervous perspiration that smelled strong. His eyes kept darting from the closed door to the table and the bag with the sample. He wanted to grab it and run. He opened the bottle of water and drank half of it.

She removed her gloves and leaned back in her chair. "What do you remember? Why do you think you might be Shaun Ford?"

"I'd rather not go into it right now." He glanced at the sample again. "Until that comes back. I will say I don't remember much about my childhood. And I don't remember an abduction. I just think I recognized the woman on television. Gail Ford."

Definitely holding back. "If you *are* Shaun Ford, it might or might not be strange that you can't remember being abducted. Trauma has a way of creating scabs, of protecting us from things. So it's very possible you would have no accessible memory."

"That stuff always seemed far-fetched to me. Like an excuse to get out of something."

"It happens. Quite a bit. Let's just see what this turns up. I'm going to put a rush on it, but that doesn't mean we'll have results right away. DNA labs are quirky. It could be days, or it could be weeks. Leave your current name, address, and phone number, and I'll get in touch with you no matter what the results are."

"That's okay." He finished the water and got to his feet, pushing back his chair with his legs, grabbing his thin coat, and slipping it on. "You don't need to. Just give me your number, and I'll call you."

He didn't trust her about keeping his DNA out of their databases, and he certainly didn't want her to know his name. What had he done? Robbery? Assault? Murder?

"DNA isn't gathered at every crime scene, you know." It was a misconception, perpetrated by television.

"Thanks for sharing that, but I'd rather be cautious."

"Did you come to Minnesota just to meet with me?"

"How do you know I don't live here?"

"Your tan. Your inappropriate clothing." She smiled. "Your accent."

"I don't have an accent."

"Of course not." She got to her feet too. "Are you going back to wherever you came from?"

"I might hang around awhile. Or I might go back."

He really didn't want to give up any information. "Okay." She gave him her card and grabbed the DNA package. "You know how to reach me. I'll escort you out."

Once he was gone, Jude wondered if she'd ever see or hear from him again.

CHAPTER 34

Alan Reed regretted giving Detective Fontaine his DNA as soon as she'd swabbed his mouth. He'd almost grabbed the sample and run off. His girlfriend said he was crazy, just looking for some reason to explain his shitty childhood, his terrible parents.

"Anybody with a past like yours would dream of being from somewhere else," she'd told him. "But you can't change who you are. You saw some lady on television, and now you wanna run off to Minnesota. That's insane." Maybe she was right.

They'd argued about it, about not having the money for the trip with a kid on the way. And when he took off, she'd screamed something about breaking up with him. He kinda got it. He mighta wanted to break up with him too.

He pulled into a station, gassed up, and went inside to use the restroom and grab something to eat. Back in the car, shivering from the unbelievable cold, he tried to call his girlfriend. It went to voicemail. Would he even have a home when he got back? Would she decide she was sick of him and his dark moodiness? He wasn't easy to live with. And having a kid on the way made him feel like even more of a loser. What kind of father would he be, somebody who'd grown up as a sexual slave? Where moving on to breaking and entering was a big step up in the world?

Before leaving Oklahoma, he'd looked up the addresses he'd need in Minnesota. He knew he should just get out of town, head south on I-35. By the time he reached Kansas City, the snow would be gone and the temperature would be warmer. He could be home in less than twenty-four hours. But he was here, and he had to know . . .

What the detective said made sense. Some traumatic event in his childhood had blocked his memories. But what could have happened that was more traumatic than the *shit he did remember*? Having sex with adult males when he was just a kid? And later, after he'd run away, becoming a prostitute? He didn't know why he hadn't told the detective that he thought he remembered the other woman too, Nanette somebody. That didn't even make any sense, because the stories were unrelated. Maybe his brain really was just making shit up.

He tried his girlfriend again. She answered, and he let out his breath in relief. "I'll be home in a couple days," he told her.

"I'm sorry I got mad."

"Nah, you were right. It was stupid. A waste of money when we got a kid on the way."

They talked a little longer, and he felt better. She was the person who'd brought him out of the darkness. Too many times, and he felt bad about that. One of these days she'd leave, and he wouldn't blame her. But for now . . .

A car honked behind him.

The station had gotten crowded while he was on the phone, and someone wanted his spot so they could fill up. He told his girlfriend good-bye and entered an address into his maps app, then started the driving directions.

The house ended up being average and boring and didn't look familiar. One and a half stories, with a dormer and pale-green siding. And since he was used to breaking and entering, the first thing he noticed was a security-alarm sign for a company that no longer existed. His professional guess? There was no alarm system.

He circled the house in his car, driving up the alley. And Jesus. The alley, with deep snow on both sides, was almost like an Olympic luge with very little sign of cars going in or out. Apparently, people parked on the street when the alley got bad. Sliding all over hell, he had no choice but to keep going, finally spotting her garage with the house number. He slowed to a crawl as he passed. Two-car, handle on the outside, so no automatic door. Everything said the place would be easy, and he was torn between breaking in or warning her.

He reached the end of the alley, turned back onto the street, and pulled to the curb a couple of houses down from the one he was interested in.

He was a patient man when it came to this kind of thing. Had to be. Impatient people got caught. While he waited for signs of activity, he ate the pizza slice and drank the Diet Coke he'd picked up at the gas station. When he was done with the pizza, he tossed the triangular cardboard box on the floor and lit a cigarette, lowering his window a couple of inches, turned on his car so he could get some heat, and saw it had dropped to a few degrees below zero. Crazy.

After a while, someone pulled up in front of the house. Older model Chevy, beige—also boring. A woman got out. Bundled up, so he couldn't get a good look at her, carrying bags of groceries. She juggled her packages and unlocked the front door. Once she was inside, lights in the house came on. He hadn't even realized it was getting dark. Five minutes later, he got out of the car and casually said hello to someone walking a dog. Hands stuffed in the pockets of his jacket, hair blowing, face freezing, he walked to the house and knocked.

The woman answered.

She wasn't what he'd expected either, even though he'd seen her face on television. This person was average too. On the drive up from Oklahoma, he'd had time to fantasize about a house in an upscale neighborhood and a grieving mother who seemed like she could be a teacher or a politician. This person seemed . . . empty. Light-brown hair that was turning gray. The hair that wasn't gray was lighter than his. That surprised him, and he felt renewed doubt about being her son.

He stuck with his plan to carry out something he'd done before, not in Minnesota but Oklahoma. Today he didn't have any props, so he decided to adjust his usual script.

"I'm looking for somebody who used to live here. Guy I went to high school with." He waited for some sign of recognition. Wouldn't a mother know her own kid, even if he was grown? Wouldn't she show some kind of reaction? She didn't. And while he was gauging her lack of response, he looked into the house, beyond her, to the kitchen, where she'd put her bags down. On the floor near the door was a mat with one pair of boots, still wet from the snow. A coat tree held a single coat, a sweatshirt, and some kind of shawl thing. The living room contained no sign of another person. That answered his big question. Did she live alone?

A cheap TV, a blanket draped across the couch. He checked the tops of windows and doors and didn't spot any sensors or cameras.

"You must have the wrong house."

She was ready to close the door, when he said, "He joined the army. Had a dog. Some kind of retriever. Does that ring a bell?"

"No."

"Okay. Sorry to bother you."

She hadn't been very nice. That annoyed him. He made one last attempt to shake a response out of her. He pointed from her to him. "Have we met?" He could be charming, something mostly done with a smile and gestures. He poured it on.

"I don't think so."

"You sure? You seem familiar."

She slammed the door in his face.

That action brought about a decision. Angry, he strode down the walk and back to his car. Inside, he turned on the heater again, sucked the last bit of drink from his gas-station soda, and waited.

CHAPTER 35

He thought he might have to wait for Gail Ford to go to sleep—he hated home-occupied break-ins. But an hour later the front door opened and she stepped out, locked up, and walked straight to her car without even glancing in his direction. Seconds later, she drove off in a cloud of exhaust. He gave it five minutes in case she forgot something and came back. That happened a lot.

Two streetlights made the block too bright, but who the hell would be outside if they didn't have to be? Head bent, hands in his pockets, he walked toward the house, circled around back, and slipped inside an unlocked three-season porch—another stupid thing home-owners did. Leaving porch doors unlocked because they weren't the main house. But unlocked porches gave burglars a nice place to hide while doing what they needed to do to get in. Like kicking at the knob a few times.

The wood frame shattered enough for him to shove the door open and enter the kitchen. Didn't appear to be any lamps on timers to even attempt to make criminals think someone was home. He told himself this would be a good lesson for her. She was lucky it was him. Someone dangerous could have broken in when she was asleep. This way, she'd come home and find the broken door, then get a security system. Many people got security systems *after* the break-in. He was once hired by a shady security-alarm dealer to break into houses just so the homeowner would install his equipment. It was a good scam. Stolen merchandise, *plus* the install and sale of the system.

A couple of night-lights helped him find his way around, one in a kitchen outlet. The light was a cardinal, maybe. Some kind of bird. Another one radiated a small amount of illumination from the living room. Neither would scare off a burglar. He didn't reach for any switches. Instead, he used his cell phone to move through the rooms.

The house still didn't seem familiar to him. Had she lived here when the kidnapping took place? He'd hoped being inside would trigger a memory, but he was getting nothing from scents or visuals. Nothing from the shitty wallpaper or the narrow hallway that led to a bedroom and bathroom.

The bedroom that appeared to be hers had a lived-in stench, kind of like clothes that had been put away when they were still damp with sweat. Combine that with a disgusting mix of laundry soap and air fresheners, and he almost gagged. His girlfriend called him an odor snob because he couldn't stand fabric softener or the smell of most laundry soap or hand soap or body soap. He bought organic products, and only certain ones.

There were no displayed photographs in the room. That surprised him. Women her age seemed to love that stuff. He opened and closed dresser drawers, then moved on.

In the living room, he hit the jackpot. Several framed photos along one wall that he'd missed earlier when talking to her at the door. A man and a woman and maybe their son, their son maybe being him. He'd done his homework, and he knew the husband was dead. But that must have been the abducted kid. And maybe she displayed the photos because they showed the happy family and what life had been like before the abduction.

He didn't even remember being lured somewhere. How did he not remember something like that? He didn't remember walking home from school, didn't remember anybody grabbing him. But he'd heard about it a lot because it was a story that tended to pop up in the news every few years. The little he did recall was probably just memories of the media reports stuck in his brain. Abducted boy.

But he remembered what came later. A dark room, chains, a ride in a windowless van. And years of sex with much older men. He got bigger and stronger and finally overpowered his owner one night and made his escape. He didn't kill him. He could have, but he didn't.

He heard a creak above his head, froze, and listened while holding his breath.

Maybe just the house shifting. Really hot weather could make a house crack and pop, the sound sometimes like a gunshot. Maybe cold weather did the same thing.

But no. Footsteps. Walking across the floor above his head.

He turned off his phone and looked right and left, not yet in a panic, but close.

He'd been involved in robberies where the owners had come home. He had only a couple of choices. Hide in the house for the night, or risk coming face-to-face with the person. From experience, he knew home-owners were usually shocked and immobilized to find someone inside. It took time for them to act. His best choice right now? Not to worry about noise and get the hell out of there as fast as he could. He lunged for the front door, turned the knob and pulled, but it wouldn't open. He tried again. It was like a cartoon, his foot against the doorframe as he tugged hard.

Footsteps were moving down the stairs. And then a voice spoke from across the living room. "I knew you were up to something when you knocked." He let go of the door and turned to face the woman he'd been talking to earlier.

Coat off, she was wearing socks, no shoes. And she was pointing a gun at him. He thought about how dark the house had been when he arrived. He'd scoffed at her lack of lights, but now he wondered if she'd set a trap for him. Had she been waiting?

"I saw you scoping out the place, looking past me into the house, mentioning a dog, checking to see if I had one. Then you didn't drive away. So I got in my car. That door is a sticky bastard, by the way. Now I'm glad I didn't get it fixed. While you were still outside, I drove around the corner, parked, and came back in through the porch."

"I'm sorry. I'll leave." He took a few steps, then stopped.

"Stay." The gun barrel didn't falter.

She was tough. He'd give her credit for that. "I know this looks bad," he said.

"It does."

"But I have a reason to be here."

She let out a snort.

"Listen, I can fix your back door. I'm handy. I can fix your front door too. And I can give you some tips about securing your house."

"I think you can just stay where you are."

It hadn't been his plan to reveal himself like this, but he had no choice. He still didn't know if any of what he suspected was true, but coming clean seemed the best thing to do in order to save his life.

"I know this is weird, but I think I might be your son."

He waited for her to gasp and put the gun away and run to him, maybe pull him into her arms, touch his face, and say how he did look like the kid she'd known and loved, now that she thought about it.

She *did* appear surprised, very surprised, but she didn't do any of the expected things the mother of a long-lost child would do. She kept the gun aimed at his head.

CHAPTER 36

You look like you could use a drink." Gail's words were friendly, but the gun in her hand didn't waver. "Let's go to the kitchen." She kept him in front of her, motioning him through the doorway to a wooden chair. Time flipped, and her breath caught as she remembered days he'd sat there, mornings before school and evenings before bed. She found herself wondering if he still liked the same cereal, and if he still liked the same superheroes. So stupid, letting her mind slip like that, getting sentimental.

She was pretty sure he wouldn't try to jump her. He was too stunned for that, but she didn't put the gun aside, managing to open a bottle of vodka with one hand, grabbing two short glasses, filling each one, sliding his across the table as she leaned against the counter with hers, watching him over the rim.

Two swallows and he was done with his drink. She set hers aside and filled his glass again. Another drink down, and he asked, "*Are* you my mother?"

She'd tried. She really had. Tried to love him. But she'd never wanted a kid. Having a kid had been Dan's idea. "You'll love your own child," he'd told her.

Didn't happen.

"I think I remember sitting here." Shaun appeared to think about it, nodded. "You bleached my hair." Obviously puzzled, because why would anybody do that to a young boy? "I sat here eating cereal with a cap on my head while the bleach processed. Is that right?"

"I've thought about this day a lot," she told him. "About wanting to see you but being afraid to see you."

Dan hadn't understood how she could do such a thing, give up her own child, their child, but it hadn't been hard. Not hard at all. And better than killing him, which had long been her secret fantasy. She'd saved him, really. But it had all been too much for Dan, because he died shortly after that, leaving her alone.

"I've actually practiced what I would do if I saw you again," she said. "I always pour you a drink, and you always take it. What I really want you to know is that I had no choice. Yes, I'm your mother. And I loved you. I still love you." It was a lie, but she wanted to give him that much after all the trouble he'd gone through to find her. "I was in a bad situation. We needed a kid, you were here, right in front of me, almost old enough, almost the right look."

"Needed a kid?" Baffled.

There was really no easy way to put it. "I sold you to someone, a man who liked young boys. He was very powerful and potentially dangerous." Not a local, and not a drop of "Minnesota nice" in him. She'd heard he'd died maybe ten years ago now.

"You sold me?" The question was really a statement, with no emotion or emphasis behind it. He was too shocked for that.

"Would you like another drink?" she asked.

He pushed his glass across the table and she refilled it while he shrugged out of his thin jacket, letting it slip behind him on the chair. He looked ready to throw up, like he wanted to be anywhere but where he was, like he wished he'd never knocked on her door. That made two of them.

"You shouldn't have come," she said. "It would have been better for both of us." At first, she'd truly thought the body found in the lake was him. She'd needed it to be him. She didn't want to think about the possibility of this day any longer.

"I saw you on the news, and then I couldn't quit wondering. I just wanted to see you. I just wanted some kind of proof." He was slurring his words, and his eyelids were getting droopy, just like that night twenty years ago. "I don't remember. Why don't I remember?"

Rohypnol could do that. Cause amnesia. She looked at his glass. The drug was tasteless, but it had a slightly blue tint.

He caught her glance and put it together, especially why the alcohol was hitting him so fast and hard. "You drugged me."

"I wanted to make it as easy as possible. Then and now."

He pushed himself up and away from the table, staggered, planted a foot on the floor to keep from falling, then dropped back in the chair, almost knocking it over.

"I hope the man was good to you." She'd always imagined him having a better life there than here. She'd never been good for him.

"Good?" His eyes opened a crack. "You freakin' kiddin'?"

"I hope he was kind. I hope you had a comfortable bed and three meals a day. Because really, isn't that what we're all looking for? Just kindness, a bed, and food?"

"You're insane." He was getting harder to understand.

"Just close your eyes and rest a little bit." She'd said the same thing to him years ago after she'd dried his bleached hair with a blow-dryer. Back then, the heat had added to his sleepiness.

"Gotta . . . go," he muttered as his chin tipped forward to rest on his chest. He looked a little like a roosting chicken. She leaned forward and inhaled. His hair smelled like some expensive, fancy product. His life couldn't be that bad.

While he was unconscious, Gail dug through his pockets and found a set of car keys. Outside, dressed for the brutal weather, she looked up and down the street, saw no signs of life because it was too cold, got in his car, circled to the alley, and pulled into her garage, closing the door behind her. Back in the house, she slapped his face and managed to bring him around enough to get him upright. Without giving him a chance to drop again, leaving his thin jacket on the chair, she put an arm around his waist and led him through the kitchen and out the back door, down a sidewalk through her fenced yard to the garage, where she urged him into the back seat of his car. He crawled in and curled up, knees to chest.

"C-cold," he mumbled, eyes closed, but still more alert than she'd like. As a precaution, she retrieved duct tape from the house and wrapped his ankles and wrists, finishing with a strip across his mouth. Then she closed the car door and locked it with the key fob. He could open it from inside, but he was probably too out of it for that.

In the house, she checked the temperature. Twenty below and dropping. The garage would be slightly warmer, but not much. Not enough for anybody to live long.

She dumped the alcohol down the toilet, rinsed the bottle, and stuck it in the recycling container, then sat at the table and waited. Several hours later, she returned to the garage. He was dead, and it didn't even look like he'd moved. She felt comforted by that. No struggle. Just went to sleep and never woke up.

"I'm sorry for being such a bad mother."

She cut the duct tape from his wrists and ankles. When she pulled the tape from his face, a little frozen skin came with it. Once night arrived again, she'd get rid of his body and his car in a way that would make it look like he'd died of stupidity.

CHAPTER 37

The road to Nanette Perkins's house was a mile of gravel running through snow-covered fields with the occasional cornstalk stubble hinting of last season's crop. Jenny Hill had spent a few summers on her aunt's farm, enough for the terrain to have a sense of familiarity. The openness after the claustrophobia of snow-crippled Minneapolis was a nice break. In the city, there were no deep breaths to be had. Even though the day was gray and overcast, it felt freer out here. Jenny inhaled. Just being able to see into the distance did her good. She could feel the tension draining from her shoulders.

Sympathy was sometimes lacking in her coworkers at Child Protection Services. They turned it off in order to get through the things they had to get through, and the awful things they had to see. But farm life was hard under the most ideal conditions, and Ms. Perkins wasn't in the best shape. Maybe she hadn't worked enough to get social security benefits, and maybe she didn't know she could get assistance through the Minnesota Family Investment Program, especially designed for people with children. Jenny would help her with that.

Yes, Nanette Perkins had left the boy outside in a storm, but she'd also left him with someone she felt would take care of him. Just misguided and desperate. Jenny's hope was to get the Perkins home approved, get Ms. Perkins financial aid, and get the child back to her. Children belonged with their parents as long as the department could be assured of their safety. Some kids fell through the cracks, but Jenny had a good track record for sorting out the bad parents from the simply desperate ones. Which was why she'd been sent to the farm today.

Someone, possibly a neighbor, had plowed the lane to the house, but snow had drifted in, and it was maybe eight inches deep in places.

The two-story sprawling white farmhouse with peeling paint looked like it had been added onto several times, with rooms that jutted from the main structure, maybe expanded years ago when farm families were huge. The house itself felt cut off and was surrounded by more fields. Hard to say how far it was to the nearest neighbor, probably over a mile. Maybe more.

There were the requisite outbuildings. A barn with a collapsing roof, a couple of silos, and a row of cement bunkers that might have been for silage. Another word Jenny had learned from her days with her aunt and uncle. *Silage.*

No sign of livestock. Records showed that the husband had died five years ago. If they'd raised livestock, Nan might have sold them off, either because she needed the money or couldn't care for them by herself. Or both. But once the livestock was gone, so was much of the income. Hence the term *cash cow.*

The place seemed abandoned except for a faint light showing through the haze of a ruffled kitchen curtain. Jenny checked the outdoor temperature gauge on her dashboard. Ten above zero. The lack of sun made it feel colder.

Shutting off the engine, she grabbed her laptop case and trudged to the door in her heavy boots. The sidewalk hadn't been shoveled. Instead, there was a narrow beaten path through two feet of snow. She'd have to check and see if anyone was available to help with snow removal. Homebound with a broken leg . . . This wasn't acceptable. The county needed to do more to help people like Ms. Perkins. If they'd been doing their job, the boy might not have ended up on Jude Fontaine's front step.

Jenny knocked, and a woman's voice shouted for her to come in.

Inside, Jenny's nose was immediately assaulted by the odor of cigarettes and an unwashed body. The house itself could use a good cleaning. Her heart took a dive. *Not good.*

The television was blaring, turned to a channel that sold items twenty-four hours a day. In her years as a social worker, Jenny had noticed that a high percentage of poor and lonely and elderly watched shopping channels. They even called in, hoping to one day talk to the sweet people they saw daily from their living room chair. Jenny was surprised to find that shopping channels even had stars with huge followings.

The kitchen was to the left, living room to the right, hallway straight ahead with the curved edge of wooden stairs peeking out.

"Sorry," Ms. Perkins said from one corner of a floral couch, walker in front of her, crutches leaning against couch cushions, leg in a walking boot she had propped on a pillow atop a footstool. "It takes me time to get up."

"Stay where you are." Jenny bent to untie her insulated boots, slipping her feet out, wondering if there was really any point, but she would never walk around in her own house with boots on, so she wasn't going to do it in someone else's, no matter how dirty the floor.

"Can I get you anything?" Jenny asked. It was a good excuse to see the kitchen or a bedroom.

"Nope. Thanks, hon. A neighbor checked on me not too long ago. Got some water right here, and an electric blanket. I just wanna get my boy back. It's so empty here without him." She lifted one arm, pinched a bit of sleeve, and wiped at her eyes. "I know it was wrong to leave him out there. Not sure what I was thinking. I don't do drugs. Test me. The only thing you'll find are the painkillers they gave me after my accident." She glanced at the overflowing ashtray next to her. "Well, I do smoke. My husband and I both smoked. But I never smoked in the house until I broke my leg."

Jenny sat gingerly on the edge of the couch, pulled her laptop from her bag, and placed it on her knees. She opened the questionnaire used for evaluating a child's living situation. She would fill everything in, then upload it to their site.

Ms. Perkins grabbed the remote and turned off the television. The sudden silence was uncomfortable. "How old are you?" she asked the girl.

"Twenty-nine."

"Just a kid."

"Not really."

Jenny went through the questions, her unease growing as the interview progressed. "Why doesn't the child have a name?" she asked.

"He was supposed to name himself. I told Detective Fontaine that. But he just wanted to be called Boy. It was a stupid idea. I should have named him when he was born. And did you get a good look at him? Did he look underfed? Not cared for?"

"He shows signs of physical abuse. And is slightly underweight."

"It wasn't me. I would never have done that. And the guy who did? He's gone. Long gone. If I could have afforded a doctor, I would have taken him in."

"Or is it possible you didn't want to get in trouble or be accused of abuse?"

"That too, I can't lie."

She asked more questions. Pages of them. Things weren't looking good, and Ms. Perkins could probably see her chances had dwindled quickly.

"I'm not going to get him back, am I?" the woman asked when they were done.

"It's too early to say." Not really. Jenny was the most lenient caseworker, but even she could see this was a bad environment for a child. "I'm only one of a team who decides. I'll upload everything to our portal. Other people will read and evaluate my report." Also not the full truth. They'd already gone over the case, and much of it hinged on the

feedback and recommendation Jenny supplied. But it was always good
to be able to hang the results on the facility as a whole rather than one
specific person. It didn't happen often, but sometimes people felt the
need to retaliate, whether it be slashed tires or something more serious,
like death threats.

She put her laptop aside and pulled out her phone, opening the
camera app. "I'm going to need to take some photos. I hope that's okay."
Getting to her feet, she began snapping pictures of the living room,
then moved to the kitchen. In the refrigerator, she found very little,
and what was there looked spoiled. The refrigerator itself looked as if it
hadn't been cleaned in years.

"Now for the boy's room," she said when she was done in the
kitchen.

"I can tell you aren't going to let me have him back. You should
just go now."

The interview had taken an unexpected turn, and Jenny knew that
what she documented from now on out was information that could
possibly end up in court. She ignored the woman's protests and moved
down a narrow hall. She took photos of two bedrooms, both packed
with junk and piles of clothing and broken furniture. One of the rooms
had a bed. The other might or might not have had a bed somewhere
under all the trash.

Jenny heard a drawer slam shut. Moments later, Nanette was standing behind her in the hallway. Jenny had been so preoccupied she hadn't
heard her coming. Ms. Perkins was holding herself up with the walker,
hands braced on each side, arms stiff. A baggy gray sweatshirt, sweatpants, hair that hadn't been washed for a while. Jenny felt a wave of
sympathy for someone who couldn't take care of herself, much less a
child.

"Where does the boy sleep?" Jenny asked. "I don't see a room that
looks like a child's."

"He sleeps with me part of the time. I know he's getting a little old for that, but he has nightmares . . ."

"Does he have a bed of his own? We require that. Is it upstairs?"

"There's nothing upstairs. Just more of the same."

"Then is his room in the addition I saw?" That would be odd and unacceptable, a young child sleeping so far from adults. "I'll have a look out there."

"You need to leave." There was no way to miss the agitation in the woman's voice. She didn't want Jenny to dig any deeper.

"Is this the way?" She spotted a door off the kitchen.

"Stop!" Ms. Perkins said. "You don't have my permission to go there."

"You gave your permission when you agreed to this meeting, when you signed paperwork at the hospital for an evaluation. *You* are the one who wants your child back." Behind her, she heard scrambling and scuffling. Ms. Perkins, following with the walker.

"Stop! Don't go in there!"

At first Jenny thought the room was locked. But after rattling the knob, she threw her shoulder against the door and practically fell inside.

No windows; the only light came from the murky hallway behind her. Jenny turned on her flashlight app and frowned. Metal cots, no mattresses, lined up against a cinder-block wall. A dog kennel to one side. The room was long and narrow and cell-like, with a heavy exterior door to her left on the driveway side of the building. On the floor near the beds stood a large propane heater, the kind used to heat an open barn, not an enclosed space.

Her first guess was that this had once been a place for migrant workers. Some farmers, ones who raised crops that needed to be picked by hand, like tomatoes or apples, hired undocumented immigrants in the fall. Not a huge surprise, and something many turned a blind eye to. But these were appalling conditions for those workers.

She was counting the beds, wondering who to report this to, when she noticed something even more alarming. There were chains attached to the wall above each sleeping space.

Were migrant workers lured here, then held captive? Was she looking at something from long ago?

"I took care of them," the woman said from behind her. "Every one of them. I was a mother to them all. I talked to them, and I read to them. They stopped crying when I was around. They looked to me for comfort."

"Are you talking about *children*?"

"I told you to stay out of here," she said. "I'm not a bad person. I wish people would understand that."

Jenny had come close to losing her life a few times. Once when the I-35 bridge in Minneapolis collapsed minutes after she'd driven across it. Another time she almost didn't see a light-rail train when she was crossing the street on foot. But even though she'd lived in the Twin Cities many years, and even though she'd also been mugged a couple of times and her money stolen, she'd never felt in danger of losing her life to another human.

Until now.

Her world shrank to the room and the palpable evil that permeated the walls and radiated from the woman standing a few feet away. And all she could think of was how this was such an awful place to die, and how sad her parents were going to be, and would anybody ever even find her? But beneath those thoughts, she wondered if she had a chance; she wondered if she could rush Ms. Perkins, who was blocking her escape. If she could get past the woman, she could most definitely outrun her. But something was happening, a sort of acquiescence. She felt a softness or weakness of her knees and an acceptance. And yet she still dredged up a feeble attempt.

"What a cute little room." Her voice was breathy and flat and so transparent. "But some artwork and maybe a plant and a braid rug over there would really brighten it up."

Her phone was still in her hand. She could press the emergency button. How did one do that? She glanced at the screen, the flashlight illuminating her feet and the wool socks she'd spent a fortune on, thinking she'd get several seasons out of them.

"Put your phone down," Ms. Perkins said.

It was over. She knew it was over. "I won't say anything," she said. "I see weirder things than this all the time. Cots? That tells me nothing. You had a Boy Scout camp or something. Migrant workers stayed here. It happens."

"I'm sorry," Ms. Perkins said. "I really am. I'm better than this."

A handgun appeared out of nowhere. Maybe from the bag attached to the walker. Yes, that would have been the perfect place to hide such a thing.

"Put down the phone."

Jenny clutched it tighter as she dropped to the nearest bed, unable to stand another second. "Don't," she whispered, not looking at the woman. "Please. I have two cats."

"I'm sorry, honey. I really am."

Jenny actually heard the gunshot. That surprised her. It was loud in the confined space. Her ears rang, kind of a *wong, wong, wong* that started long and gradually faded. Something hot and wet ran down her stomach, and her cell phone slipped from her fingers. She'd never had a serious boyfriend, but she hadn't given up on that. Now she thought about the nice guy she'd hoped to meet and the family she'd hoped to have. It seemed unlikely now.

CHAPTER 38

N an watched the blood slowly spread across the concrete.

She picked up the girl's sticky phone. The screen was locked, but the device appeared undamaged. Even though Nan was in a walking cast, she didn't like to put weight on it. Hurt like hell. She hobbled to the body, grabbed a hand, and stuck the dead girl's finger to the screen. She was in.

Thank God for fingerprint verification.

In "Settings," she turned off the screen-lock feature before stuffing the phone in her sweatshirt pocket. It would come in handy later.

Maneuvering the walker, she clumped back to the main house. In the living room, she dropped to the couch, propped her broken leg on a cushion, and pulled the girl's laptop near. The file she'd been working on was still open. Nan deleted most of the information and replaced the text with positive and harmless wording, leaving some of the young woman's comments so the evaluation would feel believable. Things like the condition of the house, changing words like *filthy* (filthy!) to *understandably messy due to the owner's injury*. At the bottom of the report was a box for the evaluator to give her own opinion. *I do not recommend returning the child to his mother* was changed to *Recommend immediate return of child to his mother with biweekly monitoring*.

The caseworker turned out to be one of those people who had her laptop set to autofill passwords. If she weren't dead, Nan would have suggested a class in online security. It was amazing with all the bad in the world that people still did such stupid things. Nan was no techie, but this stuff was easy. With a history search, Nan found the proper portal and uploaded the file for others in the department to access.

Once that was taken care of, she wiped blood from the girl's phone before opening the text messages app. The most recent message was to a coworker, sharing her plans to evaluate Nan, and her approximate time of return to the office. Nan scrolled through a couple of months of conversations, got a feel for the girl's voice. She must have had OCD, because her messages were full, punctuated sentences, more like emails. Nan typed a reply.

I'm done at the Perkins farm. Uploaded my report. Honestly, I feel we should give her another chance. With monitoring of course.😊 Nanette Perkins seems like a hardworking woman who loves her son but fell into financial problems and depression after her husband died. The abuser is no longer in her life. I'm confident of that. I also suggest we line up a therapist who can engage her in talk therapy and possibly medication to help with the depression.

Nan thought a moment, then added, *I'm also going to advise some financial aid counseling.*

The reply came quickly. Maybe the two of them were more than work friends.

Surprising outcome! I guess you were right about her, as you almost always are! I'll read the report right now, sign off on it, and get things moving on getting the child back home. 😊

Nan replied:

Thanks! I feel like I might be coming down with the flu that's
going around. I plan to head home and put my phone on DND
for the evening. I might even take a day or two off.

Reply:

You deserve it! Get some rest and watch some TV for me!

Aww, sweet girl.

Cell phones made this kind of deceit so easy.

Communication over, Nan scrolled through the past year of Jenny's
photos. So boring. There were a lot of pictures of cats. No kids, didn't
look like any boyfriend or husband either. A few taken at restaurants
with friends or coworkers, but those were old, dating back to late summer or fall. She either didn't take many pictures, or she didn't have a
social life. Nan was going to bet no social life.

She hated to waste a perfectly good phone, but keeping it was
stupid. She pulled out the battery, dropped the device to the floor, and
smashed it with the heel of her uninjured foot. Glancing out the window, she noted it was starting to snow again. Snow was good.

She levered herself up off the couch and thumped her way back to
the body, dug through the girl's pockets, and found a set of keys.

Back in the main house, Nan bundled up in a hooded coat. She
wrapped her cast in a black garbage bag and secured it with duct tape.
Grabbing a single key that hung on a set of hooks by the door, she made
her way outside, leaving the walker at the end of the sidewalk.

The girl's white sedan was unlocked. Nan slid behind the wheel,
inhaling the new car smell, and headed for the barn. A few more hours,
and she probably wouldn't have been able to get the vehicle through
the snow. She hobbled to the sliding barn door and struggled to pull it

open, leaning heavily to allow her body weight to do most of the work. Metal wheels on a metal track. Once it got going, the momentum finished the job. With the door open wide now, she drove inside, past the snowmobile, parking in a far corner near the John Deere tractor. She tossed a tarp over the car, securing the corners with bungee cords. When spring came, she'd figure out what to do with it. She might be able to get some money for it once things cooled down.

She grabbed the supplies she might need, shoving nylon straps under the padded snowmobile seat before gingerly settling on the machine as she stuck the key from the kitchen in the ignition. It took a few tries, but it finally caught. She revved the engine and drove out of the barn, parking next to the addition.

Inside the house, she ripped down the shower curtain from the bathroom, wadded it up, stuck it in the pocket of her walker, along with the other supplies, then clumped back to the body, all the while cursing the world and her bad luck.

She rolled the dead woman onto the shower curtain. Bent over, panting, leg aching, she cut off the girl's clothing with scissors. Like dealing with someone in the ER, it was easier to remove clothes with scissors, especially her bra and underpants. But when she tugged off a nice pair of wool socks, she tossed them aside to save for herself. Everything identifiable went, even the girl's tiny stud earrings. What were those? Angels? That was sad. Sleeping on the job.

Once the body was nude, Nan secured the shower curtain with duct tape. She was running low and would have to buy more on the next trip to town. Then, trying to keep most of her weight on her good leg, using the wall to support her, she dragged the body out the back door. The task got a lot easier when she hit snow. Snow was going to be her friend today.

From under the seat of the snowmobile, she pulled out the nylon ratchet strap, tied one end around the body's feet and the other to the metal lift bar at the back of the snowmobile, then she straddled the machine again.

Warmed up, it started quickly this time.

She wanted to drive like hell, full throttle, but she forced herself to move slowly across several open acres of land. She didn't want to lose her friend.

The snow was coming down thick and wet and heavy now, almost like a curtain, evening falling with it. The snowmobile lights bounced off a wall of the white stuff, hindering visibility. Nan leaned forward and squinted, finally spotting her goal—the concrete silage pit. She pulled up beside it, hobbled off, unfastened the nylon strap, and pushed the dead girl over the edge.

The body hardly made any noise when it hit. That's how deep the snow was. Just this muffled thump. Later she'd come back with gasoline and matches. In the spring, she'd bury whatever was left. Not ideal, certainly not her first choice since there was a risk of dogs and coyotes carrying off the bones.

She hobbled back to the machine. Her wrapped walking cast was slick as hell and she lost traction. Her feet went out from under her. She landed on her back, the air knocked out of her, pain ripping through her injured leg. She screamed and clamped a hand over her mouth, stopping the sound halfway, turning it down to a muffled whimper even though it was unlikely anybody would hear her.

She rolled over and crawled to the snowmobile on her hands and knees, then pulled herself up inch by inch. She didn't even try to straddle the wide seat. Sitting sidesaddle, she started the engine and drove in the direction of home, each bump a stab of white-hot pain through her leg. Halfway there, she pulled out the gun she'd used to kill Jenny Hill and gave it a heave, tossing it as far as she could into the field. Then she took off again.

Breathing heavily, almost blinded by pain, she left the machine at the front door.

Inside the house, she downed prescription medication. Once the opioids kicked in, she returned to the annex and the scene of the crime, collecting the clothing, sticking the jewelry in the pocket attached to her walker, scrubbing the blood away. In the main house, she slowly stuffed the clothing, one item at a time, into the woodstove, appreciating the warmth of the fire.

CHAPTER 39

Her cell phone vibrated. Jude grabbed it from the bedside table and glanced at the mattress on the floor, where the boy was sleeping undisturbed. Two days had passed since she'd picked him up from the foster home, but the news wasn't good. She'd heard that afternoon that he was going to be sent back to Nanette Perkins.

The call was from Ingrid. A call rather than a text this time of the night meant something serious. Jude answered as she slipped out of bed and walked lightly into the living room, partially closing the bedroom door behind her so the call wouldn't wake the boy.

"I hate to get you up," Ingrid said. "Detective Ashby said to contact you."

Uriah was going to have to tell people what was going on soon. They'd start wondering, coming up with their own suspicions, maybe things that were worse than the truth, although the truth was pretty bad and serious even though Uriah downplayed it.

"I'm on night duty and got a call," Ingrid said. "A man found frozen to death off Lyndale, between Twenty-Fourth and Twenty-Sixth Street."

Jude checked her temperature app. Twelve below zero.

"I'm sitting in my van right now, trying to get warm, but anyway, I thought Homicide might want to take a look. On the surface, it appears a straightforward death-by-exposure by someone severely underdressed for the weather. But there are a few things that made me question an accidental death."

"I'll be right there."

"I'll have some coffee for you."

Jude called Elliot. "I've got a possible crime scene I need to check out," she told him. "Can you stay with the boy?"

He sounded groggy, but said, "Be right up."

She was dressed and waiting by the time he arrived two minutes later, barefoot, clutching a pillow to his chest. White T-shirt and flannel pajama bottoms. Slipping into her jacket, Jude whispered, "Sleep in my bed. It's more comfortable."

He nodded. "It's twelve below out there. You know that, right?"

She zipped her coat to her chin and pulled on a black cap. "Yep."

"Call a cab."

"Good idea, but I'm taking my car." She wanted to be in control.

Heading downstairs, her booted feet already felt the chill seeping through every crack in the building. The inside of the foyer windows were covered in a thick layer of frost, the delicate swirling fern design made even more beautiful by the illumination from the streetlight outside. Jude pulled out her phone and took a picture of it. If she had Instagram, she could post it. Elliot was always trying to talk her into being at least a little active on social media. She tucked her phone away, hurried to the garage, and headed for the address Ingrid had given her.

It was always easy to spot the white coroner van. Right now its lights were on, engine running. A silhouette—most likely Ingrid's—in the driver's seat. A patrol car was also there, the scene in a holding pattern while awaiting input from Homicide.

Jude parked and slipped into the warm van with Ingrid. The body on the ground, illuminated by the vehicle's headlights, was covered in snow.

"Here." Ingrid passed her a carryout cup with the promised coffee. "I've got toe warmers in my boots and finger warmers in my gloves, thermal underwear, insulated snow pants, and a down jacket, and I'm freezing my ass off. And then I see photos of people in Antarctica, and it's forty below or something insane, and they're standing there smiling with no hat. And you have to wonder: *What the hell?*"

"But it's a dry cold." They both laughed, and Jude sipped her coffee. "It makes people think it's easy. Living somewhere like this."

"It wasn't easy for that guy." Ingrid pointed. "He wasn't dressed for the weather. No jacket. No hat or gloves."

There were several bars nearby. People were known to get drunk and wander off, unable to find their car, and just freeze to death. It happened. Often it was college students, but not always.

"Ready?"

Ingrid checked her phone. "It's now fifteen below, so I don't think it's going to be of any benefit to wait."

The officers in the nearby cars joined them outside, one of them giving Jude a quick rundown. "Called in by someone walking her dog. We got here, dusted off the face a little, but it was pretty obvious he was dead. Frozen solid. Just looked like another victim of the weather to me."

"I had the same reaction," Ingrid said. "Classic presentation. Young male, possibly college age. Popular nightspots all over this area. Leaves a bar drunk, gets disoriented, can't find his car, finally collapses in this dark corner of the alley. But then I looked closer. Check him out and see if you see what I see."

Someone handed Jude a flashlight. She stepped closer, crouched, and aimed the beam at the dead man's face.

And recognized him.

CHAPTER 40

The man who might be Shaun Ford.

His face was marbled and his lips were blue. His eyes looked like opaque glass. But the area around his mouth was faintly discolored in a suspicious way.

"Duct tape," Jude said. Her thoughts raced as she tried to track what had transpired in the time between his visit with her and now. "Good catch." Without revealing that she'd met him before, she stood and passed the light back to the officer beside her. "Let's cordon off the area. Get a tent up, along with some heaters." She wanted to find out where he'd gone after he left the police department less than forty-eight hours ago.

"Alan Reed." An officer standing nearby held a set of car keys and a billfold open to reveal a driver's license. "Oklahoma. No wonder he didn't know how to dress."

"We'll track down next of kin and get a few people on this," Jude said. She'd call Uriah and fill him in. "But right now, let's get inside our vehicles before we end up like him." She held out her hand to the officer. "The victim's keys." To Ingrid Stevenson, she said, "Let me know when he's ready for autopsy. I want to be there." Ingrid nodded, and they dispersed.

Back in her own car, Jude started the engine. The interior was already cold, and the vents blew icy air.

She drove around the block slowly. And bloody hell, she even lowered her window several inches while pressing the lock button on the key fob the officer had pulled from the dead man's pocket. When that didn't generate any results, she broadened her search. A car finally responded with blinking red taillights, and she pulled up behind the vehicle. Leaving her beater running this time, she grabbed her Maglite and got out, unlocking the victim's car as she approached, frozen snow sounding like breaking glass under her feet.

Still wearing winter gloves, she carefully opened the door with two fingers, shining her light around the interior. On the floor in front of the passenger seat was a single-slice pizza container. In the cup holder was an empty drink from a gas station. Wadded up on the floor near the brake pedal was a receipt.

She picked it up, holding it by one corner. Location, date, and time had been recorded with his purchase. The stop had occurred shortly after she'd taken his DNA sample.

She made a mental note of the location of the business, shut and locked the door, and returned to her car for an evidence container. Inside, she slipped the receipt into the bag and sealed it, then called Forensics to arrange a pickup of the vehicle for analysis.

CHAPTER 41

On the way back to her apartment, Jude stopped at the gas station where Alan Reed had gotten food. It was open twenty-four hours, deserted now due to time and weather conditions. Inside, she told the woman at the register she needed the names of the people on duty when Reed had stopped there. The roster was checked. "That'd be Michael or Jolene. They were both here."

"I'd like their contact information."

The woman wrote down two numbers on a tablet, tore the paper free, and passed it across the counter. Jude thanked her and glanced at the wall clock. A little after four. She'd give it a few hours before disturbing them. Back in her car, heater blasting tepid air, drying out her eyes and face, she sent Uriah a text to see if he was okay. If he was asleep, hopefully it wouldn't disturb him. If not . . .

His reply was to call. He sounded terrible, so terrible she made an instant decision to check on him. "I'm going to stop by."

"Don't. It's ugly over here."

"I'm already on my way." She disconnected and drove.

◆ ◆ ◆

"It's unlocked," was the reply to Jude's light rap on Uriah's apartment door.

She found him lying on the couch, a blanket over him, empty bucket on the floor, close just in case.

"Do I look that bad?" he asked weakly. His face was white, and he had dark circles under his eyes. His normally curly hair was flat and lifeless.

"Yes."

He tried to laugh but gave up.

"What can I get you? Something with ice? Crackers?"

"I didn't take my anti-nausea meds, because I was on call and they make me sleepy." Seeing her expression, he continued, "I finally took them, and they're kicking in." He tossed the blanket aside. T-shirt and briefs. "I'm going to take a shower."

"Do you need help?"

"God no."

"Okay." She glanced around the room. "Yell if you do."

"You'll be the last to know."

At least he could still joke.

While the shower was running, she straightened up, collecting dirty dishes and carrying them to the kitchen. In the refrigerator, she found a bottle of ginger ale. She shook it to get rid of the fizz, then poured half in a glass and added a couple of ice cubes. It would be ready if he wanted it.

The shower stopped.

She rinsed the dishes and put them in the dishwasher. In a cupboard, she found some reasonably bland food. A box of cereal she showed him when he stepped into the kitchen, dressed in gray sweatpants and a white T-shirt. "Interested in this?"

He reached for the box, looked at the image on the front, and passed it back without speaking, sitting down heavily on a chair. His wet hair was soaking into the shoulders of his shirt. She retrieved a clean towel from the bathroom and returned to find him with his eyes closed, breathing shallowly, the kind of breathing a person might engage in when trying not to throw up.

Standing behind him, she carefully placed the towel on his head and gently dried his hair. The shampoo he'd used smelled minty, and she realized it was a scent she unconsciously associated with him. The gentle head massage seemed to relax him a little, and he let out a sigh.

"My hair's falling out."

"It'll grow back."

"I keep wondering if I should shave it. Now."

"I'd wait. It's not bad."

"Never thought I'd care about my hair, but I do."

"You have great hair."

He let out a snort.

"You really do."

Once the towel had absorbed as much as it could, she draped it over his shoulders and sat down across from him.

He took a cautious drink of ginger ale. When that seemed to go down okay, he pointed to the box of saltines on the counter behind her.

His kitchen was so small she could reach them without getting up. She opened and placed the box on the table near his hand. As he nibbled on a cracker, his color improved, so much that he picked up the ginger ale and box and walked slowly to the living room, Jude following as he lowered himself to the couch, cautiously, as if lying down on a bed of glass shards.

"Would music help?" she asked. She loved how his apartment, with the dark lamps and floor-to-ceiling books and records, was a sanctuary. It felt peaceful and safe.

"Maybe something soft." He closed his eyes. "Turned down low."

She went through his albums, finally settling on an artist, placing the record on the turntable, adjusting the volume so it was soothing and ambient. "Do you want to try to sleep?"

"Maybe a little."

She turned off the lamp with the red shade. Now the glow from the kitchen was obnoxious. She crossed the room and hit the wall switch. Lights from the city kept the apartment from being truly dark. If she recalled correctly, his bedroom had black drapes. Now she understood why.

Lying on his side, Uriah scooted back and patted the small space on the couch next to him. The expression on his face was a dare he knew she wouldn't take. There was an overstuffed chair on the opposite side of the room, but she felt the need to be closer than that. But not smashed up against him. Instead, she sank to the hardwood, her back resting against the couch, Uriah behind her.

"The floor?"

"I like floors."

Since he seemed to be feeling better, she told him about Alan Reed, about how he thought he might have been Shaun Ford, and how she'd taken a saliva sample from him.

"That's extremely interesting," Uriah said.

"I know. A man comes to town, says he might be one of the missing kids. Now he's dead."

"Very unfortunate for him, but he could be just what we need to crack this case wide open."

She pulled a cracker from the box on the coffee table and took a bite. "I feel bad about it," she confessed. She didn't typically share her feelings, but the situation, Uriah's illness and vulnerability, the night, the room, made it easier. "I don't think there was anything I could have done, but . . . I don't know. I didn't take his theory very seriously. I thought it was a reach." She finished the cracker and wrapped an arm around her knee. "He told me his girlfriend was pregnant. He had a child on the way."

Uriah let out a sigh. "Like I said before, I think your captivity has made you too empathetic for your own good sometimes."

Maybe.

She felt a light touch on her head. Her hair was only a few inches long, but he was rubbing a strand between his fingers in what she suspected was an unconscious gesture.

"I don't know," she said. "My captivity might have enhanced something that was already there. When I was little, maybe seven or eight, I remember going to an event with my grandmother. Maybe a church function, I'm not sure. But one of the big attractions was a raffle for a porcelain doll. There were a lot of women there, admiring it, talking about where they'd put it if they won. They kept entering, some buying twenty tickets or more. My grandmother bought me one ticket, just for fun."

She sipped his ginger ale, offered the glass to him. He took it.

"I won. Instead of being happy, I felt horrible for the women who didn't get the doll. Every time I held it, I thought of those women and the happiness the doll would have given any of them. I kept thinking about how I wanted one particular woman to have it, someone I didn't even know, because I felt sure it would make this stranger happy. I don't think that's a normal reaction for a child to have. The doll made me feel so bad, I ended up hiding it in the closet, and I don't remember what ever happened to it."

He put the glass back on the table. "And you were a kid. Kids have dolls. That's some crippling empathy."

"Exactly."

"Was this before or after your mother was murdered?"

"After."

"It's typically the opposite. We shut down our emotions, but it's possible her death woke up an unusually strong sympathetic response in you."

That was something to mull over and something she'd never considered.

"So does that mean I should never buy you a lottery ticket?" His voice was even stronger now. Maybe the diversion had been good for him.

"That's a tough one."

"Oh, come on. If you won, would you be eaten up by guilt?"

"I think so."

"That's ridiculous."

"I know."

They both laughed, then went silent.

"You're going to have to tell everybody," she finally said. "About your health."

"I will. I plan to."

"When?"

"Tomorrow. Today, actually."

"In person?"

"I was thinking about an email."

She swung around so she could look him full in the face. From inside her head, it felt like her expression was neutral. No judging, no advice, no reaction.

He watched her a moment, then revised his answer. "In person."

CHAPTER 42

U riah called a meeting.

Jude was relieved to see he looked better than he had when she'd left him to check on Elliot and the boy early that morning. She'd found them sitting at the kitchen counter, eating cereal and talking about a character in a cartoon she was unfamiliar with. Elliot seemed up on it, and he was good at riffing, even with a four-year-old. Especially with a four-year-old. In the brief time she'd been home, she'd called the building caretaker and arranged to borrow a twin bed from an unoccupied furnished apartment. The boy would be leaving soon, but she wanted him to have a real place to sleep, no matter the length of his stay. Elliot would help set it up while she was gone.

Most of Homicide gathered around Uriah's desk for the meeting. Chief Ortega was there too, arms crossed, looking a little annoyed to have been summoned from her office. But her expression changed when Uriah shared the news of his bad health.

"It's not a big deal," he assured everyone when murmurs of concern moved around the room, almost as if a silent dread were being passed from person to person. "I might have some days when I'm working from home or when I'm not a hundred percent, but it'll be temporary." He glossed over the surgery, telling them it was routine, then they dispersed.

In the restroom, Jude heard someone crying inside a stall.

Torn between leaving the person to her privacy and offering help, she knocked lightly. "Everything okay in there?"

Detective Caroline McIntosh burst from the stall, her nose and eyes red. "Everything's not okay. Weren't you out there? He just told us he's dying."

Jude's stomach crashed at the word *dying*. "He's not dying."

"You believe that act?" McIntosh turned on water, washed her hands, grabbed a paper towel. "He's just letting us down easy. That's all. Letting us get used to the idea. I've seen it before. My dad died of cancer." She pointed in the general direction of their office. "I know that game."

Jude frowned. Was it true? She'd believed his reassurances, but now she wondered if McIntosh was right. A few minutes later she connected with Uriah at his desk, but before she could bring up his illness, both of their phones vibrated simultaneously. Like mirror images, they pulled them out and checked the screens. A text from Ingrid Stevenson.

Do you have a moment to Skype?

They walked side by side toward a private meeting room that was more conducive to video chatting. Jude sat in front of the monitor, arranging her chair, waiting for the computer to wake up. "Caroline says you're dying of cancer and just haven't told us."

"I'm not dying. Well, we're all dying, but I'm not planning on dying anytime soon."

"Are you being honest with me?"

"Two risks." He sat down beside her. "One, if the chemo doesn't shrink the tumor and they can't operate. I doubt that's an issue because the doctors think the tumor is shrinking already. Why? Because the headaches have stopped, but we'll know more once I have another MRI. The other is that the surgery is invasive and dangerous. Chances of my dying in the operating room aren't high, but chances of my coming out with some sort of neurological damage are. I didn't want to talk about this now, but I'd like you to think about stepping in as head of Homicide if that happens. If I remember right, you were interested in the position at one time."

"I don't care about it anymore." He was trying to make light of something terribly serious, and she refused to play along. "It won't happen. None of it is going to happen."

"Okay. Let's just go with that."

Ingrid answered their call from an autopsy suite, where she gave them an update on the John Doe that had finally thawed. No new surprises since carbon monoxide poisoning had already been determined. Cell phone in hand, she moved to Reed, who was lying on a table, still in the preliminary stages, no Y incision made.

"I don't understand how you're able to do the autopsy so soon," Jude said. "He was frozen like the other bodies, and they took days."

"He wasn't frozen through."

"Cause of death?" Jude asked.

"I'm going to say exposure. We've got duct tape residue around his mouth, but I also found some on his wrists and socks. I don't see any signs of trauma."

Jude leaned close as Ingrid aimed her camera at the body. "So someone tied him up and left him outside to die."

"That's my guess."

"Then removed the bonds and tried to make it look as if he froze to death," Uriah said.

◆ ◆ ◆

A few hours later, Jude decided to make a surprise visit to the gas station where Alan Reed had stopped. The girl named Jolene was working. Jude displayed her badge and pulled out the only decent photo she had of

Reed, one she'd gotten online. "Do you remember this person stopping here a couple of days ago?" she asked.

"Yep," the girl said. "Nice guy. Kinda cute. I tend to remember the cute ones."

"What time was that?" Jude typically mixed in questions she knew the answer to in order to get a read on the recall and accuracy of the witness.

The girl had it down.

"Do you remember what he bought?"

"Pizza slice and a soft drink."

Correct. "Did you engage in any small talk?"

"We joked about how damn cold it was. He said he was from Oklahoma, and I asked why he didn't just stay down there, at least till it warmed up. He said he was here to visit his mom. And as soon as he saw her, he was heading back home."

"Was he going straight to her place from the gas station?" Jude asked.

"I don't know."

"Thank you."

CHAPTER 43

That night while the boy slept in her room in the old but new-to-them twin bed, Jude sat on the couch going through the Shaun Ford case files, opening a manila folder with his photo clipped to the paperwork inside.

Shaun Ford had been reported missing at ten p.m. on a Wednesday in January twenty years ago. Later, Gail Ford told police he hadn't come home from school. There were inconsistencies in reports of the clothing he'd been wearing. First, she said he was wearing a blue jacket, jeans, and a blue T-shirt, then she said the shirt was green. Not a huge variation, and not that unusual to get inconsistencies under such emotional trauma. It was one of the unfortunate things that made kidnapping cases hard to track, because the parents were understandably out of their minds.

Jude opened her laptop and searched YouTube for content. Rather than spending hours researching newspaper archives, YouTube was now her go-to place for video research. And thanks to armchair detectives, it was becoming easier to find pre-YouTube news footage. She wasn't at all surprised to find pages of videos on the Shaun Ford abduction from various news sites ranging from local to national, but it took one local video to trigger her own recall.

She remembered it now, the event and the subsequent coverage. Jude had been about sixteen at the time, only five years older than the kidnapped victim himself. Maybe that's why it had hit her hard. She remembered feeling outraged and helpless and very sad.

She always figured she'd gone into police work because of her mother, because she'd never believed her death to be an accident. But maybe the abduction of Shaun Ford had also played a part in it. A missing child. Stranger still to think she might be working on the very case that had subconsciously directed her.

She plugged in earbuds so the audio wouldn't wake the boy.

There were interviews with detectives, some now dead, some retired, whom she made a note to try to locate. There were interviews with neighbors. And especially interviews with Gail Ford. Flash-forward to recent news reports, some just days old—renewed interest brought about by the bodies discovered in the lake, with updates on how old the victims would be today. Several sketches of what Shaun Ford might look like now. None bore much similarity to the man who was now lying in the morgue.

It took two hours for Jude to view all the videos. She sat on the orange couch sipping tea, wrapped in a down blanket, wool socks on her feet, legs crossed under her, Roof Cat sleeping on the back of the couch. Close, but not too close.

Once she'd gone through them all, she started over with just the Gail Ford interviews, yellow legal tablet braced on one knee, making notes of location and possible time of day, the clothing Gail Ford was wearing, her emotional state, and most of all, the story she kept telling.

So perfect, down to every single word.

Memorized, that memorization made obvious by the sheer number of interviews with various people, compiled in one place and easy to view one after the other within a short span of time.

Ordinarily stories morphed to some degree with each telling. New things were remembered. Some details were omitted because the teller had told them so many times before. Specific plot points dropped into oblivion. The stories were *never* the same. Never word for word.

Gail Ford had scripted and memorized these on-camera interviews. Why? Maybe because she had something to hide.

Jude watched the videos again, this time with the sound muted so she could concentrate on Gail Ford's body language instead of the words. It was interesting how the lack of sound turned off one part of Jude's brain and dialed up another. The mother broke down in every interview. Almost like a switch had been flipped. She was talking, then she was crying with no warning.

Sound back on.

Interesting. The breakdown was always at the same spot. Like many people who cried on camera, she apologized and turned away.

But there was something in her eyes that Jude had seen before in someone else—the man who'd held her captive. Just before Gail Ford turned from the camera, Jude caught a familiar flicker of pleasure.

Video could distort and magnify. It could make something more important than it was. But it could also underscore a fleeting emotion that might not be obvious in the actual moment.

Jude's heart broke for all those grieving parents who were questioned mercilessly about the disappearance or death of a child, but it had to be done.

As a professional courtesy and to keep him in the loop in case they found a dot he might be able to connect, she sent an email to Paul Savoy, updating him on the Billy Nelson and John Doe cases and asking him if he knew anything about a woman named Gail Ford. And she moved Gail Ford to the suspect position—as possibly having something to do with the disappearance of her own child. And, if the person in the morgue turned out to be Shaun Ford, possibly having a hand in his death.

CHAPTER 44

Ten o'clock in the morning. Ten below zero, brilliant blue sky. Jude could feel the cold of the steering wheel through her thick gloves, and when she turned a corner, the unmarked car creaked and the tires crunched over the snow and ice. Beside her, Uriah gripped his coffee with two gloved hands, holding it close as he tried to hide the shivers going through him. She suspected the chemo was doing a number on his metabolism. It was hard enough to tolerate the cold when you were healthy . . .

"You should try the hand warmers I left on your desk," she said. "You just slip them inside your gloves. It helps."

"I forgot." He squinted at the sky. "I think I can feel the sun through the windshield, though. Strange how it can be so cold, yet the sun still feels warm."

"Doesn't seem right, but I'm not going to complain about it."

They were heading to Gail Ford's house. It was the morning after Jude had viewed the YouTube broadcast footage on the disappearance of Shaun Ford. She'd briefed Uriah and related her suspicion of the mother. It didn't take any convincing; he seemed to trust Jude more than not when it came to her instincts about people. It hadn't always been that way.

She pulled to a stop in front of the house she'd visited not all that long ago to tell Gail Ford the body in the lake wasn't Shaun.

One-and-a-half-story cottage, green vinyl siding with a dormer. The front door had a little rounded roof, making it look cute and inviting. The element of an unannounced visit could work in their favor. She just hoped the woman was home.

"What do we know about Ford?" Uriah asked, unlatching his seat belt.

"Single. She was married when her son vanished, but, as often happens, the loss of a child led to a strain on the marriage, followed by divorce. Her ex died not long after. She's had a lot of jobs, never seems to stay at any very long. Waitress. Bartender. Clerk at Target."

She got a text and checked it before getting out of the car. A message from Paul Savoy, thanking her for keeping him in the loop.

Intriguing. I might have to visit the Twin Cities again soon. No, I don't know Gail Ford.

At the house, Uriah knocked and Jude stood back, watching windows for moving curtains or signs of activity. Someone not answering the door or someone slipping out the back. Neither of those happened. The door opened, and Mrs. Ford looked surprised but not alarmed. Understandably worried? Yes.

Uriah glanced at Jude. His brief faith in her suspicion was fading. He said hello, and Jude explained why they were there. "We're investigating something that might or might not be connected to your son's kidnapping case."

"Come in quick." Mrs. Ford motioned with her hand.

At least one good thing about the cold weather? You got invited in. Nobody was going to stand with a door open, talking to people on a front step. Inside, they removed their boots and left them on the rug near the door. In thick socks, they padded across the living room, tossing hats and gloves on a roughly cut coffee table that looked homemade.

Maybe Mrs. Ford was into crafts. Jude and Uriah sat down on the couch, their backs to the large picture window.

The house was so dark. The thick curtains were closed in an attempt to keep out the cold, but even through her coat, Jude could feel the chill seeping around and through the glass.

"We're trying to establish a timeline for a man who was found dead in a Minneapolis alley," Jude said.

Mrs. Ford sat down on a chair facing them. "Oh, I heard about that. How awful."

"It's possible he stopped by here."

An O of surprise.

Uriah jumped in. "Have you had any visitors?"

She gave that some thought. "No. I mean, nothing more than the usual door-to-door solicitor we get around here. Siding scams, cable companies, people offering to shovel or whatever. Things like that."

"It very well could have been someone posing as a siding salesman," Uriah said.

Jude disagreed. "Seems a little strange for people to be going door-to-door in this weather."

"Not really," Mrs. Ford said. "It slows down in the winter, but it doesn't stop. Especially the ice-dam-removal companies."

Ice dams. The bane of Minnesota homeowners. When the heat from the building's interior met the cold of the outdoor air, it caused thick layers of ice to build on roofs. That ice inevitably melted and leaked into walls and through ceilings if not removed. Jude was glad she lived in an apartment building and didn't have to deal with that kind of maintenance.

"Has anyone tried to email or call you, claiming to be your son?" Uriah asked.

"So that's what this is about." Mrs. Ford put a hand to her throat and froze a moment before getting to her feet and walking to the kitchen, her house slippers dragging and sliding against the wooden floor. Jude heard the flick of a cigarette lighter. That was followed by the smell of smoke. Mrs. Ford returned with an ashtray in her hand and a cigarette between two fingers. "I never smoke in the house, but . . ."

"We understand," Jude said.

The woman sat back down, sucking on her cigarette, the tip glowing red in the semidarkness. "I . . . um . . . used to hear from people a lot. At first. Like sightings from all over the country that ended up not being real. And yeah, even people coming forward to say they were my kid. I don't know if they really believed it or just wanted to be on the news."

Uriah leaned back against the couch, a sympathetic expression on his face. "It happens." He appeared to have finally warmed up, and now his curly hair was showing signs of perspiration, his face so pale the scar on his forehead stood out in pink contrast. They needed to wrap this up so he could get some fresh air.

As Jude produced the photo she'd shown the girl at the gas station, her phone vibrated. She tugged it from her coat and glanced at the screen. Her main contact at the DNA lab. "I'm going to have to take this. Excuse me." She stood and stepped away, moving in the direction of the kitchen for a little privacy. In the doorway, she raised the phone to her ear while casting a casual and furtive glance around, looking for anything out of the ordinary.

"I know you wanted those DNA results as quickly as possible," the specialist said. "Once they were processed, we ran them through the databases as you instructed. We got a hit on Gail Ford."

Jude turned her back to the others so they couldn't see her surprise. "Relationship?"

"Most likely mother."

Jude glanced over her shoulder at Uriah. He was leaning forward, elbows on knees, face still sympathetic as he engaged in conversation with Mrs. Ford.

"Thank you," Jude told him. "I appreciate your speed on this."

"No problem. I'll be following up with an email later today."

Jude thanked him again and disconnected.

She was good at the blank face. She'd employed it for so long during her imprisonment that it was her go-to expression. Unreadable. It helped with so many things. Even the checkout line at the grocery store when the person behind the counter asked personal questions about the toothpaste and toilet paper she was buying. But Uriah had somehow learned to penetrate that blankness. She saw the question in one raised eyebrow. He knew something serious was going on, and now they were both pretending. Maybe all three of them were pretending.

"I just got some bad news." Jude sat back down. She'd normally discuss a plan of approach with Uriah, but this could be their one opportunity for surprise. "The person we came to ask you about"—she picked up the photo from the table—"this man, the person we found dead in an alley, came to see me recently. He drove from Oklahoma to the police department. He had an interesting theory, interesting enough for me to act on it."

She pushed the photo across the table, close to Mrs. Ford, and watched her face, especially her eyes and mouth. "He agreed to a DNA analysis." She paused to let her words sink in. "That phone call? It was the results. The lab came up with a match."

Alarm flickered in the woman's eyes, and her mouth tightened almost imperceptibly. Then she caught herself reacting and leaned back in her chair. Casual. But Jude could see the pulse pounding in her neck.

Twenty years her son had been gone. Twenty years people searched for him. Now Jude wished she'd talked to him longer, engaged with him, asked where he'd lived since the abduction, where he'd spent most of those years. Filled in some blanks, because now it was too late.

Jude glanced at the photo. He *did* have kind eyes. She sensed he was a good guy deep down, and she hated that he was dead. She looked back up at Mrs. Ford. "I'm sorry to break this news. You were a match. The DNA suggests the person found in the alley was your son."

Jude could feel Uriah's disapproval of her bluntness. And maybe he was unhappy about no discussion of a game plan and the way she'd dumped the traumatic information in the woman's lap.

Mrs. Ford made all the right gestures and sounds. They were so good Uriah was won over, and Jude began to wonder if her suspicions were off. Cigarette abandoned in the ashtray on the table, smoke curling toward the ceiling, Mrs. Ford sobbed into her hands, face hidden.

"Can we contact someone for you?" Uriah asked. "A neighbor? A relative?"

The woman shook her head without looking up. "I need to be alone."

Jude left the photo on the table. She didn't know why, but it was intentional. Uriah picked it up. They grabbed hats and gloves and got into their boots. Outside, closing the door behind them, the temperature still subzero, they walked down the sidewalk.

"That was a little abrupt," Uriah said under his breath. "It could have been dealt with better, in a more sympathetic way."

"I realize that, but I felt I had to make a quick decision. I wanted to catch her off guard to see how she reacted."

"That grief seemed real to me."

"It could have been. Do you believe her? About no visit from her son?"

"I'm not sure about that."

Someone was coming toward them, big hood, head bent. The hair suggested female, but it was hard to tell this time of year. The bundled person in mirrored sunglasses was dressed in unisex insulated coveralls and walking a small black-and-white dog.

Jude grabbed another opportunity. "Hello, can I ask you a question?"

The person kept moving. Jude snatched the photo from Uriah's hand and ran after the dog walker, holding the photo out. "My name is Detective Fontaine, and I want to know if you happened to see this man in the area." She held out the photo.

The person paused, tipped back the fur-edged hood (female), and looked at the image in Jude's hand. Beside her, wearing rubber boots that looked like deflated balloons, the dog waited. "Yes."

"Recently?"

"Yesterday or maybe the day before. I was walking my dog and he said hi, then he walked up to that house." She pointed to Mrs. Ford's place. "I noticed him because he was friendly and cute. And he had a southern accent."

"Did anyone answer the door?" Their conversation caused a fog between them, and Jude half expected to see words freeze and fall to the sidewalk.

"A woman. I don't know if he went inside. By that point, I was past the house and it was none of my business. My dog's cold. I gotta go."

Jude thanked her, and the girl continued down the sidewalk.

In the car, Jude cranked up the heater. "So now what? Do we bring her in for interrogation?"

"We put a tail on her," Uriah said. "And I'll have our information specialist find out everything she can about Gail Ford." He pulled out his phone and gave the orders.

CHAPTER 45

That night on the way home from work, Jude stopped by one of the fancier grocery stores, where she bought several healthy items from the deli, all organic, ranging from grilled chicken breasts to rice-stuffed squash. She was vegetarian most of the time, but a child needed protein.

Up the stairs and inside her apartment, arms full of bags, she kicked off her boots and settled the groceries on the kitchen counter, then tossed her coat and laptop on her bed, followed by her stocking cap and gloves. After slipping into jogging pants and a baggy sweater, she sent Elliot a text, letting him know she was home and that she'd picked up food. Five minutes later, he and the boy were pounding up the stairs like it was a race, laughing as they burst into the apartment.

"We've had a big day," Elliot said. He grabbed plates from the cupboard, setting three places at the counter. Leaning close, he whispered, "You do know this isn't the kind of meal a kid's gonna like, right?"

She poured a small glass of milk. "He likes peanut butter and cereal, but he can't live on that." Hot tea for herself and Elliot.

"Tacos, pizza," he suggested.

"Those aren't healthy."

"You can make them healthy. But hey, this looks great. Not complaining."

The boy ended up liking the acorn squash, but he didn't care for the rice, because it had onions in it. He picked them off his tongue and wiped them on the side of his plate. Elliot gave Jude an *I told you so* look.

Later, the grown-ups washed dishes while the boy played with toys on the living room floor. He seemed to have been programmed to avoid adults when they were talking. *Keep your head down and you won't get hurt.* Heartbreaking that he'd had to learn that so early in life.

"I'm gonna head home." Elliot put the last plate in the cupboard. "Thanks for dinner."

"I want to pay you for watching him."

"Absolutely not."

"You need money. Or at least I assume you do."

"I've got some cash coming in."

"Okay, but let me know if that changes." She hung a towel on the stove handle. "Could you wait with him a minute while I run downstairs to get my mail? I forgot it earlier."

"No problem."

In the lobby, Jude unlocked and opened the small ornate metal door to her box. Two envelopes. One was a bill; the other was from the law office handling her father's estate. It looked similar to the one upstairs that she'd never opened. She disliked these formal letters, reminders of painful things. But this time she decided to tear it open and get it over with, like pulling off a Band-Aid.

It seemed to be a day for DNA results. The letter dealt with the search for her father's heirs.

> As you know from our previous letter, recent DNA tests turned up a match, and the name has now been distributed to all lawyers involved in the estate. As a courtesy, we are supplying you with the heir before we release the information to the public. It is our determination that the relationship is father/son.

That statement was followed by the name of Phillip Schilling's match, the person who would be Jude's half brother.

Elliot Kaplan.

If a chair had been handy, she would have sat down, fallen down. Instead, she dropped to the marble steps, elbows on her knees, clutching the letter in both hands, rereading it slowly, trying to make sense of it.

I've got some cash coming in. No freaking kidding.

Elliot.

It wasn't the first time he'd kept a secret from her. He'd moved into her building to spy on her, get to know her, write a book about her. Or was writing that book just another one of his covers?

And she'd let him watch the boy.

What now? Go upstairs and confront him?

It might be better to hold the information close, not let him know she knew anything, and see if he would choose to do the right thing and tell her himself. But that wouldn't undo the lie of omission. And he'd had plenty of opportunity to tell her.

In most situations she could hide her emotions, what little emotions she had left, but upstairs she found herself having a hard time going blank. She clenched the business envelope tighter, return address hidden, and when Elliot made some joke about how much the boy had liked acorn squash, she attempted a smile that caused a flash of puzzlement in Elliot's eyes.

She made up an excuse for her awkward behavior. "Sorry." She waved a hand as she practically pushed him out the door. "This case is a distraction."

That was enough to fool him.

Once he was gone, she called Uriah and told him the unsettling news. He was dumbfounded too. And angry. He offered to come over. "Also, I might just want to beat the crap out of him."

That was funny. Elliot wasn't muscular or physical, but in Uriah's present condition, it was hard to predict who'd win. "Stay home. I've got this under control."

"What's the plan?"

Now that she was on the phone with Uriah, she discarded the idea of waiting. The not knowing what he was up to would be too much of a distraction. She had to get to the bottom of this right now. "He and I are going to have a talk."

Once the child was bathed and asleep, Jude sent a text to Elliot.

Is there something you'd like to tell me?

No hesitation. No time to mull anything over. He shot back a reply: I'll be right there.

CHAPTER 46

I f the boy hadn't been sleeping a few feet away, Jude wasn't sure what she would have done when Elliot arrived. Thrown him against a wall? Unlikely. That kind of red-hot anger didn't burn in her anymore, not in defense of herself anyway. Yet the betrayal of another male relative, even one she hadn't known was a relative until minutes ago, cut to the bone.

Wordlessly, she held up the letter and pointed to his name. He'd obviously known this was coming, yet his face was ashen and he was visibly shaking, lingering near the apartment door he hadn't closed completely, ready to bolt. She was shaking too, but hers was inside.

She threw the letter at him. Reflexes engaged, he caught it, then dropped it to the floor as if stung. "What do you want?" She was done with family and all the lies and deceit and pain they brought. "Why are you here?"

He could hardly get the words out, stammering, stuttering, rubbing his arms nervously, and damn if she didn't begin to feel sorry for him.

"I was just curious about you at first," he said. "That's all. I wanted to get to know you without the layers of who I was and who you were and who our father was. I wanted it to be real."

"Jesus, sit down before you collapse."

"I'll just stay here by the door." He reached for the handle, missed, almost fell.

"Sit down."

He did. On the stained couch.

Jude remained standing, arms crossed, back to the wall. "Tell me all of it." She kept her voice low because of the sleeping boy.

She was interested only in recent history, but Elliot went way back, further than she cared to go, because his deep dive returned her to her own childhood and things better off forgotten. He told her how he'd grown up in Texas and his father, *their* father, had paid for his education. "My mother always portrayed him as a great guy. I mean, they didn't have any kind of relationship by that point, not that I was aware of, other than his taking care of me financially. And my mother convinced me you were bad, and that all of the stuff about him was a lie."

"And now what do you think?"

"I believe *he* was bad. And that's been hard for me to deal with. I know you have to feel some of the same confusion. Knowing our father was a monster. Wondering what kind of genes we have. Wondering if we should ever reproduce." He paused for thought. "But then, you're okay."

"I'm not okay."

"You were. Before."

"Maybe." Maybe not. "Did you ever meet him?"

"Not that I can remember, but I talked to him on the phone. Once a year or so. He'd ask how I was doing and what I was interested in. It made me feel good."

"Did you know about me?"

"When I got older. And of course I was curious. But I'd grown up knowing I had a secret I could never share with anyone."

Which had probably made it easier for him to continue to cover it up.

It turned out he was a few years younger than Jude. She put a timeline together in her head. Her mother had still been alive when he was born, and her father had already been murdering young girls.

"Your mother. What about her?" she asked.

He pulled out his phone and scrolled through photos, then turned the screen around. A thin woman with light hair and light skin. Elliot had an olive complexion and very dark hair. Jude wouldn't have been surprised to discover that this person was not his biological mother.

He put his phone away. "She was a good mom. She didn't beat me, but she was strict. I've come to realize she was being supported by Phillip too. I was her meal ticket."

"And that dried up when he died."

"I've been trying to help her out, and she had some money saved. And of course she can't get social security because she never paid in."

"You'll be a millionaire soon."

He flinched. "I don't care about the money, but it'll give me a way to take care of her. And there's more than enough for that. There are a lot of people in need, and I plan to spread it around. You should take your share."

"I don't need anything."

"You need a car."

"I don't know where all of his wealth came from. I'm sure some of it's blood money." But she liked Elliot's idea of philanthropy. She'd think about it. "Do you feel like a victim?"

"I had a good life. Spoiled, really."

What if the woman he knew as his mother wasn't really his mother? What if Elliot was the product of one of her father's early abductions? What if Elliot was really the son of someone his father had held hostage at his cabin in northern Minnesota? It would explain the money all those years. Paid to a woman to take care of him. Had Elliot ever thought about that?

They knew Octavia had gotten pregnant in captivity. She'd miscarried, but had any of the other captives given birth? If so, what had happened to those babies? Phillip Schilling wasn't known for having girlfriends or relationships. His "girlfriends" were his captives. So Elliot's story didn't fit with what she knew of her father.

He started crying. Quiet sobs that shook his shoulders as he buried his face in his hands. She sat down beside him and patted his shoulder lightly, awkwardly, not knowing if it brought him any comfort.

Hours ago she didn't have any close relatives. Now she had a brother she wasn't even sure she wanted.

CHAPTER 47

Child Protection Services came to take the boy away, and there was nothing Jude could do about it. Another storm was coming, and they wanted to move him before it hit.

"It's best for the child," Kim Tharp told her. At least the welfare worker had been to Jude's apartment before, so there would be some consistency. The boy didn't have to deal with a complete stranger again.

Jude knelt in front of him and zipped his jacket. Then she handed him his red knit cap, and he put it on. Red mittens with an orange cat on them were next. "Roof Cat." He pointed in delight. Pretty cute.

Her phone vibrated, and she pulled it from the pocket of her jeans. A text from Elliot.

I'll be back soon. I want to tell him good-bye.

Weird getting a communication from him, knowing what she now knew and being in the early stages of processing the information. She tucked her phone away and handed the boy the backpack. It contained his stuffed animals and flannel pajamas with pictures of Thomas the Tank Engine on them, a few pairs of socks and underwear, a hairbrush, toothpaste, and a toothbrush.

"Where's Jenny Hill?" she asked, standing back up. They'd come together before.

"Under the weather."

"I thought she'd be here. Didn't she file the initial report?"

"Yes, but we all signed off on it."

"I think the decision was made too quickly," Jude told her.

"We're the specialists." The woman's face softened. "I know it can be hard to let these children go. We get attached. But I'm sure you understand that a child is better off with a relative, preferably his mother or father, if at all possible. We'll be there to give Ms. Perkins the support she needs this time."

"I'd like to follow up on the case. Maybe visit in a couple of days." The woman looked uncomfortable, and Jude continued, "Unofficially of course."

"We discourage that kind of interaction." She glanced at the boy, lowering her voice, leaning closer to Jude. "A clean break is best. Bonding does sometimes happen between a placement and foster families, but we want the child to re-form the bond with the mother."

"When will you follow up?"

"We'll call first thing tomorrow."

"A phone call?"

"Yes."

"And the next day?"

"We'll give it a few days, then call again."

"When will you actually go there? To the home?"

"Ms. Hill will be monitoring that. We typically schedule those visits two weeks out. It gives them enough time to settle into a routine. In that way, guards are down, and what we find is a truer picture of the situation."

Jude didn't like the sound of that. She planned to give Jenny Hill a call and encourage her to visit again very soon. She also wanted to get some reassurance as to why the young woman thought the house was a safe environment for the boy when he'd been abused. Welfare services often got a bad rap. Sometimes it was deserving, and sometimes not. She wanted to make sure this case didn't end up a deserving one.

"You know what happened with his foster family," the woman said. "Before we moved to return him to his mother, we tried to find another place for him. Everybody is reluctant to step forward. Our foster families all know each other and communicate." She glanced over her shoulder again. "People were scared of him. We don't really have a lot of options."

"I'm an option. I think you're rushing this. I know he's just one of hundreds of cases, but—"

"You work full-time. You work odd hours."

"I have someone in the building who takes care of him when I can't."

"Someone who has not been approved by us."

Jude thought of Elliot's deceit and couldn't really argue. In truth, he should never have watched the boy to begin with.

"And even though you're a detective, you haven't been either. We made an exception since you're an officer, but that could end up being a problem for us, especially if Ms. Perkins were to file a complaint."

Was that one of the reasons behind their decision? She hoped not.

"We should go."

Elliot hadn't arrived. Jude wanted to give the boy a hug, but she tamped down the impulse. The woman was right. It was best not to reinforce bonds that would go nowhere and had no meaning to him.

They left.

She did not walk them downstairs. She did not watch from her apartment door, but she did watch from her bedroom window. Elliot appeared, running, then crouched in front of the boy, pulling him into his arms. Moments later, Jude heard the lobby door slam. She was glad he'd made it in time. Under all his deception, there was no denying Elliot's good qualities.

Kim helped the boy into the car. She smiled and fastened his seat belt. Was he crying? Jude hoped not.

The car door closed. As the caseworker circled the vehicle to get in the driver's seat, the child looked up. Jude wasn't sure if he could see her, but she held up her hand in farewell.

CHAPTER 48

As Jude drove south out of Minneapolis, she wished for the second or third or fourth time that she'd gotten a loan and a better vehicle. With a better heater. Because she already had a motorcycle she much preferred to ride, she hadn't wanted to spend much money on the car. Three thousand dollars, everything left from the retirement fund she'd cashed in a short time ago.

The car's vents blasted cold air, and Jude was long past feeling her feet. Even though the heater was failing, the outdoor temperature gauge seemed to be working. It was near the zero mark again, three thirty in the afternoon. Night would arrive in about an hour, and temps would continue to plummet.

Jude had tried to contact Jenny Hill with no luck, then had given it six hours, figuring that should be enough time for them to get the boy settled. She hadn't told Uriah where she was going, because she didn't want him to be complicit. And she hadn't wanted him to try to talk her out of it.

Using her phone's GPS, she found the farmhouse easily.

The landscape and remoteness were no surprise. Before leaving work, she'd looked it up on Google Maps and had been rewarded with a satellite view of a two-story white home, along with a large red barn and several outbuildings. The photo had been old, possibly taken at a time when life for Nanette Perkins had been better. At least a lot greener. Trees had their leaves, and corn in the fields had tassels. A van in front of the house that wasn't a recent model.

The long unpaved road stretched to a house with a rural emergency number—a series of digits used by fire and police to pinpoint houses that might otherwise be hard to find. The lane had been plowed recently. Both the number and the plowing were good signs—in case help for either occupant was needed. Jude wasn't sure if Ms. Perkins even had a car anymore, and wasn't sure she could drive anyway.

Past snow had built up on each side of the road, over six feet high in places. The scene was reminiscent of an old black-and-white photo Jude recalled seeing as a child—a Minnesota blizzard with snow that had been carved, creating deep white canyons for a single row of cars to squeeze through. When the temperatures stayed low, even the warmth of the sun couldn't get rid of it.

The house had a collapsing picket fence that was more gray than white, and more dilapidated yard décor than anything that served a purpose. It seemed to mark the end of the road and the beginning of the yard. It wasn't an enclosure and was open on both ends. A packed-down snow path cut around one side of the fence. At the end of the path was a snowmobile. Maybe that's how Perkins was getting around.

On one side, off what looked like the kitchen, was an awkward-looking addition, a room with a low roof and no windows. It seemed more like a livestock-confinement shed than a house, and that's quite possibly what it had been at one time.

Jude turned off the ignition and sat a moment, watching the house, absorbing minute details. Curtains were closed, and shades pulled. Not unusual this time of the year. Anything to keep out the cold. Slivers of light cut around the shades, indicating occupancy.

Jude got out of the car and walked to the house. Perkins answered her knock, no attempt to hide her surprise at the unexpected visit, but she wasn't unwelcoming. Jude hadn't seen her since the hospital, when she'd still been on pain medication. She looked better, younger. Her face even had a glow, the kind of glow winter brought. Rosy cheeks from cold and heat. But her injured leg was in a black plastic cast, and she was leaning heavily on a metal walker.

Behind her, the kitchen looked cheerful, no dishes in the sink, no food on the laminated countertops, and a tablecloth so new the folds were still evident. Obviously staged for the social worker. Now Jude more fully understood the advantage of waiting. This would not give a person the true take on the situation. And yet, Jude didn't at all like that the boy was back here, no matter how cozy the place appeared.

"You look like you're freezing."

"My heater's not working well."

"Come on in and sit down by the woodstove."

Jude stepped inside and closed the door behind her. "I'm not planning on staying." She hated lying; she wasn't a liar, but she pulled one out. "I was in the area and thought I'd drop this off." She held up a Buzz Lightyear toy. "I forgot to put it in his bag this morning."

Perkins sat in an overstuffed chair, collapsing into it rather than a slow decline, her foot propped in front of her. The white cotton wrap around her toes had turned black.

The television screen emitted a weak glow, and Jude could hear faint popping. It had just been turned off; maybe Perkins had heard her pull up.

"Sit down."

Jude wanted to get a better feel of the situation. She started to kick off her boots.

"Don't worry about that."

Jude left them on and walked across the linoleum of the kitchen to join the woman in the living room. Two walls were wood paneled; two were white. The shiny kind of paint that made Jude uncomfortable because it showed every flaw. Two dark hallways: one probably led to bedrooms and bathroom; the other might have gone to the addition. A set of stairs to the second floor. The big question: Where was the boy?

Jude loosened her scarf. The temperature in the living room must have been close to eighty. Too hot, but it felt nice for the moment. The only sign of the child was his backpack in the middle of the couch. Judging from the bulky shape, it looked as if very little had been removed.

Perkins noticed where Jude's attention was aimed and explained, "He was so tired when he got here. He's napping."

He liked to nap *with* his stuffed animals.

Without asking for an okay, Jude sat on the couch and unzipped the pack. It hadn't been opened. Everything was just the way she'd arranged it at her apartment. "He might want these." She pulled out the cat and panda.

Perkins leaned her chin against her hand, looking amused. "You really want to see him, don't you?"

Jude shrugged as if it wasn't important. "I wouldn't mind. I won't wake him up. I'll put these in bed with him, but I'll be quiet."

"Go ahead. Take a peek." Perkins pointed toward a short hallway off the kitchen. "He's in the addition."

Jude kept her expression neutral even though the strangeness of the situation was growing fast.

"It'll put your mind at ease." Perkins grabbed her walker with both hands and levered herself up, almost tipping over, then steadying herself. "Stupid thing," she muttered. "I couldn't afford one of those knee trikes. You go on, I'll catch up."

Jude felt for the holster at her waist. She fake coughed and unsnapped it at the same time, covering the sound. She didn't like buildings with secrets or narrow hallways or windowless walls. Cement floor beneath her feet, the clumping of the walker behind her. But beneath that noise, Jude caught a faint sound. A child crying.

The boy was stoic. It happened with abused children. And abused adults, so for him to cry . . . She paused and turned. "You don't need to come. I'll get him and bring him to the living room."

Perkins leaned heavily on the walker.

The crying continued.

At the end of the hall, Jude turned the knob and opened the door.

By this point, she knew better than to expect the traditional scene of a child in a sweet little bed. But she wasn't prepared for the reality of the narrow barrack-looking space with cots lining one wall, two electric heaters running, a propane heater silent, the room so cold she could see her breath.

And a dog kennel with the boy inside. Clinging to the bars, his mouth open wide, tears streaming down his cheeks. Jude ran to him, dropping to her knees in front of the cage. She felt many things: anger, sorrow, disgust, but the predominant emotion was relief at finding him hopefully unharmed. Upon seeing her, he reached up with both hands, imploring her to pick him up.

Or so she thought until he spoke. "Nana."

Jude ducked, pulling her gun from her holster at the same time. Too late. She'd allowed herself to be distracted by her concern for the boy. A blow to the side of the head sent her crashing to the floor. Her weapon flew from her hand and spun across the concrete.

"He got spoiled the short time he was with you," Perkins said with a chuckle. "You can't spoil kids. You've gotta be tough, teach 'em to be tough. It's hard, but they have to learn for their own good. Life isn't easy. I love him. Everything I've done has been because I love him. He's a sweet boy, too sweet for this world. And it's not as bad as it looks. He likes it in there."

Jude rolled, intending to kick the woman's legs out from under her. Before she could complete the maneuver, a sharp, breath-stealing pain tore through her shoulder. Perkins loomed over her with a knife. More stabs. A few feet away, the boy was screaming. Hands grabbed the front of her coat, followed by the lifting and pounding of Jude's head against the floor. She let out a choking gurgle, and lost consciousness.

CHAPTER 49

Nan watched and waited for the detective to die. She thought about stabbing her again to be done with it, but that would take some work, and Nan wasn't feeling so great. The exertion had done a number on her and caused her leg to throb. She was breathing hard, and her heart was pounding like a bass drum. No chest or arm pain, so she was probably okay.

The detective finally stopped making noise.

Nan shuffled over, picked up the stuffed animals that had been dropped during the scuffle, and wiped them across her sweatpants. Toys still sticky, she shoved them through the bars of the cage at the boy. He grabbed and hugged them to himself. It was then she noticed the detective's blood spatter on his face. She considered reaching through the bars and wiping it off, but that seemed like too much work right now.

Killed a detective. So stupid, but she'd been left no choice. Nan tested her hand, fingers spread, palm down. Bloody, but steady. That surprised her, given the way she was shaking inside. Couldn't she just catch a damn break? What a string of bad luck, from the bodies to the kid to the social worker, and now this.

She dug through the detective's coat pockets until she found a cell phone. Breathing hard, head roaring, black spots seeping into her vision while nausea and a cold sweat rushed over her, she straightened and tried to blink the spots away. She'd passed out a few times in her life and knew what was coming. Not wanting to collapse on the concrete, in the blood, she dropped to a cot and bent forward, waiting for the faintness to pass.

How much time did she have before someone started looking for Fontaine? Had she told anybody she was coming here? And what about the boy? This was all his fault.

Feeling a little better, the nausea and sweating over, she got down to business and smashed the detective's phone and stuck her car keys in her pocket.

After clumping to the main house, she dressed for outdoors—winter boots, knit cap, heavy gloves. In the bathroom, she ripped down the new shower curtain. It was white with yellow butterflies, just purchased to replace the last one. Back in the holding room, the boy was asleep in the kennel with his stuffed animals. Not bothering to strip the body this time since she needed to hurry and planned to finally take off for real, she got to work. Panting, she managed to roughly wrap the detective's body, securing it with duct tape, running out before she'd adequately bundled it. Then, walking backward, favoring her good leg, she dragged the body across the floor, pleased to see she was leaving very little blood behind. Like before, the task got easier when she hit the snow.

It was dark out, but it didn't feel as cold as it had a couple of hours ago. Glancing up at the light near the barn, she spotted a few snowflakes. Getting back to work, she wrapped ratchet straps around the detective's ankles and tied an end to the snowmobile. Thankfully, the machine started right away. Like last time, Nan drove slowly along the edge of a cornfield, resisting the urge to give the machine more gas, the twin headlights so close they seemed like one beam cutting through the dark.

At the unloading point, Nan loosened the straps, dragged the body to the silage pit, and rolled it over the side. Easy. It hit bottom with a soft but satisfying thud. Nan limped to the snowmobile, settled herself on the wide seat, and rode back across the field. It was snowing seriously now, and, as often happened when snow fell, the temperature had risen. It felt almost balmy after the bitter cold.

Snow was good. It would hide many things.

Back home, she began tossing clothes in a suitcase, pausing long enough to make a call to Gail Ford.

Not even a hello. "You're never supposed to call me," Gail said.

"Nice to hear your voice too." Nan filled her in on her shitty luck. "Just wanted to tell you I'm getting the hell out of here as soon as the snow lets up." Nan zipped her suitcase and dragged it off the bed. "I'd advise you to do the same."

"I'm not scared of the cops."

"Me either. I'm scared of somebody else." What the hell was she going to do with the boy?

Leave him. Just leave him.

"You're overreacting," Gail said. "Besides, he's not even around here."

"You sure about that? He was in my hospital room last week. Almost killed me. He's going to be after both of us. If you don't plan to mobilize, you'd better hope the cops get to you first."

"He's been calling, asking questions about the bodies in the lake. And you," Gail admitted, her voice shaking. "He said he was in California."

Good chance he was lying.

In the kitchen, Nan turned on all four stove burners, then blew out the flames. The gas made a hissing sound. "You'd better run."

Five minutes later, as snow fell thick as a curtain, Nan tossed her suitcase into the detective's car and slid into the driver's seat. A turn of the key was met by a series of clicks. Another twist, and the engine caught and died. *Jesus. Not again.*

Why in the hell didn't a cop have a decent vehicle? And one that didn't smell like mothballs? Another attempt, and the engine rumbled to life. She wasn't taking any chances, and she sure as hell wasn't going to drive off in a junker. Before it could die again, she drove it into the barn. She'd take the social worker's car. It was almost new.

Then she remembered the keys were in the house.

CHAPTER 50

The MRI machine went silent, and a disembodied voice told Uriah they were done. A whir, followed by a series of jerks and he was staring up at the ceiling, pulling the foam earplugs from his ears.

"Drink plenty of fluids to flush out the toxic dye," the technician said as she removed the needle from the back of his hand. He was told to go home. Take it easy.

Once he was dressed, he called Jude to give her a medical update. His attempt went straight to voicemail. He tucked the phone away and left the clinic, pointing his key fob at his car, unlocking the door. Nausea was still a problem, and the MRI machine and contrast agent seemed to aggravate it. But he'd taken the anti-nausea meds, so hopefully he could circumvent any severe side effects. He had a headache, but it was different from the headaches caused by the tumor.

He'd spent the afternoon trying to keep up with work through emails and by logging into their private network. He'd done a lot of behind-the-scenes research on everybody in the orbit of recent events. Over the past several hours, he'd been especially focused on Gail Ford. Right now, Molly, his information expert at the police department, was doing some deep digging for him. He planned to go home and sleep, hoping he wouldn't feel too bad in the morning and could hit the ground if not running at least strolling. When he got back to his apartment, he tried Jude again. Same result. So he called Elliot, who answered on the second ring. Uriah hadn't talked to him since the revelation of his shocking identity. This wasn't the time to bring it up.

"Have you seen Jude? I can't reach her by phone."

"Said she was going to the Perkins farm to check on the little dude. I offered to go with her, but she seemed to want to go by herself. That was hours ago. She should be home by now. I'll run upstairs and see if I can rouse her." Uriah heard feet on the stairs and a loud knock, followed by Elliot's report of no answer.

Uriah checked with a few people in the police department. No one had seen or heard from her in several hours, and she hadn't logged into their VPN recently. He got a text from Molly.

Check your email.

He pulled up Molly's correspondence. A JPEG. He opened it. A blurry photo of two women standing on a street corner next to a telephone pole, one woman light-haired, the other dark. Judging by their clothing and nearby cars, he guessed the photo to be about twenty years old. He checked the email again. No explanation, but Molly liked putting a personal flourish on her discoveries. He called.

"I give up. Who are they?"

"You can't tell?"

He looked again. "No."

"This is going to blow your mind."

"I'm sitting down."

"Gail Ford and Nanette Perkins."

He let that sink in. "So they knew each other."

"Yep. Perkins helped Ford put up missing-person flyers after Ford's son went missing."

"You're invaluable, Molly."

"Just a geek who somehow managed to find a job I love. Oh, and Detective? I'm sorry to hear about your illness."

"I'm not dead yet." He hung up and called the number they had on file for Nanette Perkins. No answer.

Then he called the tail he'd put on Ford. "How's everything going?"

"She's been in and out. Trip to the grocery store, back home. Nothing that isn't boring as hell."

"Are you sure it was her? The person who returned?"

"Well, yeah."

"Was she ever out of your sight?"

"At the grocery store part of the time."

"Go knock on the door."

"But I'm supposed to be undercover."

"Just do it. Don't hang up. Put your phone in your pocket."

Uriah heard a door slam, then footsteps crunching across frozen snow before hitting bare sidewalk. A knock, a span of a few seconds, then the sound of a door opening.

"Is Gail Ford here?"

A female replied. She sounded fairly young, with a sweet voice. "No, I'm watching her house for her."

"Do you know where she went?"

Long pause. "Hopefully where you can't find her. You newspeople are terrible. Can't you leave a grieving mother alone?"

"I'm not the news—"

The door slammed.

Ford had found some sympathetic person to switch places with her in the grocery store. Uriah called Headquarters and ordered a BOLO. Then he disconnected, grabbed a caffeine drink from the refrigerator, and headed to the elevator and parking garage. He needed to find Jude.

CHAPTER 51

Jude was dreaming about being cold. She really should get her car's heater looked at. That thought morphed into something else, and she was suddenly sitting in a car-repair waiting room. But she was still cold. Even stranger, it was dark.

Maybe she could just fly out of the repair shop, float away and find a warm room, drift skyward through the roof and past the streetlight and electrical lines, all the way to the stars. But something was nagging at her. She heard breathing very near and felt something moist against her nose and mouth. With a sucking gasp, she was out of the dream. The breathing was her own.

Between the cold and numbness and a body that felt raw and on fire at the same time, it was hard to pinpoint the source of another agony that went beyond physical. And then she remembered.

The house. The boy. Nanette Perkins.

Jude's eyes were open, but she couldn't see anything. She tried to lift her hand to feel her face and realized her arms were squeezed against her sides, so tightly she couldn't move them. She panicked and began to thrash around, her breathing coming faster, the damp warmth she'd felt in the half dream more apparent now. It took a moment longer to understand that she was bound and wrapped in plastic—she could hear it crackling.

And she was outside.

Panic bloomed. She couldn't keep it at bay. The plastic slammed against her nose and mouth with each breath, cutting off what little air she had. *She was a crime scene.* She was the body wrapped in plastic. She was the sorrow.

Heart thundering, she struggled to get her physical responses under control. She could do this. She knew how to do this. How to relax, how to slow her pulse and remove the terror from her mind.

Lying on her back, she quieted herself, relaxing each muscle, slowly, from head to toe. She was getting air, which meant she wasn't wrapped that well. Perkins, thinking she was dead, or maybe thinking she wasn't dead but would die of exposure soon, had rushed to dispose of her. Either way, she figured Jude was gone.

If you can't do something right, don't do it at all.

Calmed, her panic almost under control for the time being, Jude wriggled her arms, trying to loosen her bindings. It didn't take long to create enough of a gap to work one hand up her body in an attempt to reach her face. The tightness of the binding around her elbow stopped her. She ducked her head and maneuvered her fingers enough to grasp the plastic and pull it down, away from her nose and mouth—and felt a blast of cold air.

She gulped and blinked as snow fell against her face. She marveled at the magical beauty of the night, and she might have let out a sob of admiration. If this was where and how she died, it would be okay. Lying outside, snow falling, the sound of the flakes pattering against the plastic that still encased her. She sighed, lost in the wonder of it all, and let her eyes drift closed.

How nice to let go. Just give herself permission to say good-bye. To the pain. Not the physical pain, which was lessening, but the pain of living.

Life hurt. Living hurt. Memories hurt.

She'd tried; she'd really tried. Tried to go back to the world. It wasn't working, not when her choices were pain or nothing. She'd chosen nothing. But here now, lying by herself in the middle of nowhere, she acknowledged what she'd known all along. *Nothing* hurt too.

CHAPTER 52

I t was snowing hard by the time Uriah left the city to head south on Interstate 35. Traffic was sparse, and what cars were on the road were moving slowly. An occasional semi passed him, stirring up a tornado of white, blasting the road clear behind it for a moment before vanishing into the darkness beyond Uriah's headlights.

Forty minutes into his drive, the GPS on his phone told him to turn left. He couldn't see a road, so he took it slow, squinting through the windshield while his wiper blades smacked loudly with every downward sweep. A mile later, he dropped to a crawl and spotted a rusty, slanted mailbox and a wooden fence that had seen better days.

The two-story farmhouse was dark, the only light in the entire area coming from a single bulb high on a nearby barn. No sign of Jude's car. No tracks, but the snow was getting deep.

He tugged on gloves and a knit cap and got out of the car. Wind bit his exposed skin, and the snow clung to his boots and jeans. He knocked on the door and wasn't surprised when no one answered. He briefly thought about entering, knew better, tested the knob anyway. The door was locked. He circled the house but saw no signs of life. Back in his car, he tried Jude's phone again. Got her voicemail. Then he called Elliot.

"Still not home," Elliot said.

Uriah told him where he was.

"You better get back. I just heard they're closing I-35 because of drifting snow."

Uriah started his car. "Leaving now."

CHAPTER 53

Jude heard coyotes howling but couldn't tell if they were near or far. The sound echoed and didn't seem of this world. Trying to lock in a location was impossible. The cries seemed to come from everywhere. And there was something else, something close, a constant rustling. *That* sound had been enough to rouse her.

With stiff fingers, she brushed snow from her face and eyes and thought about the boy in the cage. He was her only regret in this scenario. Yes, there was Octavia and also Uriah, maybe even Elliot. But they'd be fine without her. They'd forget her existence soon; Elliot would take in Roof Cat, but the boy still needed someone to let him out, to rescue him from Perkins and that life. She had to hope it wasn't too late for him. With the right guidance, he might be only slightly damaged. Or he might never recover. But she'd sensed a sweetness in him. As long as he had that . . . And right now, here, lying cold on the ground, she might be the only person who could help him.

Body numb, unable to feel much of anything anymore, she forced herself to squirm within the plastic wrap, tugging at the heavy film, finally pulling it over one shoulder, freeing one arm.

The frozen surface beneath her was sloped, and the movement pitched her forward until she was lying facedown. She placed a hand on the ground, in the deep snow. And felt something unexpected.

Blindly, she felt the form beside her. Human. A thigh. A forearm. A face, half gone, probably eaten by the coyotes. She jerked away and rolled to her back.

Teeth chattering, trying to forget about the body, trying to focus on one task, she resumed her squirming, like a creature emerging from a cocoon. Surely not a butterfly, but rather some alien birth, strange and bloody.

She heard a rip. Her confinement loosened and she sat up, groped in the darkness. As she suspected, duct tape had been used to secure her. She tore the tape from her ankles, freeing her legs. Remembering her phone, she dug in her coat pocket. Empty.

She rolled to her knees and slowly pushed herself upright enough to stumble forward, hands extended in front of her, until she touched a concrete wall. She followed it, the ground rising with each step until she was out of the pit.

The rustling was louder now, and she realized she was standing in a field of corn that hadn't been picked. She felt the wind, and, beyond the blowing snow, saw a faint light in the distance. She knew nothing of farming, but suspected she'd just escaped something with an agricultural purpose. She wondered what the temperature was, wondered about frostbite. But she was feeling warmer now—probably a *bad* sign—and her teeth were no longer chattering.

She walked toward the light even though she knew it could be the light of the enemy. But it might also be the light that would lead her to the boy.

She found a trough between the corn rows and followed it, not moving fast enough for her satisfaction, the falling snow a distraction, the stalks snagging the plastic still clinging to her for some indiscernible reason. Her body felt heavy, each step clumsier, the light not appearing to grow any closer.

The wind howled, and the snow changed in tempo and sound and weight. It pelted her peculiar cape, and the pieces striking her face felt like shards of glass. She forgot what she was doing, where she was going, why she was going, and dropped to her knees. Ice was falling from the sky, yet the snow beneath her was deep and soft. Like a bed.

CHAPTER 54

U riah had told Elliot he was leaving, but he'd started feeling nauseous and had decided to drink some water and close his eyes for a little while. In the short time he'd been parked at the farmhouse, the snow depth had increased. Now it was turning to freezing rain, the sound loud against his car even though the wipers were on high, competing for his attention.

Squinting through the windshield, he drove toward the barn and an open area where he planned to swing the car around. Front-wheel drive, fairly new tires, but this was getting into chain territory, although now that the snow had transitioned to freezing rain, visibility was a little better. His headlights weren't reflecting back at him any longer.

As he completed the three-point turn, something moved across his headlights, or rather his headlights moved across an object in the field beyond the farmhouse. He paused to stare as far as the headlights allowed but was unable to lock in on any movement. He hit the high beams, clicking them back and forth in an attempt to re-create the movement.

Nothing. Probably a visual distortion caused by the headlights and the freezing rain on the windshield. He was poised to drive off when he saw something again out of the corner of his eye. A flash of white.

He turned his focus back to the landscape. A field of unpicked corn, the yellow stalks bent and broken by wind and snow, some of them folded to the ground, the ears no longer visible. Often an unpicked field was a sign of an owner's illness or sometimes death. An unpicked field also represented a loss of income and could result in total crop failure. Not something to take lightly. A single year could break an independent farmer. It might be picked in the spring, but the law of diminishing returns came into play and profit would be so low it was often better to plow it under and start over. If there was any money left to buy seed and fuel.

There.

A blur of movement.

Leaving the car running and headlights on, he grabbed a flashlight from the glove box and tucked it in his coat pocket. Out of the car, not taking his eyes from the apparition, he crept toward the house, bringing him closer to his subject and closer to cover. Maybe it was something blowing, possibly a piece of large plastic used to wrap hay bales, caught on a cornstalk. But the longer he watched, the more he was convinced it was an animal or a human. Doing what? He didn't know.

And then it vanished.

Seconds later, it rose from the ground, not tall, not like a person walking upright.

Someone crawling?

No longer concerned for his own safety, he pulled out the flashlight and turned it on, pointing it in the direction of the object in the field. Hampered by drifts up to his knees, he lumbered through the snow while continuing to bear down on his target. The freezing rain had stopped and it was snowing again. Big wet flakes that stuck to his lashes, further hindering his vision. He wiped at his face with the sleeve of his coat and continued forward.

A person.

Lying in the snow, half-wrapped in plastic, facedown. The white hair . . . Not many people had hair that color.

He dropped and rolled Jude to her back, pressing two fingers to her neck to check for a pulse.

Alive.

Blood, stark against her ashen face, her lips blue. She was wearing her black down coat, escaped feathers stuck to blood on the outer shell. Where she was injured, he had no idea.

He panned the light down her body. The plastic that had caught his attention turned out to be a shower curtain with butterflies on it, attached to her waist with silver duct tape.

She groaned and said, "Snow's warm."

People often claimed to feel warm shortly before freezing to death. "It's not, believe me." He couldn't worry about her injuries now. Grabbing her hands, he tugged her upright. "Come on. Let's get you out of here." She released a sharp cry of pain as he looped her arm around his neck.

Adrenaline and dehydration were driving concentrated toxins through his veins; he felt a rush of weakness and another wave of nausea. The sound of the plastic was deafening and disorienting so near his ear. But she was on her feet, leaning heavily against him. He ripped the curtain from her. Side by side, with his support, they staggered awkwardly into the beam of the car lights like a couple of aliens. Behind them, the freed shower curtain drifted away, then snagged in the cornstalks. It was evidence, but right now Uriah's only concern was getting Jude out of the cold and to a hospital. She was doing surprisingly well, moving forward at an awkward if steady pace, which led him to hope her wounds were superficial.

"Who did this to you?"

"Nanette Perkins." The words were faint and delivered on an exhale. "Not sure why."

He had his suspicions, but he'd share them later.

"Do you smell smoke?" she asked.

They looked toward the house and flinched just as a window shattered and flames shot skyward. He didn't know how she did it, adrenaline probably, but she broke away and ran toward the building. Uriah took off behind her. At the kitchen, she turned the knob and threw her shoulder against the door. "The boy's in there."

Using the end of his flashlight, Uriah broke a small pane of glass, reached in, and tripped the lock as Jude swung the door open and stumbled inside. Flames danced and crawled across the ceiling, the heat alone lethal. Just as Uriah realized they had to run, the ceiling crashed and a wall of fire roared at them like something alive, the sound deafening.

Instead of turning around, Jude moved deeper.

Uriah lunged after her, grabbed her by the arm.

She might have shouted no as she wrenched away. He dropped his flashlight, looped one arm around her waist, and physically lifted her off the floor. She flailed, trying to get free. Under normal circumstances, she might have been able to kick his ass, but he'd taken her by surprise, and she was injured.

Coughing, both of them close to being overcome by the flames and lack of oxygen, he turned and ran. She was tall but fairly light. Through the doorway, yards from the building, unable to carry her farther, he let her feet touch the ground, bracing himself for the second she turned, which she did, intent on going back inside.

He tripped her.

She kicked him.

He grabbed her foot and dragged her away from the house, past the dilapidated fence and into the snow-deep driveway. The heat from the house was unreal, like standing inside a blast furnace. Paint on the fence bubbled. He pulled her upright again while recognizing the acceptance and defeat in her face. But he wasn't going to let her go. With a firm grip on her arm, they ran. Two yards, then ten, moving not as fast as he would have liked because of Jude's injuries. Behind them the house exploded, the concussion throwing them to the ground, knocking his breath away.

Smaller explosions continued, flames shooting several stories into the air, illuminating the area. Fiery pieces of the building fell from the sky. Smaller pieces sizzled as they hit the wet ground. Around them, snow rapidly melted, looking like time-lapse photography, until they were surrounded by water. Black smoke rolled and billowed, filling the air with a toxic odor of noxious fumes. The house cracked and popped, walls collapsing and crashing to the ground.

CHAPTER 55

They'd failed him.

It would be too easy to blame Child Protection Services, but Jude hadn't put up a fight. She'd let the boy walk out her apartment door when she knew it was the wrong thing to do. Why hadn't she grabbed him, told them no? She should have done that. She should have stuck up for him; she should have fought harder.

Beside her, lying on his stomach, Uriah pulled out his phone and called 911, reporting the explosion. He told the operator who he was. "I need an ambulance stat."

That must not have gone well, because he barked, "I know the road is closed. Use snowplows and get people out here now."

She wasn't aware of his movement, but suddenly he was standing over her, his hand extended. She took it and he helped her up. Right now, she felt no pain from the stab wounds. Everything seemed like a dream. She turned and looked at the addition, where the kennel had been. A raging inferno.

No, the pain she felt was a different kind of pain, something deep, beginning in her chest and moving to lodge in her throat, the surroundings and this moment to be forever embedded in her brain. The heat, the smell, the sparks from the house swirling into the dark sky, mixing with falling snow. Even under the groan and pop of the building, she heard a sob and marveled that such anguish could come from her. Unexpected words followed, words that had no conscious thought behind them, yet managed to contain unarguable truth. "This world. This awful world." It felt as if they were pressing a finger to a dike. Maybe it was time to run and let the dike break.

One sob was followed by another, all control gone. She felt Uriah's hands on her shoulders, felt him wrap his arms around her and pull her close, his touch gentle, careful, maybe due to her wounds, or maybe because he knew she might not want such intimate human contact. But she leaned into him heavily and cried in a way she hadn't cried since she was a kid and her mother had died, the kind of tears that came from a place nobody should ever visit, and certainly no place a person should have to remain.

It was impossible to know how long they stood there, because grief had no regard for time. The clock in her head and heart had stopped once she knew the boy was dead, even while she felt baffled by the depth of her reaction. At some point, she pulled away from Uriah, able to stand upright on her own as her frail acceptance of the boy's death and the veil of numbness it brought kicked in. There were things that needed to be done. She had to think about what was next.

Where was Perkins?

Had she set the fire? It seemed obvious. Most likely to cover her tracks. She noted that Uriah's car was still there, not far from the barn, headlights on. The snow around it had melted.

"Your car." Her voice sounded strange, and she realized her ears were ringing from the explosion. Where was her clunker? Hadn't she parked it in front of the house? Perkins must have taken it.

"I left the headlights on when I spotted you in the field."

She took a few steps toward it, watching the falling debris floating from the house, pieces carried to the sky by the heat, then released to drift dreamily to the ground. She wondered how much damage this night would do to their lungs, not caring about herself but worrying about Uriah and his compromised immune system.

She spotted something between the house and car.

While Uriah spoke on the phone again, making demands, sounding intimidating, putting out a BOLO on Nanette Perkins, alerting the police within Minnesota and beyond, Jude forced herself to move forward, toward the object, her feet like lead until she stopped in front of it.

The stuffed panda she'd carried into the addition to give to the boy.

Without taking her eyes off the bear, she said, "Uriah." He didn't answer. She reached blindly behind her, as if fumbling for support or grasping for him even though he was far away and still on the phone.

Dizzy, she bent and almost pitched forward, but managed to slam a foot down and catch herself. Like a drunk, she swooped up the stuffed animal. It was wet and muddy from the melting snow. Being upright didn't help her light-headedness.

With an uneven gait, she walked toward Uriah's car, almost directly into the headlights.

And then something strange happened.

Like a page out of a horror novel, the engine revved and the car shot forward. Jude staggered back, ice and snow from the rapidly moving car plastering her coat and pelting her face. She shouted Uriah's name. His back was to her, phone to his ear, the sound of the burning house drowning out everything, including Jude's warning cry, as the vehicle raced straight for him.

CHAPTER 56

U riah leapt out of the way at the last moment, then ran after the vehicle as Jude replayed the episode in her mind. Yes, Nanette Perkins had been behind the wheel. She was sure of it. No sign of the boy, but the stuffed animal gave her hope that he was inside. After all, Perkins had claimed to love him.

The car roared toward the main road, away from the detectives and the burning house. When it seemed the woman was going to evade them, a pair of headlights appeared, coming down the lane from the other direction. Not the emergency vehicles they were expecting, but a white SUV. Police, Jude hoped as she moved as quickly as her injuries allowed.

The vehicle pulled to a stop, sliding sideways, effectively blocking the car's escape. Uriah moved closer, gun drawn, one arm straight out, one bent. Between the converging headlights and the burning house, the scene was lit like a stage. Just when it seemed things couldn't get any more perplexing or feel more off-script, Paul Savoy stepped from the SUV. He was dressed for the weather this time in a heavy jacket, gun braced, using his open door as a shield.

Definitely not golfing in California.

I might have to visit the Twin Cities again soon.

Maybe it was her injuries and exposure to the cold, but his presence made no sense. What had she missed? How did he know anything about Nan and this place? Had he been in touch with Uriah or someone at Homicide? That must have been it. He'd come to town, and he was here providing needed backup. Unorthodox behavior, but in this situation, not unwelcome. He'd stopped the car that might have the boy inside.

"Get out! Now!" When there was no response from the escape vehicle, Savoy shouted his command again. The driver's door swung wide and Perkins stepped out, her back to Jude and Uriah, her body silhouetted by the headlights. Before either detective could make a move, Savoy took unexpected action and fired three shots. Perkins crumpled to the ground.

Had she drawn on Savoy?

Confused, Jude limped to the front of the car in time to see Uriah roll the woman to her back. A weapon fell to the snow. Jude's gun. Perkins had been shot in the head three times. Undeniably dead, but Uriah checked for a pulse.

"You saw her. She drew on me." Savoy tucked his weapon in his jacket, splaying his hands on his hips, breathing hard, his face red, adrenaline rushing through him.

Jude didn't wait to hear his explanation of how he was even there. She swung around and opened the passenger door of Uriah's car. And immediately spotted the boy curled on the floor.

Her heart stopped, then started again when she saw he was breathing. Fortunately, Perkins was lying too near the vehicle for the boy to see her. Jude hoped he'd been on the floorboard the whole time.

"Hey there." She slid into the passenger seat, touching his shoulder. He moved enough to look up, then clambered out of his hiding spot. She ignored the pain and pulled him into her arms and held him tight. "You're such a brave little guy."

"I'm a boy."

"Yes, you are." She gave him the wet stuffed animal. He grabbed it with both hands as Uriah and Savoy stood in the headlights, talking over the body. Savoy glanced up, blinded as he looked into the car, his face illuminated.

The boy tensed. "Mean man," he stated with no emotion.

Jude's heart dropped. He must have witnessed the shooting after all.

"I don't like when the mean man comes to our house."

Her thoughts tripped. "Your house?"

"He hurts Nana. He's a mean man."

"You've seen him before tonight?"

He nodded.

"How many times?"

"Don't know."

"More than once?"

He nodded again and hugged the stuffed animal. "He hurts Nana and makes her cry."

And there it was.

Jude wasn't sure how Savoy and Perkins were connected, but now she understood why he'd flown all the way to Minnesota. Not for closure, but to insinuate himself and find out whether their investigation might expose him. The files he'd hand-delivered weren't supposed to give them any pertinent information, but rather were intended to mislead and draw them away from focusing on links between the two dead boys.

"I want you to get on the floor like you were before," Jude told the boy. "There you go. Just curl up with your bear and wait. Stay down until I come back." He was exhausted, barely able to remain awake, so he didn't argue. But then he always did what he was told.

She stepped out of the car and closed the door.

Uriah looked up, possibly to suggest she get back inside and wait for the ambulance. His words never came. He saw her face and knew something was wrong. She glanced at Savoy, then back to Uriah and gave him an almost imperceptible nod. Her partner's eyebrows lifted,

not enough to alert Savoy, but enough to transmit his limited understanding of the situation.

Savoy was the new enemy.

Jude walked closer until the three of them stood over the body.
Weakness washed through her, and she had to lean against the fender.
"There was no need to kill her."

"She had a gun."

"My gun, and I suspect she didn't even draw it." The weapon might
have slipped from Perkins's coat pocket. "My guess is she was coming
to you for help. My guess is you killed her to keep her quiet. What's
going on, Savoy?"

"That's ridiculous. You're out of your mind." To Uriah. "She's out
of her mind."

"She's probably more sane than both of us put together."

Jude appreciated his support, but she highly doubted the validity
of his words.

Another wave of dizziness hit her. She straightened and pulled in
a painful breath, attempting to clear her head. The house behind them
had settled into a steady roar, but suddenly another explosion rocked
the car.

The boy screamed, and the blast wave pitched Jude forward. A
second later, fingers yanked her hair, and Savoy jerked her against his
chest, the barrel of his gun digging into her temple.

"Keep your distance!" Walking backward, Jude glued to him, Savoy
shouted to Uriah. "It's been over for a long time," he said. "You need
to understand that."

"What's been over?" Jude asked. The cots, the boys who were so
similar . . . It had the hallmarks of human trafficking, but she wanted
to hear him say it.

"I've done good things since then. You know that. You saw my
record. I have a wife and kids. Grandkids."

"Put your gun down," Uriah said. "We'll listen to what you have to say. And people will take into account that you aren't the person you used to be."

Jude felt Savoy tense and knew he'd made a decision. "Uriah!" She shouted the warning as Savoy turned his gun and began firing. Her partner dove to the ground. Hot shell casings, one after the other, bounced, hitting Jude in the face. The air filled with the scent of gunpowder. Her knees buckled, but Savoy jerked her back up, using her body to shield his.

She blinked but couldn't see Uriah. Blackness crept into the edges of her vision, blocking out the flaming house. She wasn't sure if the roar was external or internal. Now the gun barrel was pressed to the back of her head, the metal warm from the expelled bullets. Uriah might be dead, and Savoy was going to kill her. What would happen to the boy? Savoy would kill him too and drive away. Nobody would know he'd been here tonight or had ever been involved.

And she was the only person standing between him and the child.

The passenger door to Uriah's car creaked open and the boy stepped out. "Jude?"

The arm around her neck relaxed a fraction, just a shift of a biceps muscle. Surprise was the only thing she had going for her. She dropped straight down into a squat, then shot up, slamming her head against Savoy's chin with the force of a battering ram, knocking him backward, the next shot from his gun exploding a foot from her ear. Barely taking a breath, she spun around, grabbed his arm, and slammed it against the top of the open SUV door. She felt a snap and heard his scream of pain as the weapon dropped from his hand.

And then Uriah was there, appearing unscathed, his wool coat covered in snow. He knocked Savoy facedown on the ground and pressed a foot to his spine. From the distance came the faint sound of sirens.

"About time," Uriah mumbled.

Jude kicked Savoy's gun across the ground, out of his reach. The dome light in the SUV was on, illuminating the interior. In particular, a shape in the far back. Jude circled, opened the lift door, and pulled a blanket free to reveal Gail Ford, three holes in her forehead, just like Nan. His plan had been to silence them all. He'd almost succeeded.

She returned to the boy, who was standing in the same spot. She guided him away from the scene. "Come on. Let's get back in the car."

They got inside, and the boy curled up on her lap. She put an arm around him, leaned her throbbing head against the seat, and closed her eyes.

CHAPTER 57

Concussion, hypothermia, four stab wounds, three fairly superficial. The other deep, but non-life-threatening. Forty stitches in all that I'm told you slept through. Amazingly, very few signs of frostbite, probably due to the temperatures that were hovering around freezing."

It was a lot of words to take in, all of them coming from Uriah, who stood next to Jude's hospital bed. It wasn't the first time she'd woken up in a hospital with Uriah next to her.

The room was dim, the building hushed and hinting of night, but individual lights were almost blinding, courtesy of the concussion. The boy was with Elliot, who'd been instructed not to let him go and not to allow anyone from Child Protection Services to pick him up until she was back home and they had everything sorted out.

Jude scanned the room, found a clock: 3:21 a.m. Next to the bed was an IV stand with lines that led to the needle taped to the back of her hand. She was turned slightly to her side, pillow propped behind her back. Her body was enveloped in warmth, and she realized she was covered in something generating heat, with several cords running from it and a dial that could increase the temperature. In contrast, her head was cold. She reached up, her fingers coming in contact with an ice pack held in place by an elastic bandage.

Uriah sat down and pulled his chair close. She told him about going to the farm and what had transpired there. She might have fallen asleep a few times during the conversation. "The concussion probably saved you," he said. "In Perkins's panic to get rid of your body, she thought you were dead."

She had a vague memory of embracing death. She recalled the comfort of the moment. Maybe the end was like that for many people who knew it was coming. No fear. Acceptance and even welcome.

"I was wrapped in plastic and dragged through a field. I remember that. I kept thinking I was dead when she was pulling me behind the snowmobile. Like, this is what it feels like to die." She frowned, forgetting what they were talking about. He prodded her, and she continued, "I tried to stay conscious, but I kept blacking out. Later, I actually played dead as she rolled me over and I fell. Pretty far. I don't know how much later I woke up. The freezing rain hitting the shower curtain woke me, and I was able to partially free myself of the plastic and climb from the pit. And Uriah, I think there was a body in there with me. You need to check."

"I've spoken with the county sheriff, but I'd like to get out there as soon as the roads reopen. I want to make sure they don't miss any evidence. Nanette Perkins's body is at the morgue. We've got Savoy locked up, but no statement from him yet. We have his cell phone with a call to Perkins. Also calls to and from Gail Ford. We'll know more once we subpoena his phone records and get a search warrant to Ford's house."

They both fell silent. The room was so bright. She put a hand to her head, felt stitches. "I can't stay awake. Shouldn't I stay awake?"

"The doctor said that's a myth. That sleep will help you heal faster." He was pale, with circles under his eyes.

"You don't look so great."

"When I was told to go straight home and rest after getting the MRI, this night was not what anybody had in mind."

She scooted back, wincing in pain as she patted what space was left on the hospital bed. "Turn off the light. Lie down a little bit. Close your eyes." She closed hers.

She heard the chair creak and felt the mattress dip. His hair brushed her cheek, and she put an arm around his waist. A moment later, his hand grasped hers.

"What are you going to do about the boy?" he whispered.

"I don't know."

"You could adopt him."

"He's not a cat."

"You're good with him."

"I'm never home."

"Elliot could take care of him when you can't."

A child . . . Just months ago a cat had seemed impossible, and now she found herself considering adopting a small human.

CHAPTER 58

The following day, while Jude prepared to return home to recover from her injuries, Uriah headed back to the Perkins farm in an unmarked car. His own vehicle was evidence and would not be returned to him for at least a few more days. The Dakota County sheriff and the officers from the neighboring Hennepin County Sheriff's Office were on site, along with the Bureau of Criminal Apprehension and the state fire marshal.

It was late morning, the day after the event. Roads were still bad, but better. Two fire trucks were also on location, but the blaze of last night was now a smoldering heap, a brick chimney the lone substantial element left of the structure. Mostly an open black pit, burned not only to the ground but to the basement.

Out of the car, Uriah tramped through the snow toward what little was left of the charred building, coat hitting his knees. Suddenly conscious of his shaggy appearance, he raked fingers through his hair, pulling out a few strands in the process, shaking it off his hand as he walked.

The sheriff spotted him.

"No bodies found inside yet," the officer said. He was dressed in a brown puffy coat and fur-lined cap. "But there's a lot of rubble to go through. Gas line from the LP tank and the electric are off, but we have to move with care. You said your partner was left in a field behind the house. We checked the area, and I think we found the spot. A silage pit you might want to see." He pointed and they both began walking.

Out in the open the wind was blowing maybe twenty miles an hour, and now that the snow had stopped, temperatures were falling. It seemed to be a common weather pattern. Uriah dug into the pocket of his coat, was glad to find his stocking cap, and tugged it on. Head bent into the wind, the two men trudged through the field.

The snow had been packed by foot traffic and vehicles. He spotted the concrete edges of the silage pit in the distance. It was an old method for storing chopped-up cornstalks. Once a field was picked, the stalks were threshed to create food for livestock. Sometimes those stalks were mixed with other ingredients, like expired corn syrup and even candy bars still in wrappers. The result was stored and fermented in three-sided rectangular pits about fifteen feet deep, with an opening on one end for a tractor to drive in and out. This must have been where Jude had been dumped, her fall cushioned by the snow.

The sheriff motioned him along one edge until they were looking straight down into the pit. Below was the ravaged body of a female. Animals had found her. Stomach, eyes, and half the face were eaten, bones scattered, the snow near the body, pink and brown and packed, tracks everywhere. "Coyotes." He sounded confident.

"Could be dogs," Uriah said, just to be contrary. Probably coyotes.

"Gonna take dental records to ID her. If she has enough teeth left." The sheriff shook his head.

They probably didn't get a lot of murders in this area.

"Might be hard to determine mode of death too." He glanced up. "Here they come."

Bureau of Criminal Apprehension. Striding across the field with their heavy cases, a group of men and women dressed in navy-blue jackets. It wasn't Uriah's crime scene. He would have cordoned off a large portion of the field, but he understood how tough it was to determine a boundary and how hard a scene like this would be to contain.

Maybe working from a small area was the best idea and use of limited manpower.

"I'd like to get a better look."

"Be my guest."

Uriah circled to the open end. Watching his step, he moved close to the victim and crouched, but didn't touch her.

Another frozen body. Not a kid this time, though. He'd guess her age to be anywhere from twenty to thirty-five. Light-brown hair, Caucasian. The remaining tissue and bones and skin didn't show signs of putrefaction. How long had she been there? Had she been dumped, like the bodies in the lake? He thought back to the length of time the weather had been cold enough to freeze a body and keep it frozen. Maybe a month.

He spoke briefly to the sheriff and crime-scene team. "Let me know if you find out anything." They didn't have to, but keeping him in the loop could help them all.

Walking back across the snowy field, he got a text. Expecting something pertaining to the case, he was surprised to see a message from his doctor. Talk about the collision of two worlds.

MRI looks good. Call my office to schedule surgery. The sooner, the better.

He'd respond later.

At the farmhouse, arson experts were on the scene, picking through the rubble. Uriah found the woman in charge and gave her his card, asking that she contact him if they found anything that might pertain to their kidnapping cases. He was about to leave, wanting to go home, take a shower, and find something to eat, when he decided to check the barn.

Not his jurisdiction, but he certainly had a personal interest in the case.

The giant sliding door was partway open, with footprints leading in and out, evidence of a search. Inside, the electricity was off. He passed the beam of light from his cell phone around the space. A barn could hide a lot of things with its haylofts and wooden wall ladders that led to cupolas.

He brushed some of the snow off a vehicle parked near the door and recognized it as Jude's car. Deeper inside, he checked the cab of both a tractor and a combine, then caught sight of a tarp-covered object on the far side of the building, tucked away in a corner. After stepping sideways around equipment, he released the bungee cords and pulled the tarp free, uncovering another vehicle, this one a fairly new model. Minnesota plates. Hennepin County. Perkins did not live in Hennepin County.

He tried the doors. Locked. He scanned the area and spotted several shovels hanging from nails. He grabbed one. Holding it with two hands, turning his face away, he broke the driver's window. He tossed the shovel aside and unlocked the door, reaching across the broken tempered glass to the compartment between the seats, then the glove box, finally coming up with the registration.

Jenny Hill. The social worker who'd been in charge of the boy's case. He now had a good idea who the body in the field belonged to.

He called Jude to fill her in.

"This could be how the boy ended back up with Perkins," Jude said.

"A fabricated report?"

"That'd be my guess. Perkins might have forced Jenny Hill to file it with a recommendation for returning the child."

Another text message, this one from Detective Valentine.

Savoy says he's ready to talk, and he wants you to take his statement.

CHAPTER 59

"Y ou sold children for profit."

They were sitting in a police department interrogation room, video camera high on the wall, green light on, indicating it was recording. Since Savoy had already tried to kill him, Uriah wasn't taking any chances. The retired detective sat at a table across from him, leather restraint around his waist, handcuffs attached, his ankles chained to the floor. Savoy proceeded to tell Uriah about a series of human-trafficking crimes going back forty years, long before he knew about any of it.

Some people lied and even confessed to crimes they had never committed, some wanted to brag about their wickedness, and others wanted to get the weight of their sins off their chest in what was almost a confession. Uriah wasn't sure where Savoy fell in the spectrum.

"I wasn't involved in the day-to-day, if that's what you're implying. It was a big operation, spread across the US. Buyers would request a certain kind of kid, and the company would supply it. Minneapolis was the hub, and Nan and her husband were kind of a clearinghouse. All the kids ended up there. They took care of them and shipped them out."

"To men who wanted to have sex with children."

"Not just men, but yeah, most were rich white guys." He was talking like he was telling Uriah about a vacation he'd taken, or relating some boring day in his life. A sociopath who dealt in human beings. It wasn't Uriah's job to ask about remorse, and not his job at this moment to judge. He was here to get as much information as he could, and he didn't want to say anything that might halt the discussion.

"Who were the buyers?"

"Most are dead now." Savoy leaned forward. "I want you and everybody to know this was a business. We weren't sick bastards kidnapping and raping kids. We weren't serial killers. We weren't killers at all."

Ah, that's why he wanted to tell his story. To him, it was better to call it a business, a moneymaking enterprise, rather than human trafficking. It seemed to justify it in his mind.

"But then Nan and her husband, Lyle, screwed up." Now he looked upset. Maybe it was a line he'd never wanted to cross. As he continued, Uriah realized that wasn't where the emotions were coming from. "They killed an entire shipment of kids. A month of work, product delivered from all over the country to disperse."

Product. It was hard for Uriah to keep from leaping across the table and grabbing the man by the throat. He struggled to keep his breathing even and his face impassive. Just two guys talking. "Carbon monoxide poisoning," Uriah stated.

"We shut down after that, but I kept in touch, and sometimes we talked about restarting the business. More the kind of thing you discuss over a few beers. And believe it or not, Nan used to be pretty hot. And she and I . . . well . . ." He smiled.

"What about Gail Ford?"

"She was one of the crew. The kids liked women because they were mother figures. Women kept them calm. Before the carbon monoxide thing went down, we had a buyer who'd paid in advance. A huge amount, like twenty grand, I think."

Not so huge for a human being.

"We needed a kid to replace one of the dead ones. And believe it or not, Ford had this kid who almost fit the description. And she just gave him up. Her own kid." He leaned hard against his chair back, amazement or maybe admiration on his face. "A little young, hair too dark, so she bleached it and that was it. He was sold to a customer in Oklahoma, I think."

"You don't remember?"

"There were so many. We're talking a big business." Bragging again.

"How many kids died in the carbon monoxide incident? Do you remember?"

"Ten."

Uriah moved his hands to hide them under the table. They were shaking. "We only found two. Are the rest on the farm?"

Savoy told him how it had happened in the winter, when the ground was frozen, how Nan and Lyle hid the bodies in a meat locker owned by his brother. He gave a description of the general area. "Like I said, not on me. I don't even know exactly where it is."

"What does the boy who lived with Nan have to do with any of this? The four-year-old? He's been physically abused. You do that?"

With hands cuffed together, Savoy pressed a finger against the table to drive home his point. "I'm the hero here. I want you to know that. I want everybody to know that." He looked up at the camera. "I saved that boy. She was running with him, probably would have killed him if I hadn't stopped her." He drew out his next sentence. "That kid is alive today thanks to me." He leaned closer and lowered his voice. "I could help you. I know this stuff forward and backward. I could be an asset. Think of all the work I've done to get new DNA legislation passed. I'm pretty sure that will count for something."

Uriah was disgusted. If Savoy couldn't bargain his way out of this, he'd at least try to come away with some perks. "Why would she want to kill her own child?"

He let out a snort. "He's not hers."

Not much of a surprise. "Kidnapped too? I thought all of that was over by then."

"Not really kidnapped. Secondhand, I guess you could say."

"How's that?"

"He's Phillip Schilling's boy."

Jesus. Jude's father.

CHAPTER 60

L ying in bed in her apartment, Roof Cat curled up beside her, Jude only half heard the conversation drifting from the living room. Elliot answering a knock, followed by Uriah's voice. And then her partner was in the bedroom, closing the door quietly behind him. And he had the strangest look on his face.

"What?" she asked.

He grabbed her laptop from the dresser and placed it on the bed. "Log in to our VPN and go to the most recent interviews."

"Savoy's?"

"Yeah."

"Are you going to brief me first?"

"I want you to watch it without my insight influencing your reaction."

She played the video while Uriah perched on the bed beside her, back to the headboard, close enough to see the screen. She took in Savoy's revelation about how involved he was in the business. And yes, human trafficking. They'd been right about that. She marveled at the man's delusion and how he put no blame on himself, convinced he'd done nothing wrong. Just an opportunist unable to pass up an easy way to make some extra cash. As she watched, Uriah's expression upon entering the room continued to nag her.

And then Savoy spoke her father's name.

She felt Uriah's silence beside her, sensed he was holding his breath. She did not react. The truth was, nothing about her father would surprise her anymore.

Confession unfurling, Savoy seemed unable to stop himself. "I wonder how many kids that guy has scattered around the country," Savoy said. "I don't know the whole story, but one of the girls he kidnapped got pregnant and had this kid in captivity. Schilling paid Nan to raise him. I think it was supposed to be temporary, but he never came back for him. Just kept sending her money. A sweet job. She was happy about that. That's what I understand anyway. She liked the kid. That's where she screwed up. She could have dumped him on any doorstep, but she got the idea to drop him at Detective Fontaine's because they were related."

When the interview was over, Jude closed her laptop. "He should be put on suicide watch."

"Already did it. Didn't want to find out he'd hung himself in his cell. Savoy's best punishment will be to live with the public outcry and the subsequent rejection by his family. What do you think?" Uriah asked. "Is he lying? He's lying, right?"

A light rap at the door and the boy entered, cupping a bowl with his small hands, moving carefully, Elliot behind him.

"It's ice cream," the child said. Raspberry chocolate—her favorite.

"Thank you." Accepting the treat, Jude watched the child, noting eyes that were an intense blue. Like hers. Like her father's.

She looked at Uriah, who was still waiting for her verdict. "I think it's the truth."

So strange how things intertwined in the most unexpected ways, and yet it shouldn't have been such a surprise. Last night in the hospital she'd made the decision to try and adopt the boy. This new information about his possible identity didn't change anything. He was the same person today as he'd been yesterday. He was the same abused and unsettling and charming child, who might or might not have dark tendencies, who might or might not have inherited the desire to do bad things. But she wasn't afraid.

She ate a little of the ice cream, then put the bowl aside, leaned back against the pillow, and closed her eyes. She heard Elliot usher the boy from the room. "Let's go downstairs and feed Blackie." They left, but Uriah lingered. She felt the bed dip, and when she opened her eyes again, he was lying on his side next to her, elbow on the mattress, head propped against his hand.

"What else?" she asked. She could see he wasn't done with his news.

"I got the MRI results and I've scheduled my surgery."

Now she was afraid. "When?"

"Day after tomorrow."

Her throat tightened. "That's so soon." She needed more time.

"The doctor said we should hurry. And this case is solved. Not completely wrapped up, but nothing major going on. Everybody will be fine without me."

Not true. And it was so easy to die. Too easy.

"You'll come back, won't you?"

He considered her question. The fact that he had to think about it at all terrified her more.

"You have to come back," she said. "For me."

He smiled at her as if either journey, living or dying, was nothing.

CHAPTER 61

Two weeks later, Loring Park, Minneapolis

S itting alone on a park bench facing the frozen lake, Jude folded the
copy of the *New York Times*, wishing Uriah were sitting next to her
so he could read it too. The day was a throwback to a true Minnesota
winter: temperature about twenty degrees, blue cloudless sky, sun shining, and, as happened when you acclimated to the cold, it felt warm,
almost shirtsleeve weather.

She scanned the crowd of skaters, looking for the boy, and spotted
his red knit hat. Elliot was on one side of him, Ava Germaine on the
other, both holding his hands. Occasionally, Octavia would glide past
Jude's bench, her purple scarf flying behind her, and she'd wave with
heartbreaking innocence. How Jude's father had known Nan, she wasn't
sure. It wouldn't have been a stretch for him to have been a client of
the traffickers.

Back before Uriah's terrible surgery, they'd found the meat locker
with the bodies, six in all. Two were thought to be still in the lake.
It would be spring before they could search for them, once the ice
melted. But that didn't keep the curious and morbid away, hoping to
find another child.

They might never know everything about the boy, and he might
never be able to be fully socialized. But she would deal with that. DNA

results confirmed Savoy's story. The child was not related to Nanette Perkins, and he was in fact Jude's half brother. They'd also run his DNA through their databases. No match to any of the bodies found on Jude's father's property. There could still be buried girls, killed by her father, unaccounted for. That was Jude's suspicion. She would keep looking for the boy's relatives while at the same time trying to give him the life he deserved. And a name.

In a cluster of laughter and the sound of blades on ice, all four of the skaters converged on the bench. Red cheeks, smiles, eyes that were bright. And it hit Jude that all of them, including herself, had been affected by the same evil man. But anyone who saw them today would never suspect their dark histories.

She lifted the folded paper. "This is fantastic journalism," she told Elliot. "Congratulations." He almost had her convinced to take her part of the inheritance—divided three ways now that the boy was here. The child's share would be used for his education, but she could do a lot with hers. So many worthy nonprofits out there.

"Thanks," Elliot said.

His piece, "The Body Keeper," about Perkins and Ford and Savoy, had been published at a time when it felt like nothing new would be added to the child-trafficking conversation, but the story of the bodies had reawakened outrage and reconfirmed the nation's commitment to keeping kids safe. The president had even invited Jude to the White House to discuss a task force to enhance already-existing organizations.

It was hard for her to imagine that the scale of events and the operation of years ago could happen today, what with measures implemented over the past decade, but you never knew. Unfortunately, evil would always find a way to exploit the innocent. Her father had proved that. No measures would ever be enough, but she had to believe they would help.

She wasn't really surprised that Savoy had fooled her. That day she'd picked him up from the airport, any oddity she'd detected had been filed as PTSD and the damage that happened to detectives who worked child murder cases, especially ones they couldn't solve. And it wasn't unusual for a person who felt no sense of guilt to have no tells. Many could even breeze through lie detector tests.

The group drank some hot cocoa and talked softly, then the four of them skated away, moving across the lake in a row, all four holding hands now, leaving Jude alone on the bench. She was healing but wasn't well enough to risk a fall and another concussion.

"Leroy?" a voice from behind asked. She turned to see Uriah standing there, coffee in one hand, a knit cap covering his postsurgical head. Most of his hair was gone, but it would come back.

"No."

He sat down beside her. "Jed."

"No."

"Just seeing if you were paying attention." So far, he'd suggested about fifty names for the boy. "How about Ira?"

"Hmm. Maybe. He has to like it too."

"Let me remind you that the names he's suggested so far are Kitty and Panda. Panda is kind of cool, but I don't know if it has legs. Hopefully you can find something you both agree on."

"You were gone a long time."

"The vendor ran out of coffee and had to make another pot."

"I would have gotten it for you."

"I need to do things for myself."

Almost losing the boy, followed by thinking she might lose Uriah, had changed her, lifted the numbness and cracked the protective wall she'd built around herself during captivity. Little steps. And sitting in the waiting room with his family while his brain was cut open, dreading yet needing to hear the results of the surgery, had been some of the worst hours of her life. But he was okay, and she was okay, and they were all okay.

Bittersweet, aching beauty could still be found in the aftermath of grief and evil. That's what she'd learned over the past year, over the past few months. And a lot of that realization was due to Uriah and his steady and cool and collected and unruffled self.

She touched the back of his hand and felt his small jerk of surprise. Then, without a word, he fumbled for a stronger grip, squeezing firmly, silently conveying how much she meant to him. As he held her hand, he seemed razor-focused on the skaters, but she caught a suspicious glint in his eye.

The surgery had made him more emotional, probably due to the anesthetics that could linger in a person's system. He wasn't yet a hundred percent. He tired easily, but that would pass. And she wasn't the only one coming to terms with this new life. His wife had been gone less than two years.

"Ira's a nice name," she said.

He nodded. "It means watchful. It's good to be watchful and aware. Oh, I got something for you." He reached inside his coat, pulled out a scrap of paper, and handed it to her.

A lottery ticket.

"If you win, are you going to keep it?" he asked.

"Maybe." She thought about it. "Yes."

The sun was sinking behind the city skyline, illuminating the geometric outline of the IDS Center and the gothic-looking Foshay Tower, turning the sky pink—a pastel blush that could come only in the deep heart of a Minnesota winter. Jude inhaled, pulling in crisp air, the tip of her nose cold now that evening was coming fast. And for the first time in years, she found herself looking forward to tomorrow, even if it meant another murder to solve.

BOOK CLUB DISCUSSION QUESTIONS

1. How does Jude differ from traditional female detectives? Does the difference make Jude more appealing to you?
2. In this book, we learn a little about why Jude was allowed to return to work so quickly. Should she have returned at all?
3. What would Jude be like today if she'd never been kidnapped?
4. Jude's captivity changed her. Did it make her a better cop? If so, how and why?
5. Is Uriah a good homicide partner for Jude? Why or why not?
6. Do you think Jude will ever be able to have a normal life?
7. Do you want Jude to have a normal life?
8. Have you ever been to Minnesota? If not, did the book expand your knowledge of the state beyond being the birthplace of Bob Dylan and Prince?
9. Would you like to visit Minneapolis after reading the book?
10. Did the winter setting make you wonder why anybody would ever live in Minnesota?
11. What was the most heart-pounding part of the book for you?

12. What was your favorite scene?
13. What was the most surprising part of *The Body Keeper* for you?
14. Could something like the events in the book occur today?
15. The story can be emotional. Did you react in an emotional way to events in Jude's life?
16. Did you empathize with Jude or Uriah? If so, with whom and why?
17. Did you find the suspense compelling? If so, what elements of it were particularly compelling for you?
18. What qualities of Jude do you wish you had and why?
19. If the series is developed for television, who should play Jude and Uriah?
20. The author has written books in various genres, including two critically acclaimed memoirs. She feels memoir writing taught her to dig deeper into characters. Can the experience of writing nonfiction help when writing fiction? If so, how?
21. If you've read other books by Anne Frasier, how does the Jude Fontaine series (*The Body Reader, The Body Counter, The Body Keeper*) compare to the Elise Sandburg series (*Play Dead, Stay Dead, Pretty Dead, Truly Dead*)?

ABOUT THE AUTHOR

Anne Frasier is the *New York Times* and *USA Today* bestselling author of the Detective Jude Fontaine Mysteries, including *The Body Keeper*, *The Body Counter*, and *The Body Reader*, which received the 2017 Thriller Award for Best Paperback Original from International Thriller Writers. Her other thrillers have hit the *USA Today* bestseller list and have been featured in Mystery Guild, Literary Guild, and Book of the Month Club. Among Anne's other honors are a RITA for romantic suspense and a Daphne du Maurier Award for paranormal romance. Her memoir *The Orchard* was an *O, The Oprah Magazine* Fall Pick; a One Book, One Community read; a B+ review in *Entertainment Weekly*; and one of the Librarians' Best Books of 2011. She lives in Saint Paul, Minnesota. For more information, visit her at www.annefrasier.com.